A Dead Man in
MALTA

Also by Michael Pearce

A Dead Man in

MALTA

MICHAEL PEARCE

Constable • London

Constable & Robinson Ltd
3 The Lanchesters
162 Fulham Palace Road
London W6 9ER
www.constablerobinson.com

First published in the UK by Constable,
an imprint of Constable & Robinson, 2010

First US edition published by SohoConstable,
an imprint of Soho Press, 2010

Soho Press, Inc.
853 Broadway
New York, NY 10003
www.sohopress.com

A copy of the British Library Cataloguing in Publication
Data is available from the British Library

UK ISBN: 978-1-84901-298-0

US ISBN: 978-1-56947-878-3
US Library of Congress number: 2010019577

Printed and bound in the EU

1 3 5 7 9 10 8 6 4 2

Chapter One

'Balloons.'

'Really?'

'Yes. Dozens of them. The hot-air sort. The sky was full of them.'

'And one of them came down?'

'Yes. Into the water.'

'But no one was hurt, I gather?'

'Not then, no.'

'That's the odd bit.'

'Yes.'

It was later that the German had died. When he had come down into the Grand Harbour, the basket had floated for a while, long enough for one of the water-taxis, with which the harbour abounded, to get to him. He had been standing up in the basket and waving happily. There had seemed nothing wrong with him. However, the *dghajsa*, as a precaution, had taken him to the nearby Royal Naval Hospital at Bighi. The doctors had checked him all over and found that everything was in order but had kept him in, protesting, in case there were any delayed effects. And early that evening he had died.

Like the others.

Three people now, the letter to *The Times* said accusingly, had died in the hospital at Bighi in quick succession. All of them mysteriously.

Mysteriously?

All three, when admitted, had been apparently in the best of health.

If they were so healthy, said someone sarcastically, what were they doing in the hospital?

Well, said the original correspondent, a Mrs Wynne-Gurr, one of them had injured his knee playing football, another had suffered facial abrasions in a dispute on the waterfront and was having his jaw wired, and the third was the unfortunate German. In none of these cases, said Mrs Wynne-Gurr tartly, could the condition of the patient be described as likely to lead to respiratory failure. Which was what, according to the doctors, all three had died from.

The doctors fought back.

What, exactly, was Mrs Wynne-Gurr alleging?

Mrs Wynne-Gurr was alleging nothing. She was merely pointing out that three apparently healthy men . . . etc., etc. And she thought that questions should be asked.

What about, precisely?

Mrs Wynne-Gurr hesitated but did not retreat.

'Nursing practices,' she said.

Nursing practices? The doctors reeled back.

Yes. She herself was not without experience of nursing practice and she felt that questions needed to be asked about current practices in the hospital. Were the patients left lying on their backs or on their tummies, for example?

'What?' said the stunned doctors.

'I was just struck,' explained Mrs Wynne-Gurr, 'by the similarity between these deaths and those suffered by babies in cot deaths.'

'British sailors do not suffer from cot deaths,' said the Admiral in charge of things at Malta, stiffly.

'But if they had been drinking heavily . . .' said Mrs Wynne-Gurr.

'British sailors do not . . .' began the Admiral, but then thought again.

At this point there came a foreign intervention. A German doctor wrote in saying that the German aviator had been a patient of his, that he had been a clean-living Lutheran and did not drink, that the doctor had examined him thoroughly before he had embarked on his ballooning and found him in the best of health. Before he entered the hospital.

This directed attention back to the hospital and to the question of nursing practices. Many of the nurses in the hospital were Maltese and the island took umbrage. Its umbrage was joined to the Navy's umbrage and fanned by the Maltese press. Most of it was aimed, conveniently from the hospital's point of view, at Mrs Wynne-Gurr, and in the furore the three deaths might have been lost sight of had it not been for a new development.

The mother of one of the dead sailors wrote to a newspaper (not *The Times* but a popular tabloid) saying that her son's mess mates had written to tell her they thought there was 'something fishy' about his death. When a local newshound followed this up, it transpired that the sailor had something specific in mind. They had been visiting their mate on the day he had died – and found him in excellent health and spirits – and then gone on to chat to (up) a nurse they knew. On their way back they had glanced in at their mate as they passed and seen someone bending over him with a pillow. They had thought nothing of it, that it was just a nurse making him comfortable, but then the next day when they heard that he had suddenly died, and what he was alleged to have died of, they began to wonder. Such deaths were not unknown aboard ships, they said.

'Seen it done,' one of them volunteered. And in a hospital, too. He had been sick once, out on the Singapore station, and had spent some time in hospital. One of the patients on his ward had snored heavily, night after night, and in the end the other patients had been driven to desperate measures.

'It's easy done. You just put a pillow over his head.'

Upon further questioning, the informant had backtracked rapidly; but the Maltese newspapers the next day had been full of headlines about 'Murderous British matelots'. These were soon followed by indignant denials from the Navy, the hospital and the authorities in general; so everyone believed there must be something in it.

The matter clearly cried out for investigation. But who by? The Maltese police? But the hospital, in Navy terms, was a ship and therefore not under Maltese jurisdiction. It would conduct its own investigation. The Maltese weren't having that. They called on the Governor to intervene.

The Governor, because Malta at that time was still a Crown Colony, governed by a British-appointed Governor subject to the Colonial Department in London.

The Governor appealed to the Department for guidance.

The Department deliberated.

'You need someone from outside,' they said. 'Why don't we send out someone from Scotland Yard?'

'How about that chap Seymour?' said the Navy, recalling past services. 'And, perhaps,' they added hopefully, 'he could bring his assistant with him.'

'Assistant?' said Scotland Yard, mystified. 'We don't remember him having an assistant with him in Gibraltar.'

'A mistake,' said Seymour hurriedly.

Which, possibly, it had been. But not the Navy's: Seymour's. While staying in Gibraltar, he had brought his girl-friend over from Tangier to join him. Forced once to explain her away, he had claimed that she was a Special Assistant sent out from London and had never been able to shake off the identification. The Navy had embraced Chantale with enthusiasm; not entirely to Seymour's satisfaction.

'Well, you can't have an assistant this time,' said Scotland Yard.

'Wouldn't dream of asking for one,' said Seymour.

Which was a mistake, as he discovered when he got home and told Chantale about it. Chantale quite fancied a return to the Mediterranean.

'No way!' said Seymour.

Chantale nursed her wrath and bided her time.

'This letter that started it all,' said Seymour: 'from a . . .?'

'Mrs Wynne-Gurr,' said the man from the Colonial Department.

'Maltese?'

4

'British. She is the Chair of the West Surrey branch of the St John Ambulance Association.'

'You say that as if it were significant?'

'Well, it explains what she was doing out there.'

'And what was she doing out there?'

'Arranging a visit. She'd taken it into her head, you see, to bring a party of her members out to Malta to see the origins of the Association.'

He looked kindly at Seymour. 'You may not be aware of the origins of the St John Ambulance.'

'Well, no. No. Not really.'

'You have heard, of course, of the Knights Hospitaller of Malta?'

'Of course!'

Honesty crept in. 'Vaguely.'

'They began as a community of monks set up to nurse pilgrims who fell sick on their way to the Holy Land. When it became evident that the chief threat to their health was a military one, they added knights to their number and earned an awesome reputation as defenders of the faithful. In time they became known as the Knights Hospitaller of Jerusalem.'

'Not Malta?'

'Not to start with. Actually they were thrown out of Jerusalem and had to regroup on Rhodes. When they were thrown out of there, too, they moved to Malta. They defended Malta against the Turks, most notably at the time of the Great Siege, but then they rather went downhill. Eventually they were thrown out of Malta, too, and now, I believe, the remnants of the Order are based in Rome. A British connection lives on, however, in the form of the St John Ambulance.'

'Knights?' said Seymour doubtfully.

'Nursing. The Association was set up some thirty years ago to promote the cause of first aid.'

'The people you see at football matches?'

'And public events of all kinds. They perform an invaluable service.'

'And Mrs Wynne-Gurr . . .?'

5

'Is active in the Association. Overactive, in the opinion of some people.'

'I see. And she had come out to Malta to arrange a visit . . .'

'Of her troops. Sorry, of her branch. And happened to be present on the day of the great ballooning event. Observing the balloons, however, less closely than the practices of the local St John Ambulance, who were, naturally, in attendance. On the whole, she was satisfied with them. Less so, though with the practices of the hospital.'

'How does the hospital come into it?'

'The balloonist who came down was taken there. Closely followed by Mrs Wynne-Gurr, still intent on observing procedures. Actually, she was quite satisfied with the Accident and Emergency procedures she saw and went home appeased to write a report on the day's events which she intended to give to the local St John Ambulance. It was only the next day, after she had heard about the German's death, that she decided to go back to the hospital in search of an explanation. And this time she was not at all satisfied with what she saw.'

'And so she wrote to *The Times*?'

'As you do. If you're someone like Mrs Wynne-Gurr. And opened up the whole can of worms. Or, alternatively, depending upon your point of view, stirred up a quite unnecessary hornets' nest. Some of which stung the Governor and, consequently, us. One sting leads to another, Seymour, and at the end it led to you. Go out to Malta and find out who dunnit.

'Oh, and, Seymour, there's one other thing. A lot of people are interested in this. Including other countries. Germany, especially, is asking questions. So – please – carry out your investigation with a light touch. As the bankers plead when the rest of us are trying to stop them from doing anything too awful.'

So there was Seymour, not quite a week later, standing in the Upper Barraca Gardens, looking out over the Grand

Harbour. Below and to his left was the breakwater at the entrance to the harbour. Over to his right, across the water, was Fort Ricasoli and another building which looked like another fort but must be the hospital. Directly ahead was the town of Senglea and a great mass of building spreading along the end of the harbour and blending with dockyards. There were creeks giving off the harbour, huge inlets lined with cranes and wharves and busy with tugs and little cargo boats of all kinds.

But dwarfing everything was the vast bay itself, blindingly blue in the sun and filled, for this was 1913, with warships. Little boats were nestling alongside them unloading provisions, squat tugs were bustling to and fro, and tiny water-buses, stuffed with people, and with eyes painted on their hulls, were criss-crossing the harbour in all directions, like water-beetles.

'Imagine it swarming with balloons,' said the Inspector enthusiastically. 'Dozens of them. Hundreds of them! That's how it was that day. It was a mercy they didn't collide. But there's more space up there than you think and they know what they're doing. I don't mind telling you, though, that we were really worried beforehand from a traffic control point of view. It was all right on the day, though.'

'Except for the German,' said Seymour.

As they were standing there looking out over the harbour they heard English voices behind them.

'Felix!' scolded a woman's voice. 'Where *have* you been? We have been looking for you everywhere!'

'I was with Dad. At the Grand Master's Palace. I wanted to see the Armouries but they were closed. And Dad was spending ages looking at some tapestries so I wandered off.'

'Well, you shouldn't have done. Not when you knew we have an appointment at the hospital.'

'Mum, need I go this time? We've been three times already and it's not very interesting.'

'There are *always* things of interest to see in a hospital,' said the mother firmly.

'I'll take you along to Ophthalmology,' said a man's voice conciliatorily.

'But, Dad, you took me there last time! And the time before.'

'You can learn a lot from an Ophthalmology Department,' said the mother. 'Especially if you're going to become a doctor.'

'But I'm *not* going to become –' said the boy, in exasperated tones.

'Don't set your mind too firmly against it. Not at this stage.'

'Anyway,' said the boy sulkily, 'I *was* looking at a hospital.'

'What?'

'The Sacra Infermeria. I met a doctor and he took me there.'

'Are you sure, Felix?' said the man, in a puzzled voice. 'I don't know a hospital of that name.'

'It's a very old one. Over three hundred years old.'

'Ah, well –'

'They've got lots of old instruments and things.'

'Well, I'm sure that's very interesting, Felix, but –' began his mother.

'And the Long Hall. You should see it, Dad. It was the longest ward in Europe when it was built and it probably still is. It's huge!'

'I'm not sure I'm in favour of large wards,' said his mother. 'Handy for the nurses, but bad from the point of view of spreading infection.'

'Dr Malia says it could come into its own again.'

'Dr Malia?' said the Inspector.

The boy turned to him.

'Yes, that's right. Do you know him? He's the doctor I met. And he took me over to the Sacra Infermeria and showed me –'

'Dr Malia?' said the Inspector again, in a slightly worried voice.

'Anything wrong with him?' said the father.

'No, no. Not exactly,' said the Inspector. 'He's a perfectly respectable doctor. Or was.'

'Was?'

'But that was ten years ago. Or perhaps more. He's been retired for some time.'

'You get out of touch.'

'It's not so much that. He doesn't practise much now.'

'No?'

'No. It's just that he's a bit, well, eccentric these days.'

'He thinks there's going to be a war,' put in Felix excitedly.

'War?'

'And that Malta's going to be very important in it.'

'Well, that's hardly likely, is it?' said his father.

'From the point of view of hospitals. He thinks there are going to be lots and lots of casualties all round the Mediterranean and that they'll be brought here for nursing and there'll be nowhere to put them.'

'Well, there are quite a lot of suppositions in all that, Felix –'

'I am afraid your son is right, though, Dr Wynne-Gurr,' said the Inspector. 'That *is* what Dr Malia thinks.'

'And he's making a list of possible places that could be used,' said Felix.

The Inspector nodded gloomily. 'He is.'

'Well,' said Dr Wynne-Gurr, 'there's nothing wrong with that, I suppose.'

The Inspector looked doubtful.

'Is there?'

'It's got a bit out of hand,' said the Inspector. 'He goes round everywhere making his bloody list, asking silly questions and taking up busy people's time. People get fed up with it. He came to the Police Headquarters the other day and nosed around, getting in everybody's way.'

'"There's too much space here for the work you do," he said. Well, of course plenty of people agreed with him. People are always ready to criticize the police. And, it is true, we do have a lot of people just pushing bits of paper to and fro. But –

'"You'll have to get out when the war comes," he said.

'"And *you'll* have to get out right now!" said the Chief, as mad as hell.

'Well, then he went to the Co-Cathedral. You been there? Well, you ought to go. It's a wonderful place. What with all those chapels of the langues. Amazing! So they tell me. I don't often go myself, though my wife says I should. Anyway, he went there and looked around.

'"There's a lot of space here," he said, "which could be put to better use."

'Well, you know what doctors are. Bloody infidels, the lot of them. Oh, saving your presence, Doctor! Anyway, it got the Church in an uproar. And half the island. They went to the Governor about it. But, of course, he's got other things on his plate just at the moment. This business at the hospital, for instance. So he didn't pay much attention.

'But there you have it. The old fellow's a bit cracked these days. He's got a bee in his bonnet and goes round making himself a nuisance. There's no harm in him, really. It's just that he's a pain in the ass. Saving your presence, madam!'

'He doesn't sound quite the sort of person you should be talking to, Felix,' said Mrs Wynne-Gurr.

Felix closed his lips and reserved his position.

They went down to the water together, the Wynne-Gurrs and Seymour and the Inspector, and took a water-taxi, or *dghajsa*, as Seymour was learning to call them, to the Senglea side. Down at water level, and closer to the war-ships, they looked enormous and very threatening. Seymour wondered if there could be anything in what that cracked doctor had said about a war being just around the corner. Sitting there in the sunshine in the open boat it was hard to believe it.

At Bighi they parted, the Wynne-Gurrs going in one direction, the Inspector taking Seymour in another. He led him to a small room in the hospital in which three doctors were sitting. Two of them were British, the third, Maltese.

'And let me correct, right away, an impression you may have gained,' said one of the British doctors: 'our nurses here are first class.'

The other British doctor nodded.

'First class,' he confirmed. 'Compare well with any I've seen in London. Or Portsmouth, for that matter. Cot deaths, for Christ's sake! This is a naval hospital not a bloody maternity one!'

'Yet we do have to face it,' said the Maltese doctor quietly: 'there's something that needs explaining. They shouldn't have died.'

'It does happen, Eduardo.'

'I know. But usually there's some explanation.'

'Well, there is here.'

'Three?' said the Maltese doctor. 'We haven't had a single death of that sort in the past two years. But we've had three! In not much more than a month.'

'Yes, but . . . respiratory failure!'

The Maltese doctor turned to Seymour. 'You may not be aware of medical conventions, Mr Seymour. "Respiratory failure" is a medical certificate convention. You put it down because everybody understands it and accepts it. There is no further argument, which is a handy thing from a doctor's point of view. And it is not untrue, because it is what happens when you die. You stop breathing. But it is not, of course, what causes death. That is always due to some other medical factor. But you may not want to put it down. Or, of course, you may not know. As in these cases. The problem here is that there is *no* other medical factor.'

'Shock?' suggested one of the other doctors tentatively.

'People don't usually die of shock. One has to allow for it, of course. I thought I'd better allow for it in the case of that German. I was the doctor who examined him when he was admitted, and I looked particularly for symptoms of shock. *I* would certainly have been showing them if it had been me. Going down into the water from a great height. But I couldn't find any. I thought, though, that there could

11

be delayed symptoms so I kept him in for observation. The nurses were told to keep an eye open for them. But they said there were none. Nor, I have to say, were there symptoms of anything else. I was puzzled, but about the respiratory failure there was no doubt, so I put that down on the certificate.'

'Anything in his previous history?' asked Seymour. 'So far as you know?'

The doctor shook his head.

'Nothing,' he said, 'and, actually, we do know his history. His doctor wrote to us. He's a German doctor, very thorough, and he had been keeping an eye on him because of the ballooning. He was interested in possible effects, of altitude, for instance. He had examined him both before and after ascent on a number of occasions. He said there was nothing to indicate a possibility of respiratory failure.'

The story was much the same in the cases of the other two. Here they had the medical records and again there was nothing to indicate possible respiratory failure.

Nor anything else. In each case, the doctor had been surprised when the patient had died. Each had been puzzled. Each, lacking other explanation, had put respiratory failure on the certificate. And that, after all, was what – the doctors were sure of this at least – the men had died from. But what had brought about the respiratory failure, the doctors could not say.

'I know this is unfortunate –' said one of the doctors unhappily.

'But did you not ask yourselves . . .?' said Seymour. 'When there were three?'

'Of course we did!' snapped one of the doctors.

'Not at first,' said the other British doctor. 'I mean, there was nothing to suggest that we should. They were in different parts of the hospital. The cases were quite different. You tend to think in individual terms –'

'It was only when the third case came along –'

'We went back over our notes. And over each other's notes. Even then –'

'We might not have thought there was anything amiss. I

mean, deaths do happen in hospitals. And clusters of deaths are statistically quite normal.'

'It was the fact that it was a German, I suppose.'

'And the ballooning. It made it all so much more conspicuous.'

'And that damned woman!'

'One thing we can say definitely,' said one of the doctors, 'is that this has absolutely nothing to do with cot deaths!'

'Absolutely nothing!'

'Or nursing practices,' said one of the British doctors.

'But if not . . .?' said Seymour.

The Maltese doctor nodded.

'You're right,' he said. 'You have to treat this as a possible case of murder.'

'For God's sake!' expostulated the doctor, as they stepped out into the corridor.

The man going past looked up in mild surprise.

'Dr Bartlett?' he said.

'Malia, what are you doing here?'

'I've worked here for fifty-eight years,' said the man, his tone suggesting, again, surprise at the question.

'But you don't work here now!'

'No,' agreed the man mildly. Then he stopped. 'Well,' he said, 'you could say this *is* work.'

'What is?'

'Checking on the accommodation.'

'Look, Malia, I know your theory. But you can't go round putting people's backs up!'

'I certainly wouldn't wish to do that!' said Dr Malia.

'Well, it annoys people, you know.'

'I'm sorry about that. I try not to get in the way.'

'Well, maybe, but – It's just that you're always creeping around.'

'I don't want to disturb anybody. That's why I go around quietly.'

The Maltese doctor laughed.

'You always did go around quietly, Mathias,' he said.

'Did I? I wasn't aware of that.'

'It used to frighten the nurses.'

'Oh, surely not!'

'Until they got to know you, and then they didn't mind.'

Malia looked perturbed.

'I'm sure I didn't mean to frighten them,' he said.

'Perhaps frighten is the wrong word. Disconcert, perhaps. I think you sometimes disconcerted them.'

'Because I was so quiet?'

'You used to suddenly appear from nowhere.'

'Perhaps they were busy, so they didn't notice me.'

'Perhaps.'

'Perhaps I should cough a little as I go around,' said Dr Malia, considering. 'Or sing. Just to let them know.'

'I wouldn't worry about it too much,' said the Maltese doctor. 'But, you know, Mathias, it can come as a bit of a surprise to come across you unexpectedly at all hours of the day or night.'

'I don't sleep that well these nights. You often don't when you get old.'

'There's no reason why you shouldn't get up, Mathias. But perhaps you shouldn't go around places like the hospital when you do.'

'I would have thought that was just the sort of place I *could* go around. It's a bit of a timeless place, the hospital. People are always going around. Even in the night. But I will bear in mind what you say.'

'It might make people feel happier. But, Mathias, how are you keeping in general? Apart from sleeplessness?'

'Oh, pretty well, thank you. I feel as fit as I've ever been. The important thing is to keep active.'

'Yes, I'm sure. But – it does depend a little on what you keep active doing.'

'Yes. You must keep active mentally as well as physically. I always try to do that. That's why the work I'm doing is just right.'

'The survey you're making?'

'Yes. It's physical as well as mental. I try to inspect everything in person, you see. A trained eye can tell at once if accommodation is suitable.'

'Ye-e-s.'

'And there's a social point, too. What I'm doing could prove very important if a war comes.'

'*If* it comes.'

Dr Malia laughed. 'And if it doesn't, people will just say I'm a silly old fool.'

'Well, you said it,' muttered Dr Bartlett under his breath.

'But, Malia,' said the other doctor, 'what I can't understand is what you're doing *here*. I mean, this is the one place, surely, that you don't need to come. It *is* a hospital already!'

'Of course! You're quite right. I don't really need to come here. But, you know, I've always wondered if the configuration of the wards is quite right. I'm sure it could be improved. I've been thinking about this a lot and I think I've worked out a configuration which would allow us to take in more patients. In fact, I've drawn up some plans. Would you like to –?'

'Thank you. Yes. I'd love to see them. Perhaps another time?'

'And I've got some other suggestions. We could switch round some of the units, for example. If we put Ophthalmology –'

'Oh, no!' groaned Dr Bartlett.

'It sounds very interesting,' said the Maltese doctor, deftly shepherding Dr Malia away. 'Certainly, the ideas need airing. We'll have to find a suitable time.'

'You see what I mean?' said the Inspector.

They took a *dghajsa* back to Valletta and climbed up again to the Upper Barraca Gardens. The main part of the town was on the plateau – the top of a great promontory – and from the Gardens it spread out before them. They went across to the Triq ir-Repubblika, the main street, at one end of which was the City Gate. A delicious aroma spread up all around him. The Inspector saw him sniffing.

'*Mquaret*,' he said.

The aroma came from small carts carrying shallow, bubbling oil fryers on which vendors were cooking little diamond-shaped pastry cakes filled with dates and flavoured with aniseed. It was the latter which gave the distinctive smell.

'A favourite here,' explained the Inspector.

'*Mquaret*,' repeated Seymour.

'And also you must try *kannoli*. And *kwarezimal*. And *quaghaq tal-ghasel*. It's a sort of sweet pastry made with dark treacle, semolina and candied peel.'

'Sounds –'

'– delicious,' said the Inspector. 'My wife says I have a sweet tooth. "If I do, so does everyone else!" I say.'

'*Mquaret*,' said Seymour again. And *kwarezimal*. And *quaghaq tal-ghasel*.

What sort of language was this?

'Malti,' said the Inspector with pride.

Maltese. But around him everyone was speaking not Malti but English. The doctors in the hospital had spoken English, and so had the porters and the nurses. They had spoken it naturally, as if it was their own language.

'Well, it is,' said the Inspector. 'And also Malti,' he laughed.

The shop signs were in English. The beer was English. The post boxes were the traditional English red ones. If you had been transported here by magic carpet overnight, when you woke up in the morning you would not have known you were not in England.

Except for the Malti. Which you didn't hear. And which came up only in the name of biscuits and cakes.

And there was another thing that puzzled him, too. The instructions at the port where they had docked had not been written in English. They had been in Arabic. Not in Arabic script but in an English translation of them. '*Stanna sweya*,' for instance. 'Stand to one side.' Was this for the benefit of visiting Arabs? he had asked. They had laughed at him as if he were mad. 'Maltese,' he had thought they had said; 'Malti,' he now realized, was what they had prob-

16

ably said. Had Malti some relation to Arabic? Arabic roots, or something?

He had wondered this at the port and he had wondered this again in the hospital, when he had seen the signs again. On the face of it the hospital was as English as English could be. But underneath?

Chapter Two

The German, Kiesewetter, had been put in a small room next to the nurses' office. Not in a ward.

'There was no need of that,' said the Maltese doctor. 'He hadn't, strictly speaking, been admitted. We were just putting him in for an hour or two where we could keep an eye on him. You know, to see there were no delayed symptoms. I told him we would keep him in for an hour or two and then he could go. I told him to make the most of it and have a snooze.

'"Snooze?" he said. "What is this snooze? I will take no unauthorized medication."

'"No, no," I said. "It's not medication. It's sleep. A short sleep."

'"But I do not want a sleep," he said. "I want to see if my balloon is all right."

'"It's been brought in," I said. "The police are looking at it."

'"The police?" he said. "Why the police?"

'"I expect they want to see why it came down," I said.

'"What is that to do with them?" he said. "Are they experts? A mechanic, yes, that I could understand."

'"I expect they've got mechanics," I said.

'"Ballooning mechanics?" he said. "Perhaps mechanic is not the right word. Technician, yes, that is the word. It is specialist. Yes, specialist. Specialist in balloons. I do not want ignorant oafs clambering over my balloon. People who know nothing about it. They will damage it. It costs much, a balloon."

'"I am sure they will take great care," I said.

'"It would be better if they left it alone. There are technicians back at Launch. I have my own technicians, of course. A team, yes? Specialist, all specialists. They are the ones to look at it. Not ignorant oafs, Policemen!" he said scathingly.

'"I am sure you will very shortly be reunited with your balloon," I said. "It will, meanwhile, be receiving expert care. What I am concerned about is that you should receive expert care, too."

'"But I do not need expert care," he said. "I am all right. Cannot you understand this?"

'"I very much hope that you are," I said. "I would just like to make sure."

'"But you have seen over me. Seen over – is that right? Overseen?"

'"Look over," I said. "Yes, I have looked you over. But sometimes effects don't show themselves at once. On the back, for instance."

'"Back? My back is all right."

'But I could see that this worried him.

'"Is it?" I said. "Any stiffness, for instance?"

'"Well, perhaps a little," he confessed. "But, then, my back is always like that. Always stiff, yes? A little."

'"Sometimes the effects of a jolt to the back don't emerge at once," I said. "Let's just make sure."

'Well, he went on huffing and puffing and complaining and in the end I said to him: "Look, Mr Kiesewetter, you're an expert on balloons, right?"

'"Right? Yes, that is right."

'"You know all about them, and on balloons I would not dream of contradicting you. But I, too, am an expert. On injuries and illnesses. If your balloon had landed heavily, you would want to check it. Well, you have landed heavily and I want to check you."

'Well, he saw the logic. Or perhaps it was the appeal to authority that did it. Anyway, he subsided, grumbling. But then he shot up again.

'"Where is it?" he said.

'"The balloon? Brought in to the quayside by Bighi."

'"Is there a guard on it?"

'"I expect so."

'"There must be! It must be placed at once. You must instruct the police so."

'"I'm sure it has been done, but I'll check it at once."

'He settled down, and I was just on the point of leaving when he jumped up again.

'"Boys!" he cried. "Boys!"

'"What?"

'"They're the worst. They put their hands on it!"

'"Not if there's a guard on it."

'"But is there? Is there? There will be boys. There are always boys. They come from nowhere. If there is a hole, they will put their fingers in it. They will tear it to pieces!"

'"No, no," I said. "I'll take care of that."

'Eventually, he quietened down. But it made me think that perhaps I was right to keep him in for a bit. "Boys!" he kept muttering, as I went down the corridor.'

The doctors used the room when they were on night shift. The nurses in the office adjoining would wake them if they were needed. The nurses rarely used it themselves. If they were on night shift they were usually working and there was no lying down. There were fewer nurses on duty and they were busy all the time, mostly patrolling the wards.

On the other hand they did use the office. They returned to it after every patrol to see if something had come up in their absence which required action. If no immediate action was necessary they would seize the chance to sit down and perhaps make themselves a cup of coffee or tea. It was hard being on your feet all night.

In the daytime there were more nurses around and there were usually two or three in the office. It was easy, therefore, to keep an eye on someone in the little room next door.

At least, it should have been.

Should have been?

There was a connecting door between the rooms which was normally kept open. For most of the time the German had been there it had been closed because they had thought their chatter might disturb him. But every so often one of them had looked in.

Where was the difficulty, then?

Every time they had looked in he had snapped at them. Quite rudely. So they had left him to it for a while. When they had looked in again he seemed to have fallen asleep.

In what position?

'Oh, for God's sake!' said one of the nurses, a tall, striking girl named Melinda.

Seymour was taken aback.

'When I looked in,' said the tall girl, 'he was lying on his side with his face turned away. But he was breathing. Right? I checked. That was what I was looking *for*. Right?'

What was all this about?

'And when I looked in the next time he was lying on his back. And he was dead. And it was nothing to do with the position in which he had been lying.'

After a moment he got it. She was referring to Mrs Wynne-Gurr, whose charges had evidently stung deep.

'That was not in my mind at all,' he said hurriedly. 'I was merely trying to establish the time of death.'

'You were?' said the tall girl suspiciously. 'Oh, well, it would have been sometime between three thirty and four thirty.'

'And you saw at once –?'

'You can tell. When you've had a bit of experience.'

Seymour had had plenty of experience: but that was not quite the same thing. He usually saw a body when it had been dead for some time.

'And what did you do?'

'Tried to resuscitate. And sent for Dr Docato.'

'And what did he do?'

'Joined me in trying to resuscitate. But after a while we could tell that it was useless.'

'What was his reaction?'

'He was surprised. Puzzled, I think. You could tell he was puzzled because, well, you could see him thinking. He just stood there, going through the possibilities. Eventually he shrugged and sent for the porters.'

'And what about you: were you puzzled?'

'I?' She seemed surprised.

'Yes. What did you think?'

'I don't think,' she said. 'I'm just a nurse.'

Seymour went into the other room. There was another door and he went across and tried it.

'It's locked,' said Melinda, who had followed him in. 'It's usually open, but we lock it when there's someone in there trying to get a sleep.'

'And was it locked on this occasion?'

'Yes. Especially after the German had snapped at us.'

'And what did you do with the key?'

'Put it back on the board.'

She showed him. On the wall in the nurses' office was a board hung with keys.

'This one,' she said.

'And is there another one?'

'In the porters' office.'

'So someone could have used that to get in?'

'They could,' she acknowledged. 'But why –?'

She stopped.

'I see,' she said.

Seymour smiled.

'I think nurses do think,' he said.

The porters' office was next to Reception. There were two porters.

'And that's a mistake,' said the one who was there. 'There ought to be three. I keep telling them that. You need someone to man the office when the others are out. And they're usually out, because most of what we have to do is a two-man lift.'

'What do you have to do?'

'Carry things about. Usually bodies. And that's another

mistake, because that work ought to be done by the mortuary people.'

'You move other people about, too,' said Melinda, who had gone with Seymour to show him where the porters' office was. 'When they have to change wards. Or go to a unit.'

'I don't mind that,' said the porter. 'That is the nature of the job. But even that requires two men. You might not think it, but it does. Just to get into a wheelchair. You've got to take their weight, you see. And you don't want to do that on your own, not if you want to save your back. You've got to think of these things, otherwise your back will go and you'll be of no use to anybody.'

'Stop whinging, Berto,' said Melinda.

'You'd whinge if you –'

'Bollocks!' said Melinda. 'I'm lifting people all the time. Or moving them. Turning them over.'

'And that's another thing,' said Berto. 'These nurses! They've got no respect and no sense.'

'But we do love you, Berto. You and Umberto. Berto and Umberto – they go together. A two-man whinge! And we couldn't manage without you, could we? The hospital would seize up.'

'I take back my remark about them having no sense.'

Seymour laughed. 'And you're out and about most of the time, I guess?'

'Oh, we're kept busy!'

'And while you're out the office must be unmanned and anyone could get in?'

'They could.'

'And help themselves to a key?'

'Now, wait a minute! They're not supposed to do that –'

'Do you keep a record of your jobs?'

'When people book us, we write that down. So's we know.'

'And so that you can always claim you're doing something else when we want you to do something,' said Melinda.

'Melinda, I'm going to have a word with your mother –'

Melinda laughed.

'They're quite systematic, really,' she said.

'Could I see how you book jobs in?' asked Seymour.

'How, and when,' said Melinda.

She didn't miss much, thought Seymour.

He looked at their bookings for the afternoon the German had died and, yes, they had been out of their office for considerable periods.

'Can I have a look?' asked Melinda.

'Are you setting out to move into Work Study or something?' demanded Berto.

'I'm like Dr Malia: I think things could always be improved,' said Melinda.

'Malia: that daft old bugger!' said Berto.

'So someone could have got in and taken the key,' said Melinda, handing the log-book back to Seymour.

'No they couldn't,' said Berto unexpectedly – he was another one, thought Seymour, who was sharper than at first sight. 'Because if they had tried it, they'd have Laura up their ass!'

'Laura?' said Seymour.

Laura was the receptionist. She was a middle-aged lady with her hair tied up tightly in a bun and sharp shrewd eyes.

'Yes,' she said, 'I keep an eye on things when they're out. And I wouldn't let anyone in there. What business would anyone have in the porters' office by themselves?'

'Delivering a package?' suggested Seymour.

'They would deliver it to me,' said Laura firmly.

From her position at the Reception desk she had a good view of the door into the porters' office: and also of the general entrance into the rest of the hospital.

'What is the policy about visitors?' asked Seymour.

'Most of them are sailors,' said Laura. 'This is a naval hospital,' she added with pride.

'And they can come and go pretty freely?'

'They just have to sign in.'

She showed Seymour the book. Many of them, a little self-consciously, had given their rank. Some, however, had not given their name at all, just putting down the name of their ship.

'I know all the ships,' said Laura. 'If I needed to, I could pretty soon find out who it was.'

'Not all of them are sailors,' said Seymour.

'We do take some general patients as well. Most of them are local.'

'And they sign in, too?'

'Yes.'

She showed him.

'Just their names,' said Seymour.

'I don't need anything else. They all come from around Bighi and I know their families.'

'What about strangers?'

'They have to give their addresses, look!'

And there, written in a neat, firm hand, was: 'Philippa Wynne-Gurr.' And, just beneath it, more casually: 'Dr Wynne-Gurr' with the address of a hotel.

'And son?' inquired Seymour.

'The boy? Had to be with his father. I wasn't having him wandering around the wards. Nor in the units, with all that equipment!'

'Dr Malia?'

'Oh, him! Well, he's always roaming around. But he signs in, like everyone else. Just as he used to. On the doctors' pages. He used to work here, you know. He's part of the furniture.'

'So you could tell me who was in the hospital on the afternoon of the eighteenth?'

'The day the German died?'

Here was another one who was pretty sharp.

'Yes.'

She turned over the pages.

'Can I just make a note of the names?'

'I will write them down for you.'

Seymour could see that she was a lady who liked to have everything under her control.

'Thank you. And this would be pretty comprehensive, would it?'

'The name of anyone who entered the hospital that afternoon would be here, if that's what you mean.'

Seymour looked at the book again. 'Except that there's no record of Mr Kiesewetter's arrival.'

'There is.' She showed him. 'Kiesewetter. To A and E.'

'He would have been taken straight there,' said Melinda. 'After Laura had booked him in.'

'And then he would have booked in again,' said Laura triumphantly. She looked sternly at Melinda. 'I hope.'

Melinda nodded. 'He would.'

'My guess is, though, that when he arrived, a lot of people arrived with him,' said Seymour.

'Half the island,' said Laura. 'I soon cleared them out!'

'You didn't sign *them* in?'

'No need to. They weren't going anywhere. Except out.'

'Someone must have taken him into A and E, surely?'

'We did,' said Berto. 'Umberto and me.'

'Where *is* Umberto?' asked Seymour.

Umberto was in one of the wards.

'Always on the hop, you might say.'

This time he was hopping at the behest of one of the nurses, who wanted him to move a bedside locker.

Did he remember the afternoon the German had been admitted?

He did. Not only that, he remembered his descent in the balloon. Umberto had gone outside 'for a moment' to see the balloons and he had noticed that Mr Kiesewetter was coming down. He had watched the balloon until it had come right down into the water.

'And I saw Frank get over there in his *dghajsa* and I thought: He'll bring him over here. And he did, too. I thought he might be in bad shape. Well, you'd expect it, wouldn't you, if he had come down from that height. But he seemed all right.

'In fact, a bit too fresh, if you ask me. I went to help him and he says: "Take your hands off me, my man!" His man! Who the hell did he think he was talking to? I nearly gave him a cuff instead. But if I had, they would have nailed me to the front door by my bollocks, so I just said: "Hospital staff, sir. Just helping."

'"I don't need help," he said. "My balloon came down all right."

'"It came down into the drink," I said, "and that might not have been all right."

'He pooh-poohed it. "It is neechts, my man," he said, waving his hand dismissive-like. "To come down into the trees is worse. Or on to the rocks."

'"You came down in just the right place, sir," I said. "Right in front of the hospital."

'"But I don't need –" he starts up again. Glad to get rid of him, I was.'

He turned to Melinda. 'What did the nurses do with him, love? Give him a syringe up the backside?'

'I was just going to,' said Melinda, 'when Dr Docato stopped me. I think he was sorry afterwards that he had done.'

'So who took Mr Kiesewetter to the room he was put in?' asked Seymour. 'After Dr Docato had looked at him? You, Umberto? Or a nurse?'

'Dr Docato,' said Melinda. 'With the nurse on duty. Who was me.'

'And I was sort of in attendance,' said Umberto. 'In case the bugger keeled over.'

'You put him in the little room,' said Seymour, 'and then, presumably, Umberto, you left?'

'As soon as I could,' said Umberto.

'And you, Melinda?'

'I waited until Dr Docato had settled him down and left. And then I went in to make sure everything was all right.'

'And?'

'He snapped my head off.'

'At some point the door into the corridor was locked, I take it?'

'Yes.'

27

'When was that? After Dr Docato left? Did he lock it?'

'No, I locked it. That was one of the things I was making sure was right.'

'So that he wouldn't be disturbed?'

'As I explained to him.'

'And then you put the key back on the board?'

'That's right.'

'Was the nurses' office left empty at any point?'

Melinda considered.

'If it was,' she said, 'it wouldn't have been for very long.'

'But it could have been?'

'Yes, but I don't think anyone could have counted on that. If that's what you were thinking.'

'That is what I was thinking. But I agree with you. It would have been too risky. But you see what that means, don't you? If anyone went in, it would have been by the other door.'

'Using the other key.'

'Yes.'

'If, of course, anyone went in at all. Have you thought that there might be another explanation? That he simply died of heart failure. From normal medical causes.'

But would three men have done so? In such a short space of time? The argument kept coming back to this.

The other two men who had died had been in general wards. There would have been other patients around them and Seymour couldn't see how they could have been attacked in their beds without someone seeing. If they had been attacked.

One of the two had died during the night, which made an attack more plausible. He consulted Melinda about the arrangements for night nursing.

In the bigger wards there was a night nurse on duty all the time. She had a desk at one end of the ward, at which she sat when she was not being called to one of the beds.

All the time?

Well, not quite all the time. At certain points during the

28

night when things were quiet they would slip out to the nurses' office for a quick cup of something.

Would these points be regular? That is, could the nurse be depended on to be absent at that time?

Melinda thought not. There were so many little things that might come up. You just went when it seemed the best moment.

Still, there was a point in the night when the nurse would be absent and an intruder might come in at that point?

Melinda was doubtful. They would have to be watching for the nurse to depart and where would they be while they were doing that? Anybody hanging about would be questioned by the nurse.

And how would they get in anyway? When Laura was off duty, Reception was manned by the porter on duty. But there were also, always, the nurses in A and E who worked in shifts and there was a certain amount of socializing if things weren't too busy. And on the whole they weren't busy. This was a naval hospital and the flow of patients, largely, was restricted. It wasn't, said Melinda, like a big London hospital.

And what about the porters?

Berto and Umberto took it in turns to work nights. They didn't mind working nights because there wasn't usually much to do. They could have a nice chat with the nurses and the people on Reception, come in on the cups of tea, and have a good kip, which they couldn't do at home because there were babies around and you were up half the night. Besides, said Melinda, they could call in assistance.

Assistance?

Laura's boy and his cousin. And young Fred from round the corner. And other members of the families of hospital staff. Seymour soon realized that there was a great web of family connections around the hospital. Jobs were not that plentiful in Malta and once you were in somewhere you had to do the best you could for other members of your family. It was open to abuse but it was also a source of strength. As here. For if someone fell down on the job,

Laura was on to the family in no time and then the whole family was on the offender's back. It was remarkable, said Melinda, how conscientious people became in these circumstances. So, no, there was no slackness in the system at nights. Indeed, it was the other way. For if Berto or Umberto should show signs of falling off, they would immediately be put right by young Peter or Johnnie, and that would be reported back to the family, too.

It reminded Seymour of the East End, where he normally worked. Step out of line, over a girl, say, and the next moment the sky would drop in on you.

And Melinda herself, he asked curiously: did she belong to a family, too? She certainly did; but they were up in Gozo to the north of the island, which was a long way away, and absolutely fine by Melinda, who had come down to Valletta for precisely that reason.

The impression Seymour was getting was that the human web of which the hospital was the centre spread a sort of protective film over the hospital. Everybody knew everybody – everyone was probably related to everyone – and the hospital was like not a Big Brother but a small brother whom everybody in the family had to watch over and see that it came to no harm. It was very effective. And yet somebody *had* breached the film.

If they had.

It was time, he thought, to home in on the most specific of the charges: that made by the sailors. He had arranged for them to be sent to the hospital and saw them one by one.

The first was a Londoner named Cooper. He was the one who had volunteered the supplementary information about what he had seen one night in the hospital at Singapore. Seymour had hopes of him. He had evidently a propensity to say too much.

This morning, however, he was on his guard.

'I'm not saying that's what I saw,' he said. 'I'm saying that's what I thought I saw.'

'Oh, yes?' said Seymour encouragingly.

'Yes. We went past that quickly.'

'You could see into the ward, though?'

'Yes. There was no door nor nuffing.'

'And you looked in?'

'Sort of glanced. As we were going past. I was going to give him a bit of a wave.'

'To cheer him up?'

'That's right. Poor bugger needed it, with his jaw all wired up like that.'

'You had called in on him earlier, of course?'

'That's right. We'd just dropped in to see how he was getting on, like.'

'And how did you find him?'

'All right. He'd had the wiring done that morning and his face was all swelled up. Like a football. He could hardly speak. We asked him if he'd like a fag and he just shook his head. But we gave him one all the same.'

'Could he manage it?'

'Not really. He had a puff or two and then put it by. Said he'd come back to it. So we knew he wasn't feeling too good.'

'But – how shall I put it – not too bad, either?'

'No. We said we were going to look up a little nurse we knew and asked him, by way of a joke, if he'd like to come along. "You bet!" he said. We knew he was all right, really. Still, he didn't come along. Tried to, but then thought better of it. "What's the use?" he said. "With me face in a cage?"'

'He seemed pretty all right, then. So were you surprised the next day that you heard –?'

'That he was dead? You could have knocked me down with a feather! "What, old Bob?" I said. "Why, he seemed as right as rain when I saw him yesterday!" And that's what Pete and Joe said, too. Right as rain! And then I got to thinking. "That's how he was *then*," I said. "What's in your mind, Terry?" said Pete. "If he was fit as a fiddle one day, how come he was dead as a doornail the next? It don't seem right. It doesn't happen like that." "No more it does," said Joe.

31

'So, as I say, we got to thinking. Went over it in our minds, like. And it was then that I remembered.'

'What was it exactly that you remembered?'

'Just a glimpse. That's all it was. But there was this bloke bending over him with a pillow. Well, then we went on and thought no more about it till the next day. And then my mind went back.'

'To what happened in the Singapore hospital?'

'What I *heard* happened in the Singapore hospital. There were these blokes, see. And one of them was that heavy a snorer that the others couldn't get to sleep. Night after night. It got them down. They tried everything in waking him up, putting a sock in his mouth, putting a peg on his nose – but nothing worked. And it went on night after night. And in the end it really got them down. *Really* down. So one of them says: "Look, either he's got to go or I've got to go." And they was that desperate by then that they said: "Look, give him a warning, and then if he still does it –" So that's what they did. Put a pillow over his head. And . . .'

'And?' prompted Seymour.

'Nothing came of it.'

'Nothing came of it? He didn't die? Then –'

'No, no,' said Cooper impatiently. 'He died, all right. But there was no follow-up. Nothing happened. Like here. The docs signed the certificate and that was the end of it. No one heard nothing more.'

'I see,' said Seymour.

'Happens all the time,' said Cooper expanding.

'When people are snoring –'

'No. No. When they're in hospital. People are dying all the time, and no one knows why. So they just cover it up. The doc signs the certificate and that's the end of it. No questions asked. Finis, like it says in the Bible.'

'Yes, but in this case questions *are* being asked.'

'Ah, well –'

'Partly because of what you said you saw.'

'Not saw. Heard.'

'But you said that you saw someone bending over Bob –'

'Not saw: might have seen.'

32

'With a pillow.'

'Could have been a pillow. Might not have been. It was that quick.'

'Are you sure that you saw anything at all?'

'We-e-ll . . . All I'm saying,' said Cooper, 'is that there was something fishy about it.'

'Right, well, thank you, Mr Cooper.'

'Glad to help,' said the seaman, getting up.

Seymour got up, too.

'Oh, by the way,' he said, 'can I just confirm one point in what you said?'

'Pleasure.'

'You said you saw a bloke bending over him?'

'Ye-e-s . . .' said Cooper guardedly.

'A bloke. Not a nurse.'

'Some of the nurses here are blokes.'

'Was it one of them?'

Cooper seemed for the first time genuinely to be thinking. He hesitated.

'No-o-o,' he said at last. 'I don't think so.'

'But a bloke?'

'A bloke,' said Cooper. 'Definite.'

Equally definite was the second seaman, Corke.

'Bent right over poor Bob, he was. A biggish bloke. Sort of hunched.'

'Hunched?'

'Like in the picture.'

He put his hand in his pocket and pulled out a comic paper. There, on the page, was a scantily dressed, implausibly nubile girl. And there, bending over her, was an implausibly grotesque, hunchbacked man.

'Like him.'

Able Seaman Price, fair-headed, rosy-faced, and with a marked Somersetshire accent, had actually witnessed the original fight in the bar.

'A mere bleedin' tap!' he said, in astonished tones. 'That's all it was! You'd have thought it was nothing. But the next day his face was all swelled up.'

They had taken him to the doc and the doc had said his jaw was broken.

'And then they had put that wire right round his head. Sort of to keep the jaw together.'

He had said he was all right, though, and had reckoned that he could be out the next day. But when they went to see, the next time they were in, he was still there. The doc hadn't got round yet. He had gone on with the others to find Suzie. He hadn't really noticed anything on the way back. But Terry -

'And you yourself?'

'Not, sort of, to notice. But Terry –'

It was only afterwards, when they got talking, that the thought had come.

Seymour was inclined to doubt whether any of them had seen anything.

Chapter Three

The voice was not exactly loud but penetratingly clear. It came from the Registrar's office, the door of which had been left ajar so that the air could circulate.

'There will be fifteen of us,' it was saying. 'No, sixteen now, an extra one has just joined.'

'*Sixteen*?' said another voice, a man's voice, incredulously. 'That's rather a large number!'

'Not when spread over the whole hospital.'

'The *whole* hospital?'

'Yes. They could go to different wards and then change around.' ·

'Even so –'

'And then, of course, we'd all like to see the specialist units. My husband says that the Ophthalmics here is particularly good.'

'Yes, well, thank you. Or him. We are always glad to welcome a colleague. But, you know,' – determinedly – 'a colleague is one thing, a party of . . .'

'Yes?' said Mrs Wynne-Gurr.

'Well, *general* visitors, shall we say –'

'Oh, we're not quite general visitors. We have a lot of expertise and experience among us.'

'– is another,' finished the Registrar.

'As I say, we have quite a lot of –'

'But, Mrs Wynne-Gurr, this is not really a question of First Aid, it's sort of Second Aid. All our nurses are trained and qualified –'

'Of course they are! And quite right, too! That is what I keep saying to Headquarters. Nursing should be a profession alongside other professions, and for that to happen, the highest standards must be maintained. I quite understand your concern, Mr Ormskirk.'

'Oh, good –'

'But you need have no worries on that score. We would not dream of interfering. We would just help with the humbler things. No duty too humble for us, Mr Ormskirk. We are here just to watch and learn.'

'Well, thank you. That's very nice. But –'

'Here is the list of names. There are sixteen of them now. As I said, an extra one has just joined. When she heard about the Maltese visit she was particularly anxious to come. She's from Tangier –'

Tangier, thought Seymour? *Tangier*? Surely –

'And is thinking of starting up a branch here.'

It couldn't be! Surely!

'She will be a great asset,' said Mrs Wynne-Gurr. 'And it will be very helpful for her to see another branch in action. I have written her name at the bottom. Miss de Lissac.'

Miss de Lissac? It *was* Chantale! How the hell had she managed to attach herself to the party? She was not a member of the St John Ambulance. To the best of his knowledge she had never heard of it. How had she got to know –?

He realized, with sinking heart, how she had got to know. He himself had told her.

Outside the hospital the boy was sitting morosely, looking at the ships in the harbour. He had plainly decided that he wasn't interested in them, either.

'Have they thrown you out?' said Seymour.

'More or less,' said the boy.

'Ophthalmics no good?'

'Been there, done that,' said the boy.

'What haven't you done?'

'The Armouries. They've been closed ever since we got here.'

36

'Too bad. Why are they closed?'

'They're rearranging things in the Apartments. The trouble is,' said the boy, 'they were what my project was going to be on.'

'The school set you a project?'

The boy nodded. 'As part of the deal. They would let me off a week early so that I could come out here. But I would have to do a project.'

'Couldn't you do it on something else?'

'I could, but I wanted to do it on weaponry. Dr Malia suggested I do it on the Infermeria. But I've gone off hospitals.'

He looked at Seymour. 'You're a policeman, aren't you? Investigating those murders.'

'If they are murders, yes.'

'I wouldn't mind doing a project on that.'

'You wouldn't find much to go on.'

'But that would be the point, wouldn't it? That would be real research. Not just looking up something in a book which everybody knows already.'

He walked along beside Seymour.

'I wouldn't mind being a policeman,' he said.

'It's not all like that,' cautioned Seymour.

'Are you CID?'

Seymour nodded.

'I wouldn't mind being in the CID.'

'You don't usually go there straight away.'

'Have you done other murders?'

'It's not all murders, of course.'

'Still!'

He was quiet for a moment.

'And what about these murders?' he said then. 'In the hospital?'

'We don't know they are murders yet.'

'My mum doesn't think they're murders.'

'No?'

'She thinks they're just incompetence. But, then, she thinks that most things that go wrong are just incompetence.'

'She may have a point!'

'But Dr Malia thinks they *are* murders. He says that deaths in a hospital don't happen just like that. He says the nurses are perfectly competent. And so are the doctors. They're deliberate, he says. But I say, how can they be? You've got to have a reason for killing somebody. And if you've got three deaths, you have to have three separate reasons. And that seems unlikely. But Dr Malia says there might not be three separate reasons, there might be just one reason. He says there is a certain type of person who is drawn to people lying there helpless and in certain circumstances they might want to kill them. But that's not a very nice thought, is it?'

'It certainly isn't. And while that may occasionally be true, it's not true very often.'

'But it could be true, couldn't it?'

'Oh, it *could* be true.'

'That's what I told my mum. And she said that wasn't a nice thing to think, and that I'd better stay away from Dr Malia if he's putting thoughts like that into my head.'

A girl down by the landing stage waved at him.

'That's Sophia. She's got a project, too.'

'What's hers on?'

'The Victoria Lines. But it's a waste of time, she says, because we know all about them. They were built at the end of the last century and we know who built them: the British. They were intended to protect Valletta from a land attack from the north. Sort of like Hadrian's Wall. But Sophia says that was a daft thing to do because all they had to do was sail round them.'

'Sounds logical!'

'She says they're good for walking on, though. You can see for miles. She says she'd take me. We could have a picnic.'

'It sounds a nice idea. Is she out here for a holiday, too?'

'No, she's here all the time. She's Maltese. What do you think of the Maltese?'

'They seem all right.'

'That's what I think, too. But my mum says: just be careful because they might not be. But she said that about Dr Malia too, and he's a doctor.'

'I think a schoolgirl might be all right.'

They were lying there in neat rows, a row down each side of the ward. The beds were neat, too, with the ends of the blankets tucked neatly in. Beside each bed was a small locker and they were neat as well. The tops were kept clear. A glass was allowed to stand there but only a glass. Everything else, presumably, had to be kept inside.

This was a naval hospital, of course and a disciplined place. But Seymour had a suspicion that the order was due less to the Navy than it was to the ward sister, a thin, redoubtable lady named Miss Chisholm.

'You keep it all shipshape,' he said.

She smiled.

'I do,' she said.

She said she had worked for the Navy all her life. Her last posting had been in a hospital in Cyprus. She liked working abroad, she said. The nurses were often better. There weren't many jobs around for women so you got applicants of higher quality. And, no, they didn't all run away to get married. They knew what marriage for many women was like and that they would be better off as a nurse; at least until they were thirty.

But, surely, in a place like this they would have plenty of offers?

'Oh, yes. The girls keep a league table pinned up in the nurses' room. But every nurse knows that when a man is lying there he's particularly susceptible. And that when he can get up . . .'

'Less?'

She smiled. 'It's time for him to go.'

'And you yourself . . .?'

'Bottom of the league.'

She remembered the day well, and was scathing about the seamen's suggestion.

'This was an able-bodied seaman. Able-bodied in all senses. He had just been fighting in a waterfront bar. Yes, he'd been knocked about; but are you telling me he would have let himself be overpowered by a nurse? It's usually the other way round.'

'A man, then?'

'Yes, but what man? As far as I'm concerned, there are only three sorts of men: patients, staff and visitors. We do have porters and orderlies, of course. We call them in if we want things moved around. But they don't come into my ward unless I say so. And that afternoon I didn't say so.'

'Visitors?' prompted Seymour.

'I'm not against visitors, particularly in a place like this. It often does the lads good to see their mates. But you've got to keep on eye on things. Otherwise they can get out of hand. You've no idea what they'll get up to. Or what they think is a good thing to cheer up their mates. A bottle, usually. If you don't watch out, in no time there's a party going on. So I make a point of walking through the ward when we've got visitors. And no bottles come in on my watch, I can tell you.

'I tell them, too. "Your mate wouldn't be here unless he was ill," I say. "And if you give him drink, he'll be iller. When he's out, he can drink as much as he wants. And so can you. But while you're in here it's got to be cut out. You go by my rules here. Chisholm's Rules, they call it, and while I'm in charge they're the rules we go by. Got it?" They usually do.'

'And that afternoon . . .?'

'Three visitors together. All seamen. Cooper, Corke and Price. They've been here before and they know the rules. That doesn't mean, of course, that they won't try and break them. But I'm an old hand and they respect that. Anyway,' she said, laughing, 'I know them of old. I knew Cooper when he was on the Singapore station. And I don't mind them. They cheer people up.'

'They say that on their way back, after seeing someone else, they went past the door of the ward and saw some-one bending over a patient – their mate – with a pillow –'

'Nurses are always bending over patients. And sometimes with a pillow.'

'This wasn't a nurse.'

'No?' She thought for a moment. 'Cooper, Corke and
Price are not altogether reliable, you know.'

'I didn't think for a moment that they were. Never-
theless . . .'

She thought again. 'I could ask around, if you like. The
other nurses. And the patients nearby.'

'It might be helpful.'

'Well, it might be more helpful if I did it rather than you
did it. I don't mean to be rude, but most of the patients are
seamen, and the lower deck tends to be suspicious of the
police. No doubt with good reason.'

'Might they not be equally distrustful of everyone in
authority?'

'They might,' she conceded. 'And that is why I shall conduct my inquiries through the nurses. Who are *not* viewed
in quite the same way, especially if they are young and
pretty!'

The third person to die had died during the night. Here,
again, there was a redoubtable ward sister. She was called
Macfarlane; not Mrs or Miss Macfarlane, or even Jane
Macfarlane; just Macfarlane. She seemed to be in charge of
the ward both days and nights. It was *her* ward, she
explained. Yes, there was a night nurse but Macfarlane,
who had a long naval history behind her and seemed by
now to have watch-keeping built into her, sometimes gave
her 'a turn below'.

How about on the night in question?

Not that night, in fact. She had been out with friends.
She would certainly have looked in but she had this
previous engagement. She had asked the senior nurse to
look in instead. She had done so and then reported that
everything seemed all right. The duty nurse had actually
mentioned Wilson, the injured sailor, to her. She had said
that he seemed restless, asleep but lightly, and talking in

41

his sleep. She wondered if she should administer a sedative but the senior nurse had advised not.

And then had left?

Yes, but no one had been remiss. The night nurse had made her rounds; and it was during one of these that she had found that the seaman had stopped breathing. She had immediately tried to resuscitate. It could have been, she thought, only a short time before that he had died.

And had she been aware of any intruder?

No, and there had better not be an intruder. Not even the sort that were usually smuggled in: young women. Macfarlane was fierce about this.

'Even when they're half dead, they think they can carry on as they normally do. But they can't. "Do you want to die?" I ask. "It would be a good way to go!" they usually reply. And the girls are no better. So we have strict rules against anybody entering the ward at night.'

While Seymour was wandering around the ward checking how they might have done, he noticed himself being observed by a patient close to the bed in which the seaman had died. He spoke to him but the man turned over on to his side without replying.

'I wondered if he had understood me,' he said to Macfarlane.

'Oh, yes, he understood you, all right,' she said.

'Then . . . ?'

'He's like that. About the British especially.'

'How does he manage when he's on board?'

'He's not usually on board. He keeps a small shop. We take in some patients from the locality who are not Navy. This one thought he had trouble with his appendix. It's not that, I'm afraid.'

Seymour was about to walk on when he stopped. 'Does it give him pain?'

'He says it does.'

'During the night?'

'Occasionally, certainly.'

'Keep him awake?'

42

Macfarlane hesitated. Then she spoke to the man in Maltese.

'All the time, he says. But he's a bit of a grumbler.'

'Ask him if he saw anything the night Wilson died.'

Macfarlane addressed the man. He shook his head.

'No,' she said. She hesitated, however. 'You know,' she said, 'although I speak Maltese, I do not speak it that well. I'd better get one of the nurses.'

She went off and came back with a nurse Seymour recognized: Melinda.

The man's eyes lit up when he saw her. They talked together for a little while. Then Melinda turned to Seymour.

'No,' she said. 'He didn't see anything.'

'Oh, well, thanks –'

'And says he wouldn't have told you if he had.'

'Oh? Why?'

'He doesn't like there being English on the island.'

Seymour shrugged.

'Most Maltese like the Navy,' said Melinda. 'It brings money into the island. But some don't. They don't like the British running things, they think they should run them themselves.'

'Good luck to them,' said Seymour.

'I rather think that way myself.'

'Fancy yourself as a matron?'

'I do, actually.'

'I wish you luck. But, you know, there might not be a hospital on the island if the Navy went away.'

'There would always be a hospital on the island. Although, I grant you, not so many.'

She turned back to the man in the bed.

They talked again. Then Melinda made a little gesture and turned away.

The man smiled and made the gesture, too. Then he lay back on his pillow.

Melinda led Seymour away.

'He says he saw nothing,' she said. 'But I don't think he's telling the truth.'

'I was watching him,' said Seymour, 'and I don't think he was telling the truth, either.'

'I don't think he was lying,' said Melinda, 'but I don't think he was telling the truth. Not all of it. He saw something. Or heard something. And he's not saying what it was. It may have been little, whatever it was. But whatever it was, he's not going to tell us.'

Seymour looked back at the man. He was lying there watching them. As he saw Seymour looking at him he raised a hand in acknowledgement and smiled. A smile, thought Seymour, of triumph?

She buttonholed him as he came out of the hospital.

'Mr Seymour?'

'Mrs Wynne-Gurr?'

They shook hands.

'My son tells me you are a policeman?'

'That is correct.'

'Out here to investigate the dreadful things that have been happening in the hospital?'

'If dreadful things have been happening in the hospital.'

'Are not three deaths dreadful enough?'

'Deaths are always dreadful.'

'But *three*, Mr Seymour. Three!'

'Let us not jump to conclusions, Mrs Wynne-Gurr.'

'And let us not evade the uncomfortable truth!'

'I am not aware of evading any uncomfortable truth, Mrs Wynne-Gurr.'

'Not you, perhaps,' she conceded. 'Yet. But has there not been slackness and a refusal to acknowledge facts?'

'I don't know. That remains to be seen.'

'I hope you are not going to join the general cover-up, Mr Seymour?'

'I am sure that if I did you would do your best to rip the cover off, Mrs Wynne-Gurr.'

Unexpectedly she laughed.

'I sometimes feel that I do give that impression,' she admitted.

When she smiled and lost some of her intensity she was not unattractive, Seymour thought.

'I gather you are bringing a party here,' he said.

'Yes. And one of the things I must not let us do is get distracted from the main purpose of the visit.'

'Which is?'

'To look into the origins of our Association. The St John Ambulance, you know.'

'Most interesting. But there is not exactly a direct line from the Knights to the present-day Association –'

'That is what my son says. "You're not really anything to do with the original Knights, Mum," he says. Almost accusingly. "Not quite directly," I say. "But in spirit."'

She looked at Seymour. 'And that is surely the point here, isn't it, Mr Seymour? Three men have died. *Someone* had to speak up.'

Seymour had some sympathy for her position: although he felt that it probably took a lot of living with on the part of her husband and son.

Down by the water he could see the remains of the German's balloon. It had been hauled on to the land and allowed to deflate. But now the police were reinflating it part by part and studying its surface. On the shore two men, probably Kiesewetter's technicians, were watching glumly.

'For Christ's sake!' one of them muttered. 'Don't you people know anything?'

'Keep off!' the other one shouted suddenly in anguish. 'Watch your shoes!'

The Inspector he had previously met came across to him smiling.

'Already,' he said, 'we have discovered something.'

He took Seymour over to the balloon and showed him a great rent in its surface.

'This is what brought it down,' he said. 'The question is: tear or cut?'

'Tear,' said one of Kiesewetter's technicians. 'Probably

after it hit the water. While you guys were mucking around with it.'

'Cut,' said the Inspector. 'With a knife or razor. Before take-off.'

'Ridiculous!' said the other technician. 'No one was allowed near it before take-off.'

'And we went over it,' said the other technician, 'inch by inch.'

'Do you think we would let anyone fly it if it was like this?'

'It probably wasn't like this,' said the Inspector. 'Not while it was on the ground. It was probably very small, perhaps just a little nick. Which enlarged during the flight.'

'Little nicks are what we look out for,' said one of the technicians.

'There was no nick and no tear and no cut,' said the other technician. 'Not before take-off.'

'How do you account for the hole, then?' asked the Inspector.

'Propeller blade on the *dghajsa*,' suggested one of the technicians. 'While it was towing it in.'

'Ridiculous!' snapped the Inspector.

'Why do *you* think it came down?' asked Seymour.

The technician shrugged.

'Couldn't say,' he said. 'Not until we've gone over it.'

'Could be the valve,' said the other technician. 'It came down slowly. I was watching it and it seemed all right at first. But then, when it got over the harbour, it began to drift lower.'

'I could see something was wrong,' said the other technician, 'but it looked as if he could handle it.'

'But then, at the end, it came down quite sharply,' said the first technician. 'So I reckon he was bringing it down. He knew he'd be all right on the water. One of the safest places to land.'

'And he was all right, wasn't he?' said the other technician. 'It was only afterwards that –'

'In the hospital,' said the other technician.

* * *

46

Seymour walked over to where the Inspector was standing looking down on the balloon. Half of it was in the water and half was on the land. The police were drawing it up inch by inch so that they could go over it minutely. They were, he thought, doing a thorough job.

'You think there was an attack on his life before he got to the hospital,' he said.

'I do,' said the Inspector.

'Why?'

The Inspector motioned down at the rent in the balloon's surface.

'This,' he said. 'I believe what they said, that they checked everything. They're conscientious men. They wouldn't have missed anything.'

'But they *did* miss something. You think.'

'I was there on the racetrack when the balloons were launched. Yes, they were keeping people away, but there were many balloons and lots of technicians. And just at that point they were running around like crazy. It would have been easy for a technician on another balloon to pick his moment, just as they were launching – and after they'd done the checks – and make a little cut. A little one would do. The pressure inside would do the rest.'

'So you think it was sabotage on the part of a rival?'

'I think it could be. These people are very competitive, you know.'

'*That* competitive?'

The Inspector shrugged. 'I go to Marsa racetrack every weekend. My wife likes to see the horses. Everyone likes to see the horses. Half of Malta goes. And the races! Talk about rivalry! I tell you, I see more than this –' he gestured at the rent balloon – 'every Saturday!'

'But he died in the hospital,' said Seymour. 'Are you saying that a rival followed him here?'

The Inspector shrugged. 'It seems unlikely, I know. But I've seen these sportsmen! And is it more unlikely than someone creeping into the hospital and . . . I mean, without any apparent motive. I believe in motive. In my experience, when people kill, they do it for a reason. This at least suggests a reason.'

'Two other men died,' said Seymour.

'They died, yes,' said the Inspector, 'but were they killed? Whereas in the case of the German –' he looked down at the rent balloon – 'there is independent reason to suggest an attempt to kill.'

When Chantale stepped off the boat in Valletta she was still under the spell of recovering the Mediterranean. The recovery had begun the moment the train had got south of the Loire and continued as it went south to Marseilles. The clouds suddenly cleared away, the sky became that marvellous blue that she had grown up under, the sun –

The sun. She had forgotten about the sun and the difference it made: in your bones, in your heart, in your mind. Why had she ever left it? The past winter in London had been like living in a dark tunnel with no end to it. It cramped you, chilled you, stiffened you all over. And also inside. Chantale suddenly realized that she had been stiffened inside too. Why had she ever agreed to leave Tangier?

She knew very well why she had left Tangier. Seymour. Well, she didn't regret that. At least, not deep down. For the sake of their life together she would put up with the tunnel. But, oh, it was good to get out of it occasionally!

When Seymour had told her he was being sent to the Mediterranean for a time, she had at once assumed that she would go with him. She had been unable to understand it when he had said that she couldn't. There were the rules, yes; but surely rules were meant to be broken? Or at least, slid round. She had grown up in the Arab world and in a military world and had imbibed early the understanding that to live in those worlds, particularly if you were a woman, you had to show a certain agility.

So when Seymour had told her about Mrs Wynne-Gurr and the projected visit of the St John Ambulance to Malta she had at once seen the possibilities. She hadn't been too sure what the St John Ambulance was: something to do with ambulances, obviously. Well, she wasn't against ambulances, she thought that on the whole they were a good thing, so if enthusiasm for ambulances would get her back to the sunshine of the Mediterranean enthusiastic she would be.

She then learned that it wasn't just ambulances, or even necessarily ambulances at all, but by then she had the bit between her teeth. How did you join forces with this St John Ambulance? Well, Seymour's sister explained, you joined the local Association. Just around the corner? Perfect. Well, not so perfect, actually, because this branch of the Association was not going to Malta.

The Association's Headquarters, however, was in London and she went there. A possible recruit? Excellent! and from . . . Tangier, was it? They had never had a recruit from Tangier. Might not this open up possibilities? Chantale cottoned on at once. What was in her mind, she said, was the possibility of opening a branch in Tangier.

Even more excellent! But first she would like to see how a branch operated. Might she not visit –? Most certainly! There was a very lively branch in Wigan –

Wigan?

Up in the north.

That was *not* what Chantale had had in mind. Fortunately, there was a lady visiting Headquarters at the time who came from the sunnier climes of West Surrey. She was, in fact, a member of the West Surrey Branch, tying up a few last things, in Mrs Wynne-Gurr's absence, Mrs Wynne-Gurr having gone ahead to prepare the way, to do with the scheduled visit to Malta. She and Chantale got talking.

West Surrey seemed a much more suitable place for a visit than darkest Lancashire and this was confirmed in Chantale's mind when the lady spoke glowingly of the lovely Surrey greensward.

Sword?

Obviously something to do with the Knights, although the lady had pronounced it in a slightly funny way. Dialect perhaps. Chantale spoke English well but would be the first to admit that she hadn't properly attuned to all the dialect variations of that most exasperating of languages.

But, clearly, she was on the trail. She asked the lady if she might attend the next branch meeting. Flattered, the lady invited her to come down on the following Wednesday. Among the matters discussed was the right sort of clothes to be worn for the visit. Here Chantale, with her experience of the Mediterranean, could be of great help. The thick uniform worried her, she had to admit. When she started her branch in Tangier they would have to look for something lighter –

Branch in Tangier? The ladies were all of a flutter. Perhaps it might be possible to pull Tangier and Malta together in some unspecified way. Lessons would surely be learnt.

They surely could. But, alas, – Chantale sighed – she would not be going to Malta with them.

But that was no problem! No problem at all. There was room for another one on the party. There might even be the possibility of a small grant towards expenses, given the possibilities Chantale's attendance might open up for the advance of St John in North Africa, if that was where Tangier was.

This was more than Chantale had dared to hope. She had only a very little money of her own and Seymour would go berserk if she exhausted their joint account on some unagreed private initiative.

Fired with enthusiasm for things ambulatory – if that was the right word for an adjective derived from 'Ambulance' – she even considered the possibility of actually starting a branch in Tangier. It could certainly, on the basis of her experience, do with one.

So Chantale joined the party and went with it by train across France and then by boat across to Malta.

And there, of course, on disembarkation at Valletta, she had been struck by the Arabic language all around her. She felt that, in a way, she had come home.

Chapter Four

He caught sight of her when he returned to the hotel. She was standing in the middle of a group of sensibly dressed, middle-aged women who could only be Mrs Wynne-Gurr's Ambulance Militant.

He edged towards her; she edged away.

'What do you think you're doing?' he whispered.

'Come to join you,' she whispered back.

'Yes. I can see that. But –'

'I thought you would like it.'

'Well, I do. But –'

'I thought,' said Chantale accusingly, 'that it would be what you wanted.'

'Well, it is, but –'

'*Don't* you want me?' said Chantale, putting him as usual on the wrong foot.

'Of course I want you! But –'

'You keep it well hidden,' said Chantale.

'Look, I want you. But not when I'm at work.'

'You wanted me when you were at work in Barcelona.'

'Not when I was at work. I thought I might sort of fit it in. As a break.'

'That's not what you said.'

'Briefly.'

'You said forever. And talked me into coming back with you to London. Don't you want me any more?'

'Of course I want you. But not when I'm at work.'

'I don't *often* come to you when you're at work. I don't come to you in London, do I?'

'No, and I should bloody hope not.'

51

'It's only when you work in *interesting* places. I want to share them with you.'

'Yes, well, that's very nice, and I would like to share them with you, too. But not when I'm working.'

'But that's the only chance we get to go away together!'

'No, it's not. I've suggested going on holiday together somewhere.'

'Brighton.'

'Well, that's all I can afford. We've got to be realistic.'

'Or ingenious,' said Chantale. 'All I am doing is being ingenious.'

'Unscrupulous.'

'Ingenious is the way I prefer to think of it. And it's worked. I can slip along the corridor and –'

But there's many a slip between slip and lip.

'I see you know each other,' said Mrs Wynne-Gurr.

'Run into each other somewhere,' muttered Seymour.

'In Tangier, I think,' said Chantale demurely.

'In Tangier? Oh, how exciting! I wonder if you know, Mr Seymour, that Miss de Lissac hopes to start a branch of the Association in Tangier? We're very thrilled about it. And of course, we would want to give her all the help we can. She will see a lot about our work while she's here, and it will be particularly useful to study a branch in a place like Malta. I'm sure you will learn a great deal.'

'Oh, good,' said Seymour. 'But –'

But Mrs Wynne-Gurr had done with social niceties and moved back to business.

'If you'll just come over here, dear, I'll give you the name and address of the people you're going to stay with.'

'Stay with? I'm not going to stay in the hotel?'

'Well, no. Didn't I make that clear? I'm going to farm you out to members of the local branch and let you stay with them. That way you will get to know the people of the island and form an idea, from the inside, of how this branch works. That should be especially valuable to you, Miss de Lissac, for it may be that the conditions you experience will be closer to those you will encounter in Tangier than, say, the ones you would experience in West Surrey.'

Chantale's eye caught his as she departed; disconcerted, but not, on the whole, dissatisfied.

'It may, of course, not be quite what you are used to,' said Mrs Wynne-Gurr, as they stopped in front of the door of the house. It was one of a row of identical small houses in a poor street not far from the harbour.

It was, in fact, exactly what Chantale was used to, for Seymour's pay did not extend to anything better than rented rooms in the part of London's dockland where his mother and grandparents still lived. Admittedly, coils of fog did not surround this house, as in East London they were likely to do, and at the end of the street there was a glimpse of blueness sparkling in the sun. But that, for Chantale, was an important improvement.

The door was opened by a small, homely lady full of bird-like energy, which was just as well in view of the large number of faces crowding behind her. Most of them belonged to children, small, brown-faced, dark-eyed and clearly hyperactive.

'Mrs Ferreira?'

They were shown into the front parlour. It was already occupied by a boy and a girl, both about fourteen. There were pages of writing paper scattered all over the table and books all over the floor.

'Rosalie,' said Mrs Ferreira, to one of the little girls who had followed them into the room, 'could you show the lady to her room?'

'I'd better do it,' said the girl already in the parlour. 'My things are still spread about a bit.'

'Have I taken your room?' said Chantale.

'That's all right. It's just that I've been working on a project and my stuff is everywhere.'

'I'd better clear my things, too,' said the boy apologetically. 'I've got a project, too, and Sophia has been helping me with it.'

'Isn't this the holidays?'

'The bastards are never off your back,' said the girl.

'Sophia!' said Mrs Ferreira, shocked.

The boy was clearly a little shocked too. He hastily picked up some of the books.

'Back in a moment,' said the girl. She took Chantale upstairs into a tiny room most of which was filled with school books and girl's clothes.

'Rosalie has already moved her stuff out,' said Sophia. 'But that was just dresses and things.'

She opened the door of a wardrobe. 'That end was hers and now it's for you. I'll clear the other end.'

'It's all right, I can squeeze in.'

'Is it okay if I pile the books in a corner? There isn't anywhere else for them to go.'

'That'll be fine. Just leave me some space around the edges.'

'The bed's the thing.'

'It is.'

It looked as if there was just the one bed for the two girls. 'Where will you be sleeping?'

'Oh, around,' said Sophia vaguely.

She quickly cleared the floor.

'What's your project on?'

'The Victoria Lines. They're a sort of defensive military fortification that goes across the island.'

She looked at Chantale. 'Are you English? You don't look English.'

'I'm from Tangier. But living in England.'

'I wouldn't mind going to England,' said the girl. 'But first I've got to expel the British.'

'From England?'

'Malta. Get them out of here.'

'Don't you like them?'

'Oh, I like them. But it's the principle of the thing. Do you feel like that about the French? Being in Morocco, I mean?'

'Torn,' said Chantale. 'You see, I'm half French.'

'It must make it difficult. It's difficult enough for us, depending on the British for what we do. Everyone here works for the British. Without them being here Malta would be nothing. Or so my grandfather says. He was in the British Navy. All my family work for the British in one way or another, in the docks, on the boats, in the hospital. But I say that's a bad thing. It makes us too dependent.'

'What does your grandfather say?'

'He says that education is a bad thing, if it leads to dopey remarks like that!'

She laughed. 'He's all right, really. Just behind the times.'

'I ought to go,' said Felix, as they got back downstairs.

'Oh, don't go yet,' said Mrs Ferreira. 'I was just going to make tea. *English* tea,' she said with emphasis.

Sophia made a face.

'Sophia!'

'They put milk in it. I'll bet Miss de Lissac doesn't put milk in her tea.'

'Well, no,' confessed Chantale.

'I'll make *two* pots. One, British-Maltese. The other, for the rest.'

'Please don't, just for my sake –' began Chantale.

'What will you have, Felix?' asked Sophia.

'I don't mind, really –'

'I'll bet you do. Felix will have British.'

'British-Maltese,' said Felix, fighting back.

'So will I,' said Mrs Ferreira. 'And so will Grandfather. And Sophia can join Miss de Lissac.'

'Is there any cake?' asked Sophia.

'As a matter of fact, there is. *Quaghaq tal-ghasel.*'

'You'll like this,' Sophia told Felix.

'What was that name again?' said Chantale.

'*Quaghaq tal-ghasel.* It's a Maltese speciality.'

'Maltese? The name sounds –'

'Arabic, I know. Well, lots of things here are.'

'It's got treacle in,' said Sophia.

'Delicious!' said Felix.

'Another?' said Mrs Ferreira some time later.

'I ought to go,' said Felix regretfully.

'One more. Your mother won't mind if she knows who you're with.'

'Well . . .'

When Felix did decide to go, Mrs Ferreira got up with him.

'I have to go, too,' she said. 'I work at the hospital,' she explained to Chantale. 'In the dispensary. It always has to be manned, so we work a sort of shift system.'

'Are you going to tell your mum that you've changed the title of your project, Felix?' asked Sophia.

'Well, um . . .' Felix fidgeted awkwardly. 'Perhaps not immediately. When the time is ripe.'

'Don't let Sophia talk you into anything, Felix,' advised Mrs Ferreira.

'Oh, no –'

'Nobody listens to me, anyway,' said Sophia.

'What is your project going to be about?' asked Chantale.

'Well, it was going to be on the Hospitaller Knights' weaponry. But the Armouries are closed. And, anyway, Sophia says that the Knights were a bunch of thugs. She says I ought to do it on anti-weaponry of the time.'

'Anti-weaponry?' said Mrs Ferreira, puzzled.

'Medicines,' said Sophia. 'The drugs they used to heal. Herbs and that sort of thing.'

'Do we know about them?' said Mrs Ferreira doubtfully.

'There are lists,' said Sophia. 'Bound to be. Anyway, looking for them would be the point of the project.'

'I thought, actually, of making it a bit wider than that,' said Felix. 'Anything they used to fight wounds and ill-ness. Including things like hospitals. I was think of taking the Sacra Infermeria as an example.'

'Well, that would be a very worthy thing to do, Felix,' said Mrs Ferreira.

'I hope they think that back at school,' said Felix. 'This will be the third time I've changed my project.'

When Seymour had landed in Malta the first thing he had done was, as was usual when you were seconded out, to report to his local superior. But who, in this case, was his superior? The Governor? Or the Navy? The hospital was, after all, a ship. Seymour consulted his bosses at Scotland Yard, who, after going all round the houses, advised him that since the request for his secondment had come from the Colonial Department, it was to them, in theory, that he should report. In practice this meant the Governor and it was to the Governor that Seymour went on that first morning.

The Governor was a jolly chap who shook his hand affably and made it plain that he wanted to know as little about the matter as possible. Seymour could see advantages in this. From the point of view of the Governor, he could safely be disowned if things went wrong. From Seymour's point of view it gave him a free hand.

But what about the island's police, he asked? What was to be his relationship to them? Presumably they were investigating the case already?

Indeed they were, said the Governor, and should be left to get on with it. The island was very sensitive about such things. Ought he not, then, to be liaising closely with them? Indeed he ought, but – not too closely. Keep them informed by all means but not in such a way as to make it seem that he was reporting to them. The Navy was very sensitive about things like that.

And the Navy, should they be kept informed, too? Heavens, yes, said the Governor.

It was all, really, he said, a question of relationships. To foster these he had arranged for Pickering, the island's Chief of Police, British, to drop in for a drink before lunch.

Pickering dropped in and shook Seymour's hand and said he was sure they would be able to work together. These murders, though, were a bit of a hot potato and had to be handled with deftness. Showing some of that deftness, he had, in fact, passed the matter on to an Inspector, with whom Seymour should liaise.

The Inspector was Lucca, the man he had been handed over to after lunch and who had taken him over to the hospital that first day. From him Seymour had obtained a real picture. The Navy was holding fast to the argument that the hospital was a ship and therefore not under the jurisdiction of the local police. They had, in fact, refused to allow the police into the hospital.

But, how, then – began Seymour.

How, indeed. The Inspector had been unable to interview anyone in the hospital.

'But that's –'

The Inspector nodded.

'Ridiculous,' he said. All he had been able to do, he said, was focus on Herr Kiesewetter and what had happened to him and possibly to the balloon.

'If the Navy will not lower its defences,' he said theatrically, 'perhaps we can fly over them.'

Perhaps; all the same, more traditional methods of investigation were likely to prove more fruitful and he was glad that Seymour had come.

Seymour was relieved. One of the things he had not wanted to do was antagonize the local police. He had assured Lucca that there would be genuine cooperation between them and that it was his intention that 'keeping informed' meant what it said. Everything he learned inside the hospital would be shared with Lucca.

He had hoped to thrash out some of these difficulties with the Commander in charge of the hospital on his first visit but the Commander had been away. His duties included oversight of the medical side of those ships currently in harbour and he was away in pursuit of those. In his absence Seymour had talked to the hospital's Registrar, Ormskirk.

Ormskirk was friendly enough. Yes, he agreed, things had reached an impasse, and he hoped that Seymour's arrival would help to unblock it. It was plainly unacceptable that no progress should be made on solving the murders and he could quite see that the Prime Minister had had to fire a few rockets up people's backsides. But there was another issue, too, which affected him as Registrar, responsible for the general running of the hospital, particularly. Charges had been made against the staff of the hospital, serious charges, which had badly affected morale, and until they were answered the work in the hospital generally would suffer.

He was quite sure that the charges were unjustified. He hadn't been here long himself, having been posted from Colombo only the year before, but he had been very impressed when he had arrived by the general standards of the staff and particularly the nurses. 'A lively, competent lot,' he said, who knew what they were doing. Which was not what he had to say about Mrs Wynne-Gurr.

How they had allowed that witch to get in here, and now with a supporting cast of harpies, he could not understand. It had not been his doing. A hospital was a busy, hard-working, complex place and the one thing you did not want was people coming in and getting in the way and putting people's backs up. He was all in favour of the patients having visitors or of the doctors entertaining colleagues from abroad but you couldn't have just anybody coming in. And certainly not an old busybody asking daft questions! It had all been running perfectly smoothly before she arrived, he said in aggrieved tones; as if she had somehow brought the murders with her.

The upshot had been, he said, to put the hospital on the defensive. What with the police and the press and the politicians . . .! Fortress Birgu, he said, that was what it felt like now. That was what she had turned the place into. No doubt he had noticed that, on coming in.

He certainly had, said Seymour. And it was a great pity when people were giving of their best in not always easy circumstances. But, look, things would get better only when they had found out who had committed the murders. All this daft talk would be stilled and the hospital could get back to normal.

So it could, agreed the Registrar, brightening.

And he, Seymour, would do his very best to bring that happy state about. In fact, could he start now? A little look round, perhaps? And he would try not to get in the way or put people's backs up. But it was best to get on with it. The sooner it was over and done with, the better.

The Registrar concurred absolutely: so Seymour had his entrée and had been able to make a start.

He still felt, however, that he needed to clear things with the senior officer in charge and so an appointment was made for the afternoon of the day after next.

When he got to the hospital he found that he was rather early and so he dropped in on the nurses in their cubby-hole. He found Melinda talking to a little old, gnome-like man whom he realized he had seen before.

'You should be thinking about getting home, Dr Malia,' she was saying.

The doctor looked at his watch.

'Good heavens! Is that the time?' he said. 'How time flies when you get old!'

'Have you been here all day?'

He looked at his watch again.

'I suppose I have been,' he said, surprised.

'And eaten nothing all day?'

'I had some breakfast. I think.'

'I'll bet you didn't. You'd better come in and have a cup of tea with us. And a biscuit.'

'I don't want to be a bother –'

'You're not. We're making a pot anyway.'

'Ah, but you've been on your feet all morning.'

'So have you.'

'Yes, but –'

'What is it you used to tell us? Don't go too long without getting something inside you!'

'It's the sugar. You need the sugar.'

'And so do you.'

She shepherded him into the nurses' room.

'This is Mr Seymour. No, he's not a new doctor. He's a policeman.'

'A policeman?'

Dr Malia looked puzzled. Then his face cleared.

'Oh, I know,' he said. 'It must be to do with those poor people. Have you got anywhere yet?' he asked Seymour.

'I've only just started, really.'

'Yes. And it must all be very strange to you, coming out from England.'

'Not too strange. In fact, oddly familiar.'

'Yes. That's what they all say.'

A nurse put a cup of tea in his hand.

'Hello, Dr Malia! Do you remember me? Bettina?'

'No, I don't think – yes, I do! I remember your *quecija*. You chose – I think I'm right – a thermometer. And that was right, wasn't it? Because you became a nurse.'

'Quite right! What a memory you've got!'

'Or was it your mother?'

'It was probably my mother, too,' said Bettina laughing.

'And is she well?'

'Oh, very much so. Retired now, of course. But she still wants to know everything that's going on in the hospital. I'll tell her I met you.'

'Oh, please! Yes, do that. A remarkable woman, your mother. An excellent nurse!'

'Hear that?' Bettina said to the room at large. 'It runs in the family.'

'There's been a bit of a falling off lately,' said one of the other nurses.

'Tell me about the *quecija*,' said Seymour.

'It takes place on a child's first birthday. You get together a tray of small things, a pen, rosary, thimble, or even some money, and put them in front of the child. And whatever he or she picks up is supposed to tell you what sort of future it will have. What it will do in life.'

'I see, yes.'

'Mostly, it's an excuse for a party. We're great on parties in Malta.'

'It's time we had one here.'

'It is. Would you like to come, Mr Seymour? And you, of course, Dr Malia!'

'I would very much like to.'

'And we'll invite Bettina's mum so that you can meet her again.'

'That would be very nice.'

61

'Another biscuit for you, Dr Malia?'

'I've already had one –'

'Have two. That's an order. Medical advice!'

Dr Malia laughed. 'Probably better advice than anything a doctor could give.'

'And I'll get Berto to speak to Jacopo, and he will give you a lift home –'

'I don't like to bother –'

'Ssh! Jacopo has got nothing to do. And you know he always likes to have a chat with you. *And,*' said Melinda, 'he has a new baby! He will want to tell you all about that!'

'A new one? Another? But that's –'

'Five. Perhaps you'd better give him some advice.'

'It's no good giving advice to Jacopo,' said Bettina. 'You'd do better to give it to his wife.'

'I *would* like to talk to Jacopo.'

'More medical advice,' said Melinda. 'This time from me. You're overdoing things, you know. You're looking rather tired.'

'I don't sleep as well at nights,' Dr Malia confessed.

'No, my mother doesn't either,' said Bettina. 'You don't when you get old. But she doesn't spend half the night wandering round, like you do.'

'I'm not really wandering round at night. I'm just start-ing the next day early,' protested Dr Malia.

'Well, I don't know about that,' said Melinda. 'I think you sometimes forget to go to bed at all. I've seen you wandering about in the hospital at all hours.'

'I know my way around there,' explained Dr Malia placatorily.

'You certainly do. And it's nice to see you. But I think you need to put your feet up occasionally.'

'I've got such a lot to do.'

'And your project could do with a rest, too,' said Melinda.

Dr Malia looked surprised.

'Could it?' he asked. 'Could it? You know, I've never thought about that. But perhaps you're right.'

'Both of you,' said Melinda firmly. 'You and the project. Take a break.'

'Bloody newspapers!' said the Commander.

'Very trying,' Seymour agreed.

'If it hadn't been for them – and that bloody woman, too, of course – we could have sorted things out quietly. Cot deaths!'

'Ridiculous!'

'So bloody ridiculous we would have brushed it aside. But the newspapers were a different matter.'

'But they did rather blurt it out, didn't they? The three sailors. That bit about the snoring. And the pillow.'

'They wouldn't have done if they hadn't had a drink or two first. And then been primed, I wouldn't wonder, by a few more, and not bought by them!'

'Shouldn't wonder,' agreed Seymour.

'And it's all a load of bollocks,' said the Commander. 'You get used to snores if you're in the Navy. "Put a pillow over his head,"' he mimicked. 'I'd put a boot up their backsides!'

'All the same, they might have seen something,' said Seymour.

'They didn't see anything! They were so slewed they wouldn't have seen anything if the whole hospital had gone down! No, they made it up. It was the beer talking. And then the newspapers blew it up, made more of it than they should have done. And once they'd shouted it out from the hilltops everyone got in on the act. And it was all unnecessary.'

'Unnecessary.'

'We would have looked into it. We *were* looking into it. Only quietly. We would have taken any action that was necessary. If any action was necessary. We'd have given the police the tip-off. If it was murder, which I doubt.

'But it all got out of hand. And then that damned woman came along and made things worse. And in no time at all we had a Force Eight gale blowing up. And all the time they were missing the point.'

'Missing the point?'

'Yes. The Type XK 115.'

'I'm sorry?'

'The Type XK 115. The new destroyer. Just in from Portsmouth. First time out. That's what they wanted to see.'

'Sorry, who wanted to see?'

'The Germans. That's what was the point of it all. That's what they were up there for. Those balloons. Getting a good shufti at our fleet. And especially the new Type XK 115.'

'Spying?'

'Yes.'

'Surely not all of them. I mean –'

'No, no, not all of them. Just the German. And, do you know, the bugger was cheeky enough to come down right beside them. So that he could get a closer look! I'd have clapped him in irons, but, instead, they took him to the hospital. So that we couldn't get our hands on him. Fortunately, somebody else did.'

According to Inspector Lucca the place to go in Valletta on a Sunday was the Marsa racetrack.

Not church?

'Church, too, of course,' said Inspector Lucca. 'Mass in the morning, then a good lunch, and then, when it gets a bit cooler, the racetrack. I go every Sunday.'

And so, evidently, did a lot of other people. When Seymour made a rough count, he reckoned that there were over four thousand people in the stadium, many of them in their Sunday best. There was a general air of festivity. Two bands were playing simultaneously, one on each side of the stadium.

'Where's the third?' said Inspector Lucca, worried. 'Ah!'

Pushing its way through the crowd was the missing band, brass – most Maltese bands were brass – instruments gleaming in the sun.

'This is where there's sometimes a bit of trouble,' said the Inspector.

Every Maltese band – and there were dozens, if not hundreds, of them – identified strongly with its own locality, and pride, and passions, ran high. This was fine when the band was playing in its home patch but not so good when it was playing in the patch of another. As, of course, it had to when it was accompanying a march (political) or procession (religious) both of which were frequent in Malta; and practically every route took it through some rival territory. Disputes, according to the Inspector, frequently broke out. Not infrequently they turned into pitched battles and the police, and sometimes the army, had to be called in.

It sounded, thought Seymour, not at all unlike the marching season in Northern Ireland – where religious processions marched at, rather than through, the local inhabitants whenever they were of an opposing faith.

The Marsa racetrack bordered on the territories of several bands and all asserted a claim to perform whenever there was a meeting. Blowing turned to blows and eventually the Governor had to intervene. After prolonged negotiation a compromise was reached whereby the bands took turns. This proved unsatisfactory since it was so long before your turn came round. To speed things up it was decided that two bands should play simultaneously but on opposite sides of the track.

This worked well for a time but then another difficulty arose. Many of the attenders at the racetrack came not from Valletta proper but from across the bay, from 'the three cities' of Birgu, L'Isla, and Bormla, each with its own band, and they asserted *their* right to play at Marsa. After a long period of bloody conflict a compromise was reached whereby 'the three cities' would take it in turns to supply a band, which would play on alternate Sundays on the third side of the racetrack, leaving, as the Inspector pointed out, just the one side for you to stand if you wanted a bit of peace.

Peace, though, and the Maltese did not necessarily go together. The later compromise was not universally accepted, as 'the three cities' found when they tried to assert their claim. It was not uncommon for them to have to fight their way through to the station assigned them. Not that they necessarily minded that.

Hence the Inspector's concern.

'But it all adds to the fun,' he said philosophically.

Seymour knew about that sort of fun. There were no racetracks in his part of London but police were regularly drafted to other parts where there were race meetings. Some professed to relish it – the open air, escape from the city, the prospect, for those from the more sedentary parts of London, of the excitement of a 'bundle'. But in the East End, where Seymour served, there were 'bundles' a-plenty. Admittedly, as a member of the CID you were more likely to avoid them. Even so, the prospect of a day at the races was not one which filled Seymour with enthusiasm. However, when the Inspector had invited him he had accepted with alacrity. He had his own purposes.

At once, though, he had a surprise. For the racing at Marsa was not the sort that he was used to, horses belting round a track. Instead, it was horses pulling a cart, or, as the Inspector put it, two horses and a trap. For the great passion of Malta turned out to be pony-trotting.

Chantale was not enthusiastic about going to the racetrack either. But Mrs Wynne-Gurr had drawn up a programme and the programme had to be adhered to. Today they were going to the racetrack to observe how the local branch of the St John Ambulance went about its work. The Valletta St John was regularly in attendance at the races and this Sunday was no exception.

The English visitors were distributed around the track at the various points which the Ambulance manned, one English visitor to two Valletta members. The two ladies Chantale was with seemed very pleasant and the duties not onerous. For the most part they seemed to consist of tending spectators who had succumbed to the heat. Once, however, said one of the ladies, 'a wheel came off and the driver was thrown out right in front of me and I was able to practise my slings'. Today, however, there was no such excitement.

As the evening moved on, though, there was another sort of excitement. Chantale had been stationed at the interface between the territory of one of the Valletta bands and that of the band from 'the three cities', and soon a trickle of people suffering from knife wounds began to arrive.

About slings and fainting Chantale knew very little, but about knife wounds – coming from Tangier where she had run a hotel – she knew a lot and soon was happily working away.

'Miss de Lissac,' said Mrs Wynne-Gurr approvingly, as they were going home, 'was a credit to the West Surrey St John's.'

Also at the racetrack was Felix, theoretically in the charge of his father. Dr Wynne-Gurr, however, had met an Ophthalmic colleague from the hospital and soon was far away, mentally at least. This became physically when Felix was hailed by Sophia and lured away by her. She had much to show him: the place where the pony-traps assembled and where the horses, skittish and sometimes resentful, were brought to wait and where there was always the chance of one horse biting another or kicking its owner; and the refreshment tent, which you could sneak round behind and find a gap through which to put your hand and grab a *mquaret* or a piece of *quabbajt*.

They had been doing this when they noticed a roped-off piece of ground behind the tent on which was spread out a great length of grey, rubbery material. 'Keep off!' said a handwritten notice; so, naturally, they went over to look.

Two men, on hands and knees, were bent over one corner of the material.

'Bugger off!' said one of the men, without looking up.

''Op it!' said the other. 'Bugger offski!' As if talking to some Slav foreigner.

'*You* bugger offski!' retorted Sophia, flaring up.

'What are you doing?' asked Felix politely. At his public school voice, ridden with class authority, the technicians looked up.

'Checking it over,' one of them said.

'And what have you found?' said Seymour, coming up at that moment with the Inspector.

'It's a cut,' said the technician shortly.

'Not where your lot were looking,' the other technician said to the Inspector. 'That was definitely a tear.'

'But this was definitely a cut,' said the first technician, showing it to Seymour.

'Why didn't it enlarge?' asked Seymour.

'It's where it is. Close to the seam. The fabric is doubled at that point and there's a tuck-over.'

'So it wouldn't have been seen?'

'It would have been seen on the first inflation. We inflate it a little and then go over it thoroughly. We actually check the seams. It wasn't there then.'

'So when was it cut?'

'During or after the second inflation. When we fill it up just before launch.'

'We do a second check then, but it's pulling away at that point, and if it's small we could miss it.'

'Are there people around?'

The technicians hesitated.

'Well, there are always people around. Working on the other balloons. We launch them at about the same time.'

'So someone could –?'

'They could,' said the other technician, 'but –'

'We're all in the game together,' said the first technician. 'We just don't do that sort of thing.'

'It's sort of honour among technicians,' said the second technician.

Chapter Five

Things had looked up at the St John Ambulance aid point. Business had tailed off and Chantale had had plenty of time to watch the racing. The point was in a conspicuous position at the edge of the racetrack and she had a good view of the pony-traps hurtling past. Like Seymour she had been surprised to see the racing take that form. She hadn't gone to races when she was in Tangier – women didn't – but on one or two occasions she had gone to see pig-sticking, which was, in some respects, especially among the Tangier colonial community, Tangier's nearest thing. Horses pulling carts, though, seemed a pallid equivalent.

There was a little flurry in the crowd and a man pushed through. He was supporting another man.

'Another stab wound for you, Miss de Lissac,' said one of the Maltese St John's workers.

'The bastards!' said the man doing the supporting. 'They've stabbed a bandsman. That's not right! We're supposed to be neutral!'

He was a bandsman, too, dressed for the occasion and with a trumpet slung across his back.

'They'll look after you, Luigi,' he said, easing the man into a chair.

He had spoken in Arabic and, without thinking, Chantale did the same.

'Where is it?' she said.

'Here.'

The man felt his ribs.

Chantale inspected the wound.

'Lucky you!' she said. 'It hit the ribs and ran along them. Not between them, otherwise you'd have been a goner.'

'I saw who did it,' said the wounded man. 'I'll know who to look for.'

'You'd do better to know where to look out,' said Chantale.

'That, too!' said the man who had brought him. He looked curiously at Chantale.

'Are you Arab?' he said.

'Of course she is!' said the wounded man. 'She's speaking Arabic, isn't she?'

'I come from Tangier,' said Chantale.

'I've been to Tangier,' said the other man. 'Nice place.'

'What are you doing over here?' the wounded man asked Chantale. 'Came over for a job? Like the rest of us?'

Chantale guessed that, despite his Italian-, or Maltese-, sounding name he was an Arab of some kind but where from she could not tell. Although she could understand it, the Arabic was unfamiliar to her.

'Came over to get a husband more like,' said the other man.

'I've got one,' said Chantale, stretching the truth a little. 'In England.'

'England?'

'Yes.'

'Oh!'

Chantale patched the man up and sent him away.

'Get that looked at by a doctor,' she called after him.

'I will,' the man promised. 'Thanks.'

'I didn't know you spoke Maltese, dear,' said Mrs Wynne-Gurr, stopping on one of her patrols.

'I don't,' said Chantale. 'At least, I think I don't.'

The Inspector, busy, genial and relaxed, had begun to move through the crowd chatting to people. He seemed to know everybody. Then Seymour realized: he probably *did* know everybody.

The space cleared for the technicians to work on their

balloon was behind some low stands raised just sufficiently to enable those at the back to get a view of the racing. On the day of the launch the course itself had been taken over by the balloons. There had been between fifty and a hundred of them, spread out through the stadium, some big, some small, some huge ones tugging at their pegs, others unable to get off the ground at all. The stadium had been full of people, most of them connected with the balloons in some way, technicians, ferryers of parts, fuel and provisions. Among the balloons were hand carts, mules and the occasional car and truck, although there were not many of these, the motor-car not having really hit Malta yet.

And there had been, of course, lots of onlookers. These had in theory been kept back by ropes which had marked the stadium off from encroachment; in theory, because in practice they had just stepped over the rope and pressed forward to satisfy their curiosity. The police had been too few, the technical staff too busy to stop them.

And, of course, they had trespassed on the workspace. And it would have been possible to tamper with the balloons. When the balloons were launched, an effort had been made to clear the space and the Inspector claimed that it had succeeded. At the moment of launch the space around the balloon had been clear. That was why he felt certain that any last-minute interference must have been carried out by somebody from the balloon crews.

Some of the people now watching the racing might well have been present on the day of launching. That was why he was going round talking to everyone. People had their favourite spots, he said. Like the bands, they were territorial. And someone might have seen something.

Seymour found a steward who had been present at the launching of the balloons and asked him to describe what had happened.

It had been on a Saturday, the man said, so that as many people as possible could see it and so that the stadium would be clear for races the following day. They would have had the whole of the Sunday morning to dismantle the balloons and pack them away. Of course, while they were doing that they would not have been able to go to church but the organizers had assured everyone that the balloonists would have been able to attend early Mass if they wished to. In any case – carried away – was not the experience of ascent itself akin to a religious experience? A moment of uplift? The Church did not think so. Seymour saw, however, how the Church was a continual point of reference in Malta, even for those who were not themselves devout.

But so, for many, was the racing at Marsa. It was a great social occasion. Many people brought picnics and towards the end of the racing spread out over the grass.

He had joined up with Chantale and was about to leave when Sophia came running up. Surely they were not going to leave without joining in the family picnic? This, too, was a considerable occasion. About twenty or thirty people had gathered and were laying tablecloths on the grass, and in the middle of them Mrs Ferreira was beckoning vigorously.

Not to be refused. Especially when the dishes started to be distributed on the cloths. '*Fenek*,' said Sophia, 'and *torta tal lampuki*.' *Lampuki* were fish and the *torta* was when they were made into a pie covered with spinach and cauliflower and olives. But the rest, she assured him, was *fenek* in its various forms, fried, casseroled or roasted with chips. *Fenek* was rabbit, very popular in Malta. He hadn't seen many wild rabbits, and perhaps that was why.

'A regular *fenkata*,' said one of the relatives, grinning, seeing him looking at the dishes.

A *fenkata* was, apparently, a rabbit occasion, when rabbit, in various forms, was the chief dish. It was a popular evening out.

And also, of course, there were the usual piles of sweet cakes and biscuits, some of which he had already met: the aniseed-flavoured *mquaret*, the ricotta-filled *kannoli*, like huge cigars, the treacly *quaghaq*, the *kwarezimal*, honey-and-almonds, and various almondy cakes. As he had previously spotted, the Maltese were very keen on almonds.

The names, which interested him, he did not know at all. On the other hand, the names of the beers – Hopleaf Pole,

72

Farson's Shandy, and Blue Label – were always comprehensible although not always familiar.

For the most part the group was talking in English although here and there he could hear Malti. Chantale picked out the Malti, too, mostly because she was conscious of the Arabic in it. It wasn't just a question of incidental words. Some of the most basic were Arabic: *la* for instance, no, although the Maltese pronounced it 'le', *iva*, yes, pronounced 'eeva', *inta*, you, usually, though, without the 'a' on the end, 'int'.

Mrs Ferreira brought them into a circle which included her parents. Both had worked at the hospital, her father briefly before joining the Navy and going to sea, as a porter, her mother as an assistant in the dispensary. It seemed that most of the family had worked at the hospital at some time. Quite a few others had worked for the Navy in some capacity or other, as stewards, as nursing assistants, or as seamen, often down below in the engine room. There was quite a naval confraternity, apparent in the frequent casual references to ships and conditions on board.

At some point a little group of musicians turned up, bandsmen with their instruments. They put their instruments down in the grass and joined the groups around the tablecloths. Apparently they were members of the family, too, and had been playing until the bands dispersed.

One of them came and sat next to Chantale. He was introduced as Uncle Paolo.

'But we've already met!' said Chantale.

It was the man who had brought the knife victim.

'Luigi,' explained Paolo, as if they all knew him.

'How is he?' asked Chantale.

'All right; but I sent him home. I told Marta to see that he lay down for a bit,' he said to the others around him.

'Not badly hurt, I hope?' said Mrs Ferreira.

'Badly enough,' said Paolo. 'It's come to something when bandsmen get knifed.'

'They're an easy target,' said someone.

'Yes, but that's why they shouldn't be attacked,' said Paolo. 'They're playing for everybody. They're sort of neutral.'

'I don't know what things are coming to,' said Mrs Ferreira's mother, shaking her head.

'But Madame, here, patched him up,' said Paolo, turning to Chantale. 'For which we are very grateful.'

There was a little murmur of acknowledgement around the tablecloth.

'But what a thing!' said Mrs Ferreira. 'She comes to Malta to see how the St John does its work, and what do we show her? Someone being stabbed! What must she think?'

'It happens, Madame,' said Chantale. 'I know from Tangier.'

'Ah, yes,' said Paolo, 'you come from Tangier.'

'Tangier is one thing,' said Mrs Ferreira's father, 'Valletta is another.' He raised a glass to Seymour. 'Valletta is like the beer: English.'

'Even in London there are stabbings,' said Seymour.

'I have never been to London,' said Paolo.

'But you have been everywhere else,' said Mrs Ferreira.

'Only in the Mediterranean,' said Paolo. 'I work the liners,' he explained to Seymour.

'Now,' said Mrs Ferreira's father.

'I've changed around a bit.'

'He was in the Navy,' said Mrs Ferreira proudly.

'Once,' said her father.

'And now I work the liners,' said Paolo easily. 'More pay.'

'Seasonal,' said Mrs Ferreira's father dismissively.

'Sometimes I am between ships.'

'As now.'

'Fortunately,' said Mrs Ferreira. 'For then he comes to see us.'

Her father snorted. Evidently he did not altogether approve of Paolo.

There was an awkward pause.

'You speak Arabic excellently,' said Chantale. 'May I ask how that comes about? Not by touching in briefly at Tangier, surely!'

'Ah, well –'

'It came about like this –' began Mrs Ferreira.

'Oh, no!' cried Sophia. 'She's going to give us the family history now!'

'My sister –' continued Mrs Ferreira determinedly.

'This could take a long time,' muttered Sophia.

'– Debra,' said Mrs Ferreira's mother.

'Debra,' continued Mrs Ferreira,' married a Libyan –'

'– and went to Tripoli,' said her mother.

'A big mistake,' said her father.

'– which she soon realized,' said Mrs Ferreira, 'and came back home.'

'– with her son –'

'Me,' said Paolo.

'– and then she married Uncle Piero.'

'Me,' said a man at the next tablecloth.

'Don't think you're going to get off lightly,' said Sophia. 'You're just at the beginning. Our family's a big one.'

'Sadly,' said Uncle Piero, 'Debra died, having her second baby –'

'– third,' said Mrs Ferreira's mother.

'Don't forget me!' said Paolo.

'We didn't know what to do,' said Piero.

'Well, *you* didn't –' said Mrs Ferreira.

'Well, Christ, a newborn baby –'

'Me!' called a voice from another tablecloth.

'So I took her over,' said Mrs Ferreira.

'– but you already had Nico and Carlo and Rosalie and –'

'– me,' said Sophia.

'– so we were a bit stretched.'

'It took me all my time to look after Roberto,' said Uncle Piero, 'and, of course, I couldn't spend all my time looking after him because I had to work. So –'

'So he called in Liza.'

'Are you still with us?' asked Sophia.

'His sister. But she already had three children of her own. Roberto, she could manage. But Paolo —'

'Too much, as always,' said Paolo.

'— went to a cousin —'

'Keep hanging in!' advised Sophia.

'— who lived at Medina. Medina is an Arab town. At least, we call it the Arab town.'

'It *is* an Arab town,' insisted Mrs Ferreira's father.

'— because it belonged to the Arabs a thousand years ago. We don't forget these things in Malta.'

'Could you hurry it along, Mum?' pleaded Sophia.

'She had many friends —'

'Look, let's keep it to relations, *please*,' said Sophia.

'— who had family —'

'Oh, no, please!' said Sophia.

'I'm sorry, I haven't quite got this bit —' said Felix, who had been listening earnestly.

'— in Tripoli. Which was where Paolo's father had come from. And they happened to know him, and told him about Paolo. And he said he would take Paolo back.'

'Got it?' Sophia asked Felix.

'I think I'll have to write it down,' said Felix.

'You could draw a chart. Look. I'll show you,' said Sophia.

'It's quite easy, really,' said Paolo. 'I was born in Tripoli, came to Malta, then went back to Tripoli —'

'We could put arrows on the lines,' said Felix.

'— and then sort of drifted around,' said Paolo. 'But I grew up in Tripoli.'

'And so you speak Arabic,' said Chantale.

'Phew!' said Sophia. 'Got there at last!'

The Inspector went round the tablecloths shaking hands with everybody. He kissed Mrs Ferreira.

'Hello, Maria!' he said. 'As beautiful as ever!'

'Flattery will get you anywhere!' said Mrs Ferreira.

'The most beautiful woman in Valletta!'

'What about me?' said Mrs Ferreira's mother.

'And me?' said Sophia.

'You may grow into it,' conceded the Inspector.

He seemed to know the whole family.

'You back?' he said to Paolo, shaking hands.

'Until the *Ascania* gets in.'

'She's coming in next week, so you'd better make the most of it while you can.'

'I have been.'

'It's time you settled down. Found yourself a good wife. Don't you think so, Maria?'

'I keep egging him on. But every time I find him a nice girl, he runs away to sea!'

The Inspector came to Chantale and looked puzzled.

'Medina?' he said.

'London,' said Chantale.

'She's staying with me,' said Mrs Ferreira. 'She's with the Ambulance.'

'Oh! Just visiting, then?'

'She's been making herself useful. She's the one who bandaged Luigi.'

'On her first day here!' said Mrs Ferreira. 'What impression of Valletta will that give her?'

'I think Valletta is a very nice place,' said Chantale.

'Yes, but a bandsman!' said Paolo, still aggrieved. 'They're supposed to leave us alone!'

'Well, they do, usually, don't they?'

'Yes, but they cut Luigi. Why did they do that? You ought to look into it!'

'I will. But I've got other things to look into as well.'

'Where were you when they went for Luigi?'

'On the other side of the racetrack. Doing my job. I can't be everywhere.'

'But you knew there was likely to be trouble there. You ought to have put someone there.'

'I had to put them somewhere else. There's always trouble somewhere or other.'

'Yes, but you ought to keep a particular eye on the bands. I mean, that's where there's likely to be trouble.'

'There is, Paolo, if you're around.'

'People ought not to be allowed to get at the bands.'

'I'll bear your advice in mind, Paolo.'

The Inspector wandered off.

'It's not right!' insisted Paolo.

'Okay, Paolo, calm down!' said Mrs Ferreira's father.

'I thought you were going to see how Luigi was?' said Mrs Ferreira.

'I am, I am! I'm going now!'

'He always feels so deeply!' said Mrs Ferreira fondly.

'Felix!' said Mrs Wynne-Gurr. 'It is time we were going home.'

'Can't I stay a bit longer, Mum?'

'You've trespassed on Mrs Ferreira's hospitality long enough.'

'Not at all –' murmured Mrs Ferreira deprecatingly.

'And where is your father?'

'I think he met someone he knew. Someone from the hospital.'

'A doctor?'

'A nurse, I think.'

'A nurse!'

'And a doctor, too,' said Sophia quickly. 'I think there was a little party of them. Come to see the races.'

'I do wish your father wouldn't go off without telling me!'

'Shall I go and look for him?' asked Felix hopefully.

'Then we would lose you, too!'

'I could go with him,' said Sophia. 'Then I could bring him back here. Or to the hotel if you wanted.'

'I do wish he wouldn't wander off like this. There are things I have to do. Like planning tomorrow's programme, for instance.'

'I thought you'd done that?' said Felix.

'Well, of course I have. But I like to go through things in case a late adjustment is necessary.'

'I'll bring them back very quickly,' promised Sophia.

'I think I ought to go myself,' said Mrs Wynne-Gurr.

'No, no, I think that would be a bad idea,' said Sophia hurriedly. 'I mean, when you've got things to do.'

'If you're sure you know where to find him –'

'Oh, I'm sure. I'm quite sure!'

'Well, then – if you wouldn't mind. And, Felix, don't let yourself be lured away again. You must be back by eight thirty. I've arranged an early dinner, especially for you.'

'Gee, thanks!' said Felix. 'On my own?'

'We will have ours later. But I think you could do with an early night.'

'Could Sophia have dinner with me?'

'No, no, no –' began Mrs Ferreira.

'That would be nice,' said Sophia.

'Surely you don't need another meal,' said Mrs Ferreira. 'After what you've just had?'

'They're all the same,' said Sophia *sotto voce* to Felix. 'Mothers!'

'Just a little one,' coaxed Felix. 'After all, I've been battening on Mrs Ferreira all day.'

'Yes, indeed. It has been most kind of Mrs Ferreira. Yes, perhaps she could. And that would probably ensure that the pair of you were back at a reasonable time. Eight thirty is the time I have booked.'

'Eight thirty it will be,' promised Sophia.

'And if you're sure about finding my husband –'

'I know the person he's with,' said Sophia. 'He's one of the doctors in Ophthalmics.'

'Oh, good. That would be very kind of you, Sophia. I really do need to go through the programme for tomorrow. I'm spreading us all around the hospital, you see,' she explained to Chantale. 'This is a good chance to see a hospital in action. A foreign hospital.'

'Most interesting,' murmured Chantale.

'And I've reasons of my own for wanting to take a good look at some of the practices in that hospital,' said Mrs Wynne-Gurr grimly.

'I shall be over there myself tomorrow,' said Seymour. 'Which ward will Miss de Lissac be in? Perhaps I could look her up.'

'Ward C, I think,' said Mrs Wynne-Gurr.

'Would you mind if she switched to Ward J?' asked Seymour. 'I have a particular reason for asking.'

'That is the ward where one of those poor men died,' said Mrs Wynne-Gurr.

'Yes,' said Seymour.

Mrs Wynne-Gurr smiled.

'I understand,' she said. 'I was thinking of going there myself. However, if that is where you are focusing your inquiries, I shall go to the other one – the other one where a patient died.'

'I look forward to comparing notes,' said Seymour.

'The racing has all stopped,' said Felix.

'But the drinking hasn't,' said Sophia. 'And that's where we'll find your father.'

'I don't think he's much of a one for drinking,' said Felix doubtfully.

'But Dr Cassar is,' said Sophia, 'and that's the doctor he was with the last time I saw him.'

Around the racecourse, set back from the track and behind the seats, were stalls where quick food and drink could be purchased, and around the stalls, particularly around the ones selling beer, was a seething mass of people. Finding anyone in the mass seemed impossible but Sophia wormed her way through to the counter in each case and looked around. Felix saw her arm wave and there, yes, was her father talking earnestly.

'Dad, you've got to come back to the hotel.'

'Sure, sure,' said Dr Wynne-Gurr, and went on talking.

'This is the first time of asking,' said Sophia. 'We'll go away and come back in ten minutes. And then five. And then we'll keep coming until we're such a nuisance that you'll have to come with us.'

'This girl knows how to get what she wants,' said the man Felix's father was talking to. 'Hello, Sophia!'

'Hello, Dr Cassar,' said Sophia. 'And you'd better come away, too, or Anna will get very fed up with you.'

'One last drink,' stipulated Dr Cassar.

'I think I've had enough,' said Felix's father.

'So have I,' said Dr Cassar. 'So we'll make this the last one. One for you, Melinda?'

'I'm back on duty in three-quarters of an hour, so I'd better not,' said Melinda. 'I saw your Uncle Paolo, Sophia. Is he back on shore?'

'For a bit,' said Sophia.

'I wanted to catch him, but he disappeared.'

'He was going to see how Luigi was.'

'Luigi?'

'A friend of his. In the band. He got knifed.'

'Badly?'

'Badly enough for him to go home.'

'That band is the cause of a lot of trouble,' said Melinda. 'Or, at least, it attracts trouble. A pity, because it's not at all bad. And better still when your uncle is playing.'

'He ought to stick to that,' said Sophia.

Felix had seen Dr Malia, not in the crowd around the beer stall, but by the *mquaret* stall. He went across to him.

'Hello, Dr Malia,' he said. 'I didn't realize you were one for the races.'

'I like to see them occasionally,' said Dr Malia. 'And on a Sunday you can't get into a lot of the places I want to go to.'

'Nor me,' said Felix.

'The Armouries won't be open for a long time yet,' said Dr Malia.

'I know. So maybe I ought to change my project. Sophia says so. She says I ought to do so anyway. She says I ought to be looking at anti-weaponry.

'Anti-weaponry?'

'Medicine. Hospitals. And such.'

'Well, now, that's not a bad idea.'

'Yes, but that's your project, not mine.'

'I could share it,' said Dr Malia.

Sophia came through the crowd. 'Dr Malia, you're needed over by the bandstand. Someone's got hurt.'

'Another one?' said Felix.

'It happens all the time,' said Sophia, dismissively.

'What's wrong with him?' asked Dr Malia.

Sophia shrugged. 'There was some fighting. Cuts and bruises, I think.'

'If it's more than that, they ought to go to the hospital.'

'They don't want to go to the hospital.'

'In case too many questions get asked?'

Sophia kissed him.

'Got it in one,' she said. 'You're the man they want.'

'Yes, but they don't want me for the right reasons,' said Dr Malia. 'Anyway, I'm not really up to it these days.'

'You're the one everyone wants.'

'I haven't got my bag,' Dr Malia objected weakly.

'If you need it, they'd send someone to fetch it.'

'I suppose I ought to go,' said Dr Malia. 'Where, exactly –'

'By the bandstand. The Three Cities bandstand.'

'There always trouble there!'

'Yes. Luigi got stabbed there earlier this afternoon.'

'Where is he?'

'Someone took him home. Uncle Paolo has gone to see him. I think you ought to go and see him, too. You'd be much more use.'

Dr Wynne-Gurr was extricated and delivered. Mrs Wynne-Gurr meanwhile had been reviewing the day with the ladies of the Ambulance and pronounced herself satisfied. That she attributed to the superior organization of St John's and also to the fact that women played a significant part in it.

'If you want a job done, give me a woman every time,' she said. 'Especially one who has had the experience of running a family. Don't you agree, Mrs Ferreira?'

Mrs Ferreira said she did.

'Especially a large family,' she added.

'One is enough for me!' said Mrs Wynne-Gurr.

Sophia rose in Felix's defence.

'Boys are more manageable than girls,' she said. 'At least, that's what my mother always says.'

'I was thinking of you, dear,' said Mrs Ferreira.

They all left together. Seymour and Chantale, the Wynne-Gurrs, and a substantial part of the Ferreira family. As they were leaving they ran into music. One of the bands was leaving, too, not quietly, as the Three Cities band had done, but in a blare of triumph.

Sophia knew the members of that band, too, and waved to them as they went past.

'That's our band!' she said proudly.

The band recognized the Ferreiras and gave an extra puff. Mrs Ferreira ran along beside them excitedly like a small girl.

'If this is your band,' Felix said to Sophia, 'why doesn't Uncle Paolo play for it?'

'He lives in Birgu,' said Sophia.

'Birgu?'

'That's what it used to be called. It's called Vittoriosa now.'

'It's not just that,' said Mrs Ferreira's father. 'That's where his heart is. Not with Valletta.'

'When you said "heart",' said Dr Wynne-Gurr, 'do you mean he has a wife there? Or, perhaps, a girlfriend?'

'If only,' said Mrs Ferreira.

'I mean, he likes them not us,' said Mrs Ferreira's father.

'Now, Father. That is too hard! You know it is. Why, he's only just been eating with us.'

'And then he went away.'

'To see how Luigi was.'

'And that's another waster,' said her father.

Chapter Six

The next morning the West Surrey St John Ambulance were at the hospital in force, including a less than happy Chantale. Mrs Wynne-Gurr lined them up and then posted them around the places she had assigned them. Chantale went dutifully to Ward J; although what she was supposed to do there, and why Seymour had asked for her to go there, she did not know. She had seen him in the distance but he had not spoken to her. The only person who had spoken to her was the ward sister, who indicated a place for her to sit down and said, not exactly welcomingly:

'You're here to observe, I gather. Well, at the moment we're doing the bed pans so observe away as much as you like.'

The nurses were cool and Chantale had the impression that she was being deliberately made to feel uncomfortable. She guessed that she was catching some of the resentment they felt for Mrs Wynne-Gurr. She settled down in her corner and wished she had brought a book.

Mrs Wynne-Gurr appeared after about half an hour to see that things were proceeding according to plan and handed her a printed sheet of instructions.

'Just put a tick every ten minutes,' she said. 'Apart from that, ask them where you can be of most use.'

Chantale did and got the feeling that the place where she could be of more use was somewhere else. She shrugged and thought of returning to her corner, but then one of the nurses said she could clear away the breakfast things when the patients had finished. There was a sort of scullery to which the dishes were being taken and in it two elderly Maltese ladies were doing the washing up. Chantale wondered whether she should offer to assist but they plainly did not need assistance.

Someone asked her to put the trays away. She looked around for a place to put them. At the end of the ward was a door. A cupboard, perhaps? She opened the door and went in.

Inside, on the floor, was a mattress; and on the mattress a woman was lying. She was young and not over-dressed. In fact, she was not dressed at all.

She opened one eye and looked at Chantale.

'Oh!' she said.

Then she sat up, reached across to a pile of clothes on the ground beside her, and began to put them on.

Chantale, taken aback, retreated and shut the door.

But then she stopped, wondering what to do? If anything? The young woman had seemed quite at home.

The routines of the ward were going on all around apparently as usual. Was the young woman part of these routines? A night nurse, perhaps, taking a break? Or a day nurse about to come on? If the nurses had been more forthcoming she would have asked one of them. But somehow it didn't seem right to ask the ward sister.

In the end she shrugged and went back to her corner. If this was part of the scheme of things in the hospital, who was she to intervene?

She kept an eye on the door, however, and after a while the woman came out, fully dressed and self-possessed. She went to the end of the ward and walked out.

About halfway through the morning Mrs Wynne-Gurr came along and switched everybody round to different wards, rather to Chantale's relief. Just before then, however, she had gone for a walk round the ward.

'You're Arab, aren't you?' said one of the patients.

'Yes,' said Chantale.

'What are you doing here?'

'I've just come to watch and learn,' said Chantale. 'I'm with the St John Ambulance.'

'Those people who are at the racetrack?'

'And other places. Yes.'

'Where are you from? Medina?'

'England,' said Chantale.

'England?' he said, astonished.

'Yes. I'm just visiting Malta. I'm with a party from England.'

'But you're an Arab!'

'Yes,' said Chantale, not wanting to embark on complicated explanations.

'What are you doing here?'

'As I told you, I'm here to watch and learn. I'm with the St John Ambulance. The English St John Ambulance.'

'And you've come to learn?' He gave a short laugh. 'Well, there's a thing! To come here to learn. From us!'

'There's always something you can learn,' said Chantale.

'Yes, but from us!'

'Why not from you?'

He didn't reply at once but seemed to be thinking.

'Well, I suppose,' he said, 'that if you're an Arab, you've got a lot to learn.'

'And if you're Maltese,' said Chantale nettled.

'If you're Maltese, too, yes. And if you're English?'

'They've got things to learn, too.'

'They certainly have! But will they learn them?'

'That's what they're here for,' said Chantale quietly.

He thought it over. 'That woman with the loud voice, is she one of them?'

'The one who was in here earlier? Yes.'

'She has come to learn?' he said incredulously.

'One can always learn.'

'Not if you're like her! Not if you're British!'

'It was her idea,' said Chantale loyally.

'Well, I'm surprised,' said the Maltese. 'Very surprised!'

'Are you being difficult again, Mr Vasco?' said Sister Macfarlane, appearing at that point.

'Yes, I am being difficult,' he said. 'I want a nurse. A Maltese nurse. Send me Melinda!'

'Melinda's busy. You can have Bettina.'

'I don't want Bettina. I want Melinda.'

'Why don't you want Bettina? She's very nice and sensible. And Maltese.'

'I want to send a message to my brother. And it's no good asking her because her family and mine don't get on.'

'No one gets on with you, Vasco,' said Bettina. 'And the reasons why is that you're such a pain in the ass.'

Unexpectedly Vasco laughed.

'I'm not saying you're wrong,' he said mildly. 'All the same, I want to see Melinda. I want to send a message to my brother.'

'I'll ask her,' said Bettina. 'But I think it's quite possible that she'll tell you to stuff it.'

She went out of the ward.

'Happy now, Mr Vasco?' said Macfarlane.

'No. I'm bloody not!' said the Maltese. 'My stomach is giving me real trouble this morning!'

'I'll get you something.'

She went off.

He lay there watching Chantale not suspiciously but doubtfully.

'So you're an Arab,' he said.

Chantale did not reply.

'You can't be!' he said suddenly. 'Not if you're from England!'

'There are Arabs there, too,' said Chantale. 'And Maltese.'

'Well, there bloody ought not to be. Maltese ought to stay at home. But Arabs – they get everywhere, don't they?'

Melinda came in.

'Are you being unpleasant again, Vasco?' she said sternly.

'No, I'm not. I'm just saying that the Arabs get in everywhere. Even here. Even into the hospital!'

'Not many,' said Melinda. 'And why shouldn't they?'

'I don't mind them,' said Vasco weakly, the energy suddenly going out of him.

'Well, you don't want to mind this lady,' said Melinda. 'She bandaged up Luigi when he got stabbed.'

'Luigi got stabbed?'

'Yes. At Marsa.'

'The buggers!'

'You want me to take a message?' said Melinda.

'Yes. To my brother.'

'A sensible message, I hope?'

'Yes, yes,' he said indignantly. 'A sensible message. Why are you always on at me, Melinda?'

'Because you're always making trouble. You and your lot.'

'I don't make trouble for you, do I?'

'No, and you'd better not.'

'Nor for the Arabs. I've got nothing against Arabs.'

'Sophia!' said Laura sternly. 'What are you doing here?'

'Nothing,' said Sophia.

'Well, go and do it somewhere else!'

'I'm looking for my mother,' said Sophia, too obviously at random.

'Well, you know where to find her. And it's not here.'

'Actually, it's Ophthalmics I want.'

'Why?'

Felix stuck his head cautiously in at the door.

'Ah, there you are!' said Sophia, and went across to him. 'You managed to get away, then?'

'Easy,' said Felix. 'Actually, I don't think it mattered much. They're all busy looking at some new equipment that's just come in. A something-o-scope. And I don't think they're really bothered about me, so long as I keep out of the way.'

'Okay, then,' said Sophia. 'Let's go.'

'Where are you going?' asked Laura.

'Mum won't mind,' said Sophia.

'But Felix's mum might.'

'We'll be around,' said Sophia airily, and hauled Felix through the door.

'In the hospital?' Laura called after them.

'Yes,' said Sophia. 'More or less.'

'It's all right for her,' Laura said to Seymour. 'She knows her way around. But he doesn't. The hospital's a big place and it's easy to get lost.'

'I think he'll be all right,' said Seymour, 'if Sophia is with him.'

'She's quite responsible,' Laura conceded. She looked up at Seymour. 'Can I help you?'

'I'm looking for the porters.'

'They're out the back,' said Laura. 'Unloading some equipment. Do you want me to send for them?'

'No, no. Perhaps you can help me. I was wondering which of them was on duty on the night of the twenty-fifth.'

'The night the first one died?'

'Yes.'

'Well, I can tell you. Umberto. I can tell you because he had asked my son to be with him.'

'Why was that?'

'Usually you don't need two on at nights. One can do it. But sometimes the doctors say they want a patient turned over at intervals during the night and if he's a big, heavy man, it's better if there are two do to it. But that's all you need two for and it doesn't seem worth getting an extra man in full-time. So they get in a lad, someone who's big and strong like my Mario, and they'll do it for a few bob.'

'And that's how it was that night?'

'Yes. I remember it because when Mario came home for breakfast he told me about it. That a man had died. He was quite shocked. I don't know why, because he'd been there before when someone had died. He's even had to help move the body, because it's better to do that when every-one is still sleeping.'

'And this time?'

Laura hesitated. 'I don't know if he had to move the body by himself. He didn't say. Maybe he did. He was certainly a bit upset, which isn't like him. I don't like him having anything to do with dead people, he's not ready for it. I know he's got to learn, but he's only fifteen. They know how I feel, Berto and Umberto, I mean, and try not to let it happen. But sometimes if you're on duty at night and there's no one else around, they've got to. But he didn't say he'd had to do it this time, so maybe it was something else.'

A young boy came in.

'Do you know where Dr Docato is?' he asked Laura. 'He's not in Emergency.'

'He may be in Orthopaedics,' said Laura. 'Try there. Do you know where that is?'

The boy laughed. 'Do I know . . .? Mum, I know every inch of this hospital.'

'All right, all right. But they've just moved a section from Orthopaedics and I wondered if you knew about *that*.'

'Of course I knew. I helped to move it.'

'I just wondered. That was all.'

'You reckon he might be there? In the new section?'

'Try it.'

The boy looked at Seymour.

'This is Mr Seymour,' said Laura.

'Oh, yes, the policeman from England.'

'And this is my son.'

'Hello, Mario,' said Seymour.

'Sir!' said Mario politely. They shook hands.

'I'd like to have a word with you, Mario, if I might.'

'Certainly, sir. I'll come back. Only I've got to find Dr Docato first as otherwise they'll be held up. There's some new equipment for Dr Docato,' he explained to his mother. 'But it's in a crate and the crate is too big to get through the door, so they'll have to unpack it. And they don't like to do that unless the doctor it's for is there, so that if there's something missing, they can't be blamed for it.'

He hurried off.

'An extra boy, just for a crate?' said Laura, pursing her lips. 'I'll have to have a word with Berto. Of course, it may be a big crate.'

'You keep a sharp eye on them,' said Seymour.

'I'm a bit of a dragon,' said Laura. 'They're all right, but they need to be kept up to the mark.'

Seymour took Mario into the porters' room, empty at the moment, with the porters out the back. He was plainly nervous.

'Don't worry, Mario,' said Seymour encouragingly. 'It's nothing very important. I'm just trying to get a general picture of the way they do things in the hospital. I wanted to ask you about nights. You do occasionally work nights, don't you?'

'Yes, sir.'

'I wanted to ask particularly about the night the sailor died. You were here then, weren't you?'

'Yes. I was here.'

'Helping Umberto?'

'That's right, yes.'

'To do what, particularly?'

The boy hesitated.

'You do remember that night, don't you?'

'Oh, yes. Yes, I remember.'

'And what did Umberto want you to do?'

'Oh, this and that,' muttered the boy.

'Exactly, please.'

Mario looked unhappy.

'I don't remember,' he said unwillingly.

'Were you needed to turn someone over?'

'Not that night.'

'Or move something? Carry something around?'

Mario looked even more unhappy.

'Not much on that night, was there?' said Seymour, guessing.

'No,' said Mario, suddenly relieved.

'Then why did he ask you to come in?'

Mario was tongue-tied.

'Did he think there *might* be a need for you, for some reason?'

'Yes, that was it,' said Mario, relieved again.

'What was the reason?'

'I – I don't know. Some reason,' said Mario unhappily.

Seymour thought. Mario sweated.

'Something you don't want to tell me,' said Seymour.

'No, no.'

'No?'

'It's just that I forget.'

'I don't think you do forget. I don't think you're a boy who forgets things.'

He waited.

Mario said nothing.

Seymour took a chance. 'What I'm trying to find out, Mario, is whether it was possible for someone to get into the hospital at night unobserved.'

Mario suddenly looked stricken.

'But this would be difficult, wouldn't it, if the porters were there?'

Seymour waited. 'They would see anyone come in, wouldn't they?'

Mario, it seemed, could only nod.

'If they were there,' said Seymour. 'Were they there, Mario?'

Mario looked intensely miserable.

'All the night? Or did you have to go off somewhere? Together? The two of you.'

'No,' said Mario, with surprising definiteness.

Seymour was puzzled. 'No?'

'Not the two of us.'

'Just one of you, then?'

'*Iva.*' So low that Seymour could hardly hear him. Malti for yes.

'Which one of you? Umberto?'

'*Iva.*'

'He had to go off somewhere, leaving you on your own?'

'*Iva.*'

'Do you know why he had to go off?'

Mario was silent.

'He had to check on somebody, perhaps?'

After a moment there was the briefest of nods.

'Or was it something else?'

Mario's face was wooden.

Seymour tried a different tack. 'You were left on your own, then, Mario. Did you mind?'

Mario looked puzzled. 'Oh, no.' After a minute he volunteered: 'I'm used to it.'

'It often happens?'

'Not often.'

He corrected himself. 'Quite often.'

'So you were on your own, then?'

Again, after a moment, the nod.

'So you were the only one who was there, then, when they discovered that the sailor had died?'

'*Iva.*'

'On your own?'

'The doctor was there. And the nurse. Two nurses. I didn't have to . . . do anything. They decided to leave him there. Until another doctor came in. It was just that they thought . . . that he might have to be moved. That is why they called . . . a porter.'

'You?'

'Me, yes.'

After a moment he said: 'They usually do move them. If it's at night. So that in the morning it's gone. When everybody wakes up.'

'But not on this occasion?'

'No.'

'It wouldn't have been easy, anyway, if you were on your own. Were you still on your own?'

'*Iva.*'

'Umberto wasn't back?'

'*Le.*' No.

'When did he come back?'

'Later,' said Mario unwillingly. After a moment –

'I haven't told my mother,' he said. 'She would be angry.'

'With you? Or with Umberto?'

'With both of us. If she knew.'

* * *

93

Chantale feared that this was going to be a long day. Apart from the excitement of the girl in the cupboard, and the rather different interest provided by the difficult Mr Vasco, nothing, but nothing had happened. It was much the same in the new ward. And that seemed likely to be the way that it normally was in wards. Unless there was some sort of crisis. Or unless there was a murder, of course.

She wondered what was the point of her being there. What was she supposed to see? What was she expected to be observing?

As the morning wore on she began to feel more and more mutinous.

It was a relief when Seymour put in an appearance, although also an irritation in that the nurses paid much more attention to him than they had to her. This was true even of Macfarlane, that old, cold stick. How had he managed to swarm his way through the defences of even that pillar of Scottish rectitude? And then Chisholm in the other ward.

Nor was her irritation mollified when she was allowed to take him into the nurses' room and offer him a cup of tea, for she saw the nurses' league table on the wall, and when she had worked it out, felt an unusual, and, possibly Arab fit of much disapproval overtaking her. League table of proposals indeed! They were, she told herself, just a bunch of randy schoolgirls.

Mrs Wynne-Gurr appeared on one of her rounds just before lunchtime.

'A very profitable morning!' she said with satisfaction. 'I have learned a lot.'

So had Chantale; and two of the things she had learned were, first, that she would never make a nurse, and, secondly, that the idea of securing her passage by enrolling in the St John Ambulance had been a dreadful mistake.

Seymour had somehow, typically, oiled his way through the hospital's defences and secured permission to take her out for a quick lunch. Her spirits rose but then fell again when it became apparent that what was envisaged was a brief sandwich in a bar. Blasted away by Chantale's fury, Seymour had hastily proposed that they make up for it by a really good Mediterranean meal that evening. 'Paella,' he had suggested temptingly. 'Or maybe a good mullet.' Since Chantale had tasted neither of them since she had been in England, she was prepared to make concessions; and in the end they had eaten a sandwich lunch sitting on a sea-wall looking out over the harbour. Where they could see the ships, said Seymour.

Chantale pointed out that they were all warships. 'How typically British!' she said. 'Well, they've got to go somewhere,' said Seymour. But Chantale, sensitive to expressions of imperial power, whether British or French, felt uncomfortable. Maybe it had been a mistake coming to Malta.

Her spirits were slightly cheered by a *dghajsa* passing near them on its way across the harbour to Valletta. The eyes painted on its bow seemed to be watching them as it passed but she didn't mind them, they were cheerful eyes, seeming almost to wink as they went by.

'Why don't the British paint eyes on their warships?' she asked Seymour.

'They can see all right without them, I suppose,' said Seymour.

'They make the boats more human,' said Chantale.

However, this encounter with the human had cheered her up and she began to tell him about her morning. She told him about the girl in the cupboard and cheered up still more when he didn't believe her.

And then she told him about Mr Vasco.

'What the nurses have to put up with!'

'Yes. I've come across him myself,' he said. He was interested, however, in what she told him about Vasco's ambivalence over her being an Arab.

'Another one with crazy, mixed-up ideas about the Arabs!' she said.

'I can understand it,' he said. 'With the Arabs being so close. You wouldn't know whether to be for them or against them.' Chantale, half Moroccan, half French, found that position entirely understandable.

Seymour thought he should follow up Chantale's tale of the girl in the cupboard. He found the cupboard but, alas, no girl inside it. There were, however, signs of occupation. A mattress was there, leaning against the wall; and evidence suggested that it had not been used just for sleeping.

He asked the nurse in the ward about it.

'Oh, it's just used for storing,' she said, and looked him straight in the face as if defying him to advance any other hypothesis.

Coming out of the ward he ran into the three sailors, Cooper, Corke and Price, whose account of what they had seen, or half seen, in the ward has sparked off such a furore in the newspapers.

They were just going in.

'Now, what brings you here?' he said.

'Just visiting,' said Cooper.

'Your mate, of course, is no longer here.'

'We've got other mates,' said Corke in a slightly hostile tone.

'We like to visit the sick,' said Cooper unctuously. 'It's a sort of errand of mercy.'

'Oh, yes!' said Seymour sceptically.

'No, really!' Cooper insisted. 'There are a lot of our boys in here, and we like to come round once or twice a week to cheer them up.'

'Give them someone to talk to,' said Price.

'So it wasn't just Turner you came to see?'

'No, no. We like to do the rounds.'

'We're like that,' said Cooper.

'But Turner was a special mate of yours?'

'Yes. Yes, you could say that.'

'You were with him when he got injured, weren't you? Or, at least,' he said, turning to Price, 'you were.'

'We all were.'

'In the bar?'

96

'Yes. Just having a peaceful drink – after the match.'

'You had been to see a match, had you?'

'Yes, we like to see a match. They have them in the evenings here, when it not so hot.'

'And then you went on to the bar?'

'For a peaceful drink,' Cooper insisted.

'So how was it that they didn't get to be so peaceful?'

'A bunch of Maltese came in. Well, it was all right at first. They were on one side of the room, we were on the other. Just talking normally, like.'

'So how did it start?'

'Someone must have said something.'

'One of *them* said something,' said Cooper.

'After the match?'

'Well, no,' said Price. 'That's what I couldn't understand. If it had been, I mean, well, you might have understood it. But it wasn't that.'

'Some of them hadn't even been to the match.'

'And then one of them said something?'

'Yes. It was that little bloke,' Price said to the others. 'He came in after the others and seemed to have something against Terry, because he just stood there looking at him.'

'I didn't see him,' said Cooper.

'Well, no, you wouldn't have,' said Price, 'because he was sort of standing to one side. My side. And I saw him staring at Terry, and I thought: Hello, is he a long-lost friend? But he didn't look that friendly. And then he said something to the others, and one of them said something, to poor old Bob, I think it was. And then Bob said something, replied, as it were. And then the next moment someone had hit him!'

'Them was the aggressors,' said Cooper.

'I don't think he hit him that hard. Just a tap, really. But Bob was off balance and went down. And, of course, once you're on the floor anything can happen.'

'Boots!' said Corke briefly.

'Well, we weren't having that,' said Cooper. 'Not to our mate!'

'And the next moment it was a sort of free-for-all!' said Corke.

'You've no idea why he took against you?' Seymour asked Cooper.

'No.'

'Come across him before?'

'Never seen him before in my life.'

'Once it had started, I lost sight of him,' said Price. 'Just disappeared!'

'Ran off, I think,' said Corke.

'Having started it!' said Cooper.

'Didn't see him again,' said Price.

'And then the police came,' said Corke.

'And then our very own little blue-eyed boys!' said Cooper. 'And beat the hell out of us. They shoved us on to their boat – they've got a special boat, you see, for the likes of us. And they were pushing us on board, when one of them sees Bob. "He looks in a bad way!" he said. "Sick bay for him!" "Hadn't we better get him to the hospital?" another of them says. "It's just round the corner." Well, I thought this was our chance. "Let us take him," I says. "Me and my mates. We were nothing to do with all this," I said, "and we knows the hospital." "You were nothing to do with it?" says the Petty Officer. "You boys bloody started it!"

'Well, there was a bit of an argument at that point, but then someone shouted: "There's trouble at Antonio's!" and they thought they'd better get there. So they said we could take poor Bob to the hospital, and if they had any more trouble from us that night, they'd kick the hell out of us. So we went.'

They passed on into the ward and when he looked in a little later Seymour saw them assiduously going round the beds chatting to their incumbents.

'Quite touching, really,' said Sister Chisholm. 'They come every week, twice or three times a week, and go round religiously to everybody. And not just this ward!

They usually look in on Macfarlane's ward. They've got mates there, too. I don't mind them coming round, they bring a bit of life into the place. Of course, you've got to keep an eye on them. God knows what they'd get up to if you didn't! Although, as a matter of fact, I do know what they'd get up to; they'd never leave the nurses alone. So I always make a point of being here when they visit, and that keeps things decent. I suppose I've got a bit of a soft spot for them. I've known them for a long time. They were out on the Singapore station with me.'

'The Singapore station?' said Seymour. 'Ah, you must have been there when –'

'Yes, I know,' said Sister Chisholm, 'when Cooper was in hospital there and witnessed, or heard about, the famous snoring incident. Well, I'm sorry to disappoint you, but that story is an old chestnut which regularly makes the rounds every time a new ship comes in. It wasn't true then and it's not true now. But everyone in the Navy takes it for Gospel.'

Chapter Seven

'And this,' said Mrs Wynne-Gurr, 'is where it all began. Where *we* began.'

The ladies were impressed.

'The headquarters of the Knights of the Order of St John of Jerusalem, the Grand Master's Palace.'

'Actually, this is not, strictly speaking, where they began,' said Felix, tagging along for once, with some interest. 'They started in Jerusalem.'

'Thank you, Felix –'

'And then they moved to Rhodes.'

'Yes, well, thank you, Felix –'

'The Palace wasn't started till 1520. But the Order had been set up in 1085.'

'If I may continue,' said Mrs Wynne-Gurr resolutely, 'when the Order was first established *on the island of Malta*, this was its headquarters. It is, as you see, a very grand building, and even grander inside. The principal apartments are on the first floor, the *piano nobile* as it is called. They are built around the courtyard and include the Council Chamber and the Supreme Council Hall –'

'And the Armouries,' said Felix, 'although they're at the back.'

'I do recommend you, while you are here, to find an hour in your busy schedule to visit them.'

'You won't be able to get into the Armouries,' said Felix. 'They're closed.'

'I don't expect you'll be wanting to visit *them*,' said Mrs Wynne-Gurr crushingly. 'As I say, the Grand Master's

Apartments are worth a visit. However, the main focus of your interest will be the Sacra Infermeria, the Holy Infirmary, which was, at the time it was built, in 1574, the most modern hospital in Europe. And the largest, with over five hundred beds.'

'Five hundred and sixty-three,' said Felix, 'which could be increased to nine hundred and fourteen. Dr Malia says that this is very important.'

'Yes, well –'

'Most of them would be in the Long Hall.'

'Which we shall go and visit now. If you would follow me –'

'Five hundred and eight feet,' said Felix. 'The longest room in Europe.'

'Thank you, Felix.'

'Do you know, they used to boil their surgical instruments?'

'Did they? Well, that was very advanced of them –'

'Oh, they weren't doing it to sterilize them. Dr Malia says they thought it would reduce the pain. But it would have helped, wouldn't it? I mean, it would have cut down the numbers dying.'

'I expect so, Felix. Now –'

'They were fed off silver dishes.'

'Really?'

'Sophia says, though, that when the French were on the island they seized all the silver and melted it down so that they could pay for Napoleon's wars.'

'Well, there you are. That's the French for you.'

'Fed off silver?' said one of the ladies. 'Everybody?'

'I think so,' said Felix. 'Though maybe not the lunatics.'

'Lunatics?'

'Lunatics and galley slaves were treated on the first floor.'

'But they *were* treated?' said the lady who had spoken before. 'Well, I consider that very enlightened.'

'Yes, but Sophia says that the structure of the organization reflects the class-ridden society of the time. Slaves at the bottom, knights at the top.'

'Felix,' said Mrs Wynne-Gurr, 'would you like to go off on your own somewhere? You've been over the Infermeria several times already and I'm sure you would like to give it a miss this time.'

'Oh, no, Mum. I'd be very interested to see it again. You notice different things each time you go through it.'

Mrs Wynne-Gurr sighed.

Chantale, still tired from the journey from England, although hardly from the exertions of the day, fell asleep as soon as her head touched the pillow; but then, almost immediately after, or so it seemed to her, she was woken by an ear-splitting noise. At first, in her dazed state, she thought it was in the room with her, but then she realized it came from outside.

It sounded like a concert. Right under her window. But not exactly a concert. A performance, by a band of some sort. The instruments were mostly brass and the music was stirring. Martial, you could have said. It was a bit like the music the bands had been playing at the Marsa racetrack.

It *was* the music the bands had been playing at the Marsa racetrack.

She looked out of the window. It was one of the bands, too. The band was parading up and down the street, not just under her window but under everybody else's, too. Many of the inhabitants of the houses had come out to join in the fun. The street was packed with people. Not just grown-ups but children, too, who in England would have been in their beds hours before. Young, old, men, women – everyone was there!

Chantale soon realized that if you couldn't beat them, the best thing was to join them. She threw on her clothes and some sandals and went downstairs. The front door was open and Mrs Ferreira was standing outside.

'Our band!' she said, turning a blissful face to Chantale.

All her children were there, except, for some reason, Sophia. Even Mrs Ferreira's father, that solid, slightly dour, man with his feet very much on the ground, was there.

There, too, were many of the relatives she had seen, the uncles, the cousins and the aunts, not all from her house but from the houses round about, all excited and pressing around the band as it paraded up and down.

There was Paolo, with a young woman –

Chantale stopped. It couldn't be! But, yes, it was. She was sure. The woman he was with was the young woman she had come upon in the cupboard in the hospital. Her face was now not sleepy but animated. She was waving her arms and clapping her hands above her head, shouting excitedly to the band, possibly singing with it.

Paolo, too, without any instrument but beating time, was cheering the players on.

And definitely with the young woman she had seen in the cupboard. He had his arm around her and once, delighted by the rendering of a particular piece of music, she threw her arms about his neck.

But everyone was throwing their arms about each other, and jumping up in an attempt to see the band better, and waving rapturously.

'Our band!' said Sophia with pride, materializing suddenly.

'What are they celebrating?' asked Chantale.

'Oh, they're not celebrating anything in particular. They've just been rehearsing, and I suppose they got a bit carried away.'

She broke off to wave to someone.

'Perhaps they *are* celebrating a little,' she said. 'Mrs Mumtaz has had a baby. And the Boys' Under Fifteen has won a match. In fact, they've reached the semi-final.'

'Do they always carry on like this?'

'Always,' declared Sophia.

She waved to someone else, a girl of about her age, but dressed in a different kind of school uniform.

'I saw your Uncle Paolo,' said Chantale.

'Oh, yes? It's not his band, but, of course, he knows lots of people in our street.'

'He was with a girl.'

'No, I don't think so,' said Sophia.

'He was. He had his arm around her.'

'This would be a first!' said Sophia.

'That was not my impression,' said Chantale.

'No? Oh, well, things are looking up, then.'

'That girl over there.'

'Oh, that girl. Suzie. She doesn't count.'

'Why doesn't she count?'

'Well, he's not going to marry her, is he? And from the point of view of my family, that's all that counts.'

'Why isn't he going to marry her?'

Sophia laughed, but said nothing.

'I saw her yesterday in the hospital.'

'She works there. Sometimes.'

'She's not a nurse?'

'Oh, no.'

'An ancillary worker of some kind?'

Sophia laughed again. 'You could call it that.'

'Is she a . . . a prostitute?'

'Not exactly. A lady whose virtue is particularly easy, my grandfather says. She sleeps around but she only goes with you if she likes you, and it's not always for money. She's just very casual. She works in the hospital laundry but she's very casual about that, too, so much so that they got rid of her. But sometimes they need her when there's a lot of work to be done and then they take her back. But she never stays long. She doesn't like being tied down. A bit like Uncle Paolo, I suppose. Though he's not really like that. Casual in that sense, I mean. He's deadly serious except about marrying.'

The girl saw them looking at her and said something to Uncle Paolo. Then they worked their way through the crowd across to them.

'You saw me, didn't you? In the cupboard.'

'Yes,' said Chantale.

'They never go in there so I use it sometimes.'

'I saw you come out.'

'You didn't say anything, though, did you? I half expected that you would. In fact, I more than half expected

104

it. I was sure you would give me away. So I put my clothes on pretty quickly. But then you didn't.'

'No.'

'Thanks.'

'Actually, I couldn't think what I ought to do, so I did nothing.'

'I wouldn't do anything to hurt the hospital, you know. I work there. In the laundry. But sometimes I have had to stay on because there's so much washing to be done. They make me do the sheets and sometimes I don't finish them until quite late. It's not worth me going home so I sometimes stay in the cupboard. Especially if I've been in there already.'

'You oughtn't to be doing that in there,' said Paolo.

'Oh, I don't know.'

'Not regularly. And not with British sailors.'

'They're all right.'

'Well, they're not all right. There was that business with Luigi.'

'They had nothing to do with it. Not with the stabbing.'

'Not with the stabbing, no.'

'Anyway, thanks again,' said Suzie.

'This lady is the one that bandaged Luigi up,' said Paolo.

'Did you?' said Suzie, surprised. 'Well, thanks for that, too. Luigi is my bloke. Some of the time.'

On his way to the hospital Seymour ran into Lucca.

'Hello!' he said. 'How are things?'

'Bad,' said Lucca. 'I've had a man from the German Consulate in with me all morning asking questions. About that German who died. He's got to write a report. He went on and on and in the end I said: "Look, Herr Backhaus, I don't know about you, but I've been up since five and on since six and I've hardly had a bite. So if it's all right with you, I'm stopping for one right now!"

'"It is a long time, perhaps," he said grudgingly.

'"It bloody is," I said.

'So we stopped and I had a beer and a sandwich. But he didn't have anything. He just stood there watching me, waiting to get on with it. "How about you, Mr Backhaus?" I said. "Can I get you something?"

'"Perhaps a glass of milk," he said.

'Milk is not what I would go for in Malta. Or, indeed, anywhere. But if that was what he wanted, he could have it. So I got him one.

'But then I thought: look, I don't mind standing anyone a beer, but this is not like that. This is an expense incurred in the line of duty. So when I got back I banged it in as expenses. And the bloke in the office looks at me and says: "Are you having me on, Lucca? A glass of milk?" "It was for him!" I say. He purses his lips, cold, accountant lips, and says: "Are you sure, Lucca? Are you sure you're not trying to take the piss out of me?"

'And he bloody disallowed it!'

'Suzie?' said Sister Chisholm. 'She works in the laundry.'

'Not just the laundry,' said Seymour.

Sister Chisholm was silent for a moment. Then she sighed.

'All right,' she said. 'I know what you mean.'

'Here, for instance.'

'Not here,' said Sister Chisholm. 'Not actually in the wards.'

'Where, then?'

'In a place like this there are lots of odd corners. And Suzie would know them all. She's been here a long time. In fact, you could say she grew up here.'

'Grew up here?'

'In a manner of speaking. She was born here. And then she sort of stayed. She's been here so long that she's part of the place. Part of the shipboard fittings, as they call it. That's how she began. As the result of a shipboard fitting. Her mother was a cleaner in the hospital, her father – well, a passing seaman, I suppose. He passed, and she was left with the baby.

106

'Of course, they all knew about it. Both the hospital staff and the seamen. But they were very good. About it and to her. The sailors, I mean. They gave her money, enough to live on, and the hospital was reasonable, too. It kept her on as a cleaner.

'Well, the baby grew up, and the seamen remembered and used to ask after her. They brought her presents, toys when she was small, then perfume and things like that. Money, sometimes. They looked her up when they were in port. She grew up thinking she was part of the Navy. And that was how they saw her, too, as part of the Navy. They still looked out for her. Only, as she grew up, they looked out a bit too well and she became a shipboard fitting.

'That's how it was when I got here. She was part of the furniture I inherited. I received strict instructions from my predecessor to keep her up to date on birth control and to check regularly that she kept free from disease.

'Well, there you have it. You could say we condone her plying her trade. Only no one sees it as that, and I don't think she does. No money passes – she insists on that. They're nice to her and she's nice to them, that's how she sees it. But they still make a donation on her behalf every time they get into port. Sometimes they give it to Laura. "For Shipboard Fittings," they say. I think that a lot of them, especially the new ones, don't know what it means. And I'm not entirely sure that Laura does, either.'

'I thought you'd come looking for me sooner or later,' said Suzie.

'Yes,' said Seymour.

'That girlfriend of yours, the Arab one, she saw me, didn't she?'

'Yes.'

'She didn't do anything about it. I thought she might.'

'She told me.'

'Well, I thought she would once I realized that you were together. But when she didn't do anything about it, I rather hoped that you wouldn't, either.'

'I still might not.'

'Depending on what?'

'Depending on what you tell me now.'

Suzie nodded.

'What do you want to know?' she said, after a moment.

'You know why I'm in Malta, don't you?'

'Yes. You're the police.'

'And you know what I'm doing here?'

'Yes,' she said, in a small voice. 'It's those blokes, isn't it?'

'The ones who were murdered, yes.'

She flinched. 'I don't like it when you say it like that.'

'It's true, though, isn't it?'

'I suppose so.'

'One of them was in the ward where the cupboard is.'

'Yes.'

'Were you there that night?'

She hesitated.

'Part of it,' she said. 'The early part. Then I moved somewhere else.'

'Why?'

'I heard them talking. I'd been asleep, and then I woke up. There were several of them and I was surprised at that because it's usually just the nurse, and sometimes another nurse comes in to see her. But this time there was a man's voice, one of the doctors. So I thought maybe he'd been called in because there was an emergency. But it didn't sound like that. Then I realized and I didn't like it. I wanted to get out quick. So I waited until I got a chance and then sneaked out. I thought there might be a search, you see.'

'Why should there be a search?'

'I heard them talking. Someone said: "Like the other one."'

'Turner?'

'I don't know his name.'

'Go on.'

'Well, there'd been a lot of talk. Not just in the laundry room but all over the hospital. People knew the doctors were puzzled. And someone said they were wondering

108

if – well, if it might not have been an accident. And so, when they said: "Like that other one," it gave me the creeps. I mean, the thought that there might be some crazy bugger, and that he might have been in the ward next to me – Christ, he might have come in!'

'And you thought they might start searching?'

'Yes. I thought I'd better get out. Right out. I didn't feel like staying in the hospital at all. So I left.'

'How?'

'How?'

'How did you get out? Without being seen?'

'Oh, it was easy. I got out by the coal chute. It goes down into the boiler room. No one's there at night, so it was easy.'

'Do other people know about the coal chute?'

'They must do. But it's not the sort of thing you think of, is it? I mean, they know that coal is delivered and gets down to the boiler room, but they don't go beyond that.'

Seymour took his time, and then said: 'Suzie, there's one other thing I've got to ask you, I'm afraid: were you alone in the cupboard that night?'

Suzie didn't reply at once. Then –

'No,' she said, very softly.

'Did he leave before you did?'

'Yes,' even more softly.

'You know why I have to ask you this?'

'Yes. But it wasn't him. He'd gone long before.'

'By the coal chute?'

'Yes.'

'You've told him?'

'Yes.'

'Are you sure he went straight there after leaving you?'

Suzie was silent for quite some time. Then she said: 'You can't be, can you? But it wouldn't have been him. He couldn't have done – what you're thinking.'

'Why not?'

'They were friends. Mates. Him and the one in the bed.'

'You know that, do you?'

'Yes.'

109

'How?'

'He'd been in to see him. To see how he was. Because they were mates.'

'Can you tell me his name?'

'I don't remember his name. But it wasn't him. I know that.'

'Look, when the boiler is working, it's working. Right? We don't need to be there all the time. It does all right without us. And it does all right without us at night. We go off at eight and set it so that it carries on without us. Until we come in at six the next morning. If anything goes wrong, I'm just around the corner. From my house I can come in less time than it takes to walk from one side of the hospital to the other. Umberto has only got to give me a call.'

'All right, all right,' said Seymour. 'I'm just checking on security, that's all. I was wondering if someone could get into the hospital using the coal chute.'

'It would be easier said than done. Look, I'll show you. There's a flap on the chute, see? It may not look much but it's as stiff as a board. Particularly if you were trying to get in from outside. It takes a big load of coal to push that open. A man on his own couldn't do it.

'And even if he could, he wouldn't be able to get far. Not if he had a normal pair of shoulders on him. I know. I've tried it.

'If you were a bit smaller? Even then you'd have a job. Just take a look. There's a bend in it, see? The coal sort of slips past, but a man, well – As I say, I've tried it. We had a load which got stuck once. All right, there's bendier people than me. And maybe if you took your clothes off, so you were bollocks naked, and greased yourself all over, like I've heard some of those Africans do. You could do it. But who's going to strip himself naked in the streets of Birgu and grease himself all over? And then crawl over the lumps of coal at the bottom?

'One of those sailors? Yes, I know they're like monkeys, they can wriggle their way in anywhere. But don't forget about the flap. It's like a big, heavy board. Maybe if you got some help from inside you could manage it. Or if you had wedged it open beforehand. But if you'd just come along and tried to get down it, well, you'd have a job on.

'Getting out from inside? Well, it's possible, I suppose. Especially if there were two of you.

'A woman? Bloody hell, mate, what sort of woman is that? But if she's going to strip off, just pass the word, mate, and I'll be along to watch.

'But getting out, rather than in? Climbing up the bloody coal chute? A woman? Christ, mate, what sort of imagination have you got? You worry me, you really do!'

'I'm not getting anywhere on my project,' said Felix gloomily.

'Nor am I,' confessed Sophia. 'I've got the conclusions. It's just the bit before that's missing.'

'I haven't got anything,' said Felix. 'Neither the conclusions nor the bit before.'

'Let's put our heads together,' said Sophia.

'Hello!' said Mrs Ferreira. 'What are you doing here?'

She was just going out of the dispensary with a trolley. Every morning she went round the wards with the prescriptions for the patients. It took her most of the morning and then, if she was still on duty, she would go round again in the late afternoon.

'We've come to see if there's anything here that would help Felix with his project.'

'What was the project on, again?' asked Mrs Ferreira.

'Anti-weaponry,' said Sophia.

'I don't think there's a lot here –'

'Medicines,' said Sophia.

'Ah, well, those we do have.'

'They have to be old medicines,' said Felix.

'Some of the medicines here are pretty old,' said Mrs Ferreira's assistant.

111

'Twelfth-century,' said Sophia.

'But not quite that old,' said Mrs Ferreira.

'We thought there might be some old books,' said Sophia.

'They would be in a library. And not ours,' said Mrs Ferreira. 'The Cathedral Library, perhaps. Or you could try the Infermeria?'

'Hello, Dr Malia!'

'Why, hello, Sophia!' said Dr Malia, startled. 'What are you doing here?'

'We've come to look for some material. For Felix's project.'

'What was the project on, again?'

'Anti-weaponry.'

Dr Malia seemed taken aback. 'I'm not sure there's much –'

'You see,' said Sophia, 'what we were thinking was that when you talk about knights, you think of bashing people up. But the Knights Hospitaller weren't like that, or, rather, not just like that. They tried to heal people as well as bash them. Well, that's the side Felix wants to do his project on.'

'Oh, very good!' said Dr Malia enthusiastically. 'Hospitals, you mean?'

'Actually, we were thinking of medicines. They're sort of anti-weaponry.'

'Well, yes, they are, I suppose. But isn't the title rather misleading? It sounds a bit – if that's the title of the project, I mean.'

Felix knew at once what he meant. It *did* sound a bit – He could just imagine what his teachers would say, especially old Mackereth. 'Anti-weaponry? Death-rays, is it? I'm not sure the Board will rate comics as highly as sources as you do, Wynne-Gurr!'

'Perhaps we could change the title,' he said.

'But keep the argument,' said Sophia sternly. 'I like Felix's slant.'

'It is certainly an original way of looking at it,' said Dr Malia.

'We were wondering if there were any old books here that we could draw on.'

'Well, as a matter of fact, there are. Two certainly. One is a very early herbal. The other, yes, I think you could call it that, a treatise on medicine.'

He went into another room and came back with two worn, leather-bound books.

'I think these will help you,' he said.

Felix and Sophia looked at them.

'But –' they both said.

One was in Latin; the other in –

'Arabic,' said Dr Malia happily. 'A lot of the early work in medicine was in Arabic.'

'I think I would find that a bit tricky,' said Felix.

'We could ask Uncle Paolo, I suppose,' said Sophia.

'Or maybe that lady who is staying in your house,' said Felix. 'She's half Arab.'

Sophia was looking at the other book.

'This is in Latin,' she said. 'You're doing Latin, aren't you, Felix?'

'Yes, said Felix, 'but –'

But not this kind of Latin. He could barely understand a word.

'It has some excellent illustrations,' said Dr Malia.

Perhaps he could copy them, thought Felix. That would at least be something. But –

'Beautiful!' said Dr Malia enthusiastically. 'And so accurate! You can see at once what they are. This one for instance.'

He showed it to Sophia.

'I'm not good on flowers,' said Sophia. She looked hopefully at Felix.

'Well, I can see it's a poppy,' said Felix.

'Yes, that's right,' said Malia. 'I suspect they made a great deal of use of opium.'

'You could stick a poppy in your project,' suggested

Sophia. 'Press it between the pages. Teachers always like that sort of thing.'

Maybe they did. But not Mackereth. Mackereth would go berserk if Felix did that. 'What's that?' he would squeak. 'A *flower*? Take it to your mother, Wynne-Gurr, not to me! What is that meant to show? That you can pick a flower? Oh, and recognize it, of course, which, I admit, is unexpected. But where does it get you? What does it lead to? Conceptually?'

'Well, I could,' said Felix. 'But where would it lead to? Conceptually?'

This floored Sophia for the moment.

'It takes time for the concept to develop,' said Dr Malia. 'Take willow, for example. They knew, even in the twelfth century, that it has medicinal properties, but it's only comparatively recently that we've been able to isolate them and derive aspirin. That would be a very interesting process to follow, Felix, and make a worthwhile subject for your project.'

'I know!' said Sophia excitedly. 'You could show how the Knights would have made opium. There are lots of poppies around. I can show you some. There are lots over by the Victoria Lines. We could pick some and then you could make it. A sort of practical project.'

'A laboratory project?' said Felix considering.

'Yes.'

'But I haven't got a laboratory!'

'You can use a kitchen.'

'I haven't got anywhere in the hotel.'

'Our kitchen. That's the place!'

'I'm not sure –' began Dr Malia uneasily.

'Drugs, is it, now?' said Sophia's grandfather.

'Medicine,' said Sophia. She could see that another of those arguments with her grandfather were about to begin. '*Medicine.*'

'Oh, yes?' said her grandfather sceptically.

'Dr Malia says he thinks it likely that the Knights Hospitaller made a lot of use of opium.'

'And alcohol, too, I'll bet,' said Grandfather.

'Father –' began Mrs Ferreira.

'It was used,' said Sophia, picking her words with care and enunciating them with emphatic clarity, 'as an anaesthetic.'

'They didn't have anything else, you see,' said Felix.

'So when they were cutting people's legs off, they would give them a dose of opium first,'said Sophia.

'I'll bear that in mind,' said Grandfather, 'the next time I'm having my leg cut off.'

'This is a serious historical project,' said Sophia, glaring at him.

'Sophia –'

'Actually,' said Chantale, intervening hastily on the side of peace, 'we used to use opium like that in Tangier. Or, at least, pregnant women did. To alleviate the pain of childbirth.'

'We used to use it here, too,' said Mrs Ferreira. 'But we don't any more.'

'We found it in an old herbal that Dr Malia showed us,' said Felix. 'You know, medicines the Arabs derived from plants.'

'Dating from the twelfth century,' said Sophia, embroidering the truth slightly.

'And of course, the fact that the book was in the Infermeria is significant,' said Felix. 'It suggests it was there for use.'

'So we're on to something,' said Sophia. 'Despite what some people might think,' she added, looking at her grandfather menacingly.

'Arab?' said Grandfather.

'Yes. Apparently the Arabs led the world in medicine at that time. Or so Dr Malia says. He says a lot of the early words we used in science came from the Arabic. Alcohol, for instance.'

'Are you going to make that, too?' asked Sophia's grandfather.

'No, just the opium.'

'Here, in the kitchen?'

'Felix, can I have a word with you,' began Mrs Ferreira.

'Opium *and* alcohol? It wasn't like that when I was at school!'

'Science didn't exist when you were at school!' said Sophia crushingly. 'Things have moved on a bit since then.'

'I'll say!'

'Felix, can I have a word with you?' said Mrs Ferreira. 'I wonder if this is really quite the right project for you?'

'But –'

'I really think you ought to consider changing it.'

'Oh, no!' said Felix. 'Not *again!*'

Chapter Eight

The next morning Mrs Wynne-Gurr announced a change in the programme.

'It has occurred to me,' she said, 'that in view of the importance of religion to our original founder, we should not, while we are here, overlook that side of their lives. The Order was, after all, often referred to as The Religion. I propose, therefore, a visit this morning to the Co-Cathedral, aptly, for us, the St John's Co-Cathedral.'

Felix thought for a moment that his mother had stuttered, but then, when she repeated it, decided that she had not.

'Why are you saying "Co-Cathedral"?' he asked.

'Because that's what it's called. I do not know why, exactly –'

'Because it is a Conventual Church,' said one of the ladies.

'What is a Conventual Church?' asked Felix.

'You can look it up later,' said Mrs Wynne-Gurr firmly. 'Now let us press on, as there is something I wish to show you all.'

She stopped by a blank wall in which there was a single window.

'This is very special,' she said.

The ladies and Felix examined it gravely.

'What's special about it?' asked Felix.

'This is the wall of one of the Grand Inquisitor's prisons. And in it were kept two English ladies. Ordinary ladies like ourselves. But Quakers. They had been put in the prison because they were trying to save the island from Catholicism.'

'I'm a Catholic myself,' said one of the ladies.

'As were most of the inhabitants of the island,' said Mrs Wynne-Gurr. 'So these ladies were up against it. However, they made such a nuisance of themselves that the Grand Inquisitor locked them up. Nothing daunted, the ladies continued their efforts from within the prison. Through this very window. They continued to address the passers-by.'

'In English?' said Felix.

'Certainly.'

'But –'

'They refused to be deterred. Just think of it: two ordinary elderly ladies, in prison in a strange land, refusing to give in. Determined to spread the Word.'

'But in English?' said Felix.

'Yes. Every day and all day.'

'Did the Maltese speak English then?'

'I expect so,' said Mrs Wynne-Gurr, slightly flustered. 'The point is, they were standing up for what they believed in.'

There were mutters of approbation.

'It is an example,' declared Mrs Wynne-Gurr in ringing tones, 'which has always meant a great deal to me. An example to us all!'

Felix wondered about this as they walked on to the Co-Cathedral. Was it? It seemed a bit sort of misguided to him, haranguing passers-by out of a window and not even in a language they could understand. It wasn't likely to be very effective.

Effective, that was the word. Felix liked things to work. And then he liked to see how they worked. But he couldn't see how this was likely to work. Surely people would just take no notice?

He could see, however, the point that his mother was making, that it was a stand on behalf of a principle. The Wynne-Gurr family was hot on principles and Felix was too much his mother's son not to feel the force of an appeal to it.

All the same, though, it had to work. He put the point to Chantale as they were walking along.

'What about martyrs?' she said. 'And these ladies probably thought of themselves as martyrs. They were prepared to suffer for their beliefs.'

What about his mother, wondered Felix? Was she prepared to suffer for her beliefs? As opposed, he thought, to making him suffer? He thought she probably was.

And then another thought came into his head. What about Sophia? Would she be prepared to suffer for her beliefs? Would she, in the right circumstances, be willing to become a martyr?

He thought she would.

And he, Felix, would he be prepared to suffer for his beliefs? Not if it wasn't going to work. What would be the point? You would be dead, and nothing would have changed.

'At the time, I suppose,' said Chantale, 'you don't know it's not going to work. In fact, you probably think it *will* work. But I've always thought there was a kind of cussedness to being a martyr, that, perhaps, they think to themselves: Right, you bastards, I know I'm going to lose, but I'm not going to give you the satisfaction of admitting it.'

'That sounds like my mother,' said Felix.

Felix found the Co-Cathedral more interesting than he had expected. There were marble tombstones all over the floor which were covered with heraldic coats-of-arms with many quarterings, some of which he tried to work out. And there were lots of inscriptions commemorating battles, some at sea. There was also, downstairs, a big picture of St John being beheaded, which Felix thought was pretty good.

But – St John? Was he another loser? The Wynne-Gurr family was not strong on the Bible and nor was Felix. Was St John one of the Twelve Apostles? Felix thought he probably was. But what happened to the Apostles afterwards – after all that bit in the Gospels? Did they all end up like St John? He would have to ask Sophia. She would certainly know.

But, look, this was bad. The founder of the Order of St John – no, no, that wasn't right, the person around whom the Order was founded – was not effective. He couldn't have been if his head had been cut off. Did that mean that the Order of St John wasn't likely to be effective, either? And, certainly, they didn't seem to have been very effective. They had been chucked out of Jerusalem and out of Rhodes.

On the other hand, they seemed to have made a success of their move to Malta. They had beaten off the Turks, after all. So maybe the St John Ambulance had more going for it than he had thought.

'At least they beat the Arabs,' he said to Chantale.

But then he remembered that Chantale was an Arab and thought: What a crass thing to say!

'I'm sorry!' he apologized.

'Why?' said Chantale, surprised. She had been walking along with her mind elsewhere, taking in the effect of the golden light. A lot of the buildings in Valletta were of honey-coloured stone and the effect of the light on them was magical. It was as if they had been dipped in honey. But inside the Co-Cathedral everything was grey. Not the cold, reducing grey of the churches in London which absorbed the light and then didn't let go again, but somehow a cool, sharp grey which refreshed after the brightness outside and which brought out the richness of the heraldic symbolling.

'You being an Arab,' said Felix.

Chantale laughed.

'I'm only half Arab,' she said. 'The other half is French. And, anyway, I'm not sure the Turks count as Arabs. They were Muslims, certainly. But Turks are different from Arabs.'

'Of course they are!' said Felix mortified. He knew that, really.

'However, they were all lumped together as Saracens. I'll give you that. But who beat them, anyway? Exactly who were the Knights? I've been looking at the chapels. Each one belonged to a different langue, as they called them. A different language, I suppose, or a different nationality. There was one for France, one for Italy, one for Germany, and so on. There was even one for England. The Knights were pretty international. The one thing they weren't, though, was Maltese. There isn't a chapel, or a langue, for Malta.'

'Do you think they mind?'

'I would if I was them. Of course, perhaps they think that since the whole Cathedral is Maltese, it takes in all the other nationalities.'

'That's a nice thought,' said Felix. 'And it's good that the Knights came from all over the place. It's good to see the different countries working together,' he added, echoing something his father frequently said.

'Yes, but they were working together against the Turks. And the Arabs. They had just been at the Crusades. Some people,' said Chantale, teasing him, 'say that the only time the Europeans work together is when they're working against the Arabs.'

Felix let it pass but took it in. He thought he might try it out on Sophia.

After the visit to the Co-Cathedral, Chantale walked over to the Upper Barraca Gardens, where she had arranged to meet Seymour when he got back from the hospital. Felix went with her, hoping to meet Sophia, who had half promised to be there. And when they got there, she *was* there, talking happily to Seymour, who had just crossed over from the Birgu side.

'The sky was full of them!' she was saying excitedly.

'It must have been an amazing sight,' said Seymour.

'It was,' said Sophia.

She had watched things that day from a position down by the sea where her grandfather had taken her. Above had been the balloons, dozens of them, and below had been the grey, sleek Navy ships, clustered in the harbour for the occasion.

'Like sitting ducks,' Umberto had said.

'Ducks with guns,' her grandfather had said scornfully. 'Balloons would be useless if it came to a fight.'

'They wouldn't be used for that,' Uncle Paolo had said. 'They would be used to bring an army here, land them inland, over by the Victoria Lines, say, and the Navy's guns would be useless.'

'An invasion is it, now?' her grandfather had said. 'Christ, boys, we'd better look out. The Arabs are coming!'

'It's not the Arabs you've got to worry about,' Uncle Paolo had said. 'It's the British. And they're already here.'

It was about then, Sophia remembered, that the balloon had started to come down.

'My God!' said Grandfather. 'The invasion's already started!'

They had watched the balloon descend lower and lower. At first they had thought it was intentional but then they had seen that it was going to come down into the sea.

'You'd better get back to the hospital where you're supposed to be,' Grandfather had said to Umberto. 'You could be needed.'

Umberto had scuttled off and they had watched the balloon settle down on to the water. A bit like an elephant sitting down, Sophia had thought.

Grandfather had had a programme and he had checked the number on the balloon to see whose it was.

'It's German,' he had said.

'Then they'd better get their act together at the hospital,' Uncle Paolo had said. 'The Germans won't like it if things go wrong.'

But they hadn't gone wrong, thought Sophia. The balloon had settled down quite gently on the water and in a moment the *dghajsas* had been racing over to it. The basket beneath the balloon had given a jump when it had hit the water and the man standing inside it had disappeared from view. But then he had stood up again and begun shouting at the *dghajsas* as they closed in.

'I don't know what he's shouting about,' Grandfather had said. 'He's got off very lightly.'

'The Germans are like that,' Uncle Paolo had said. 'They do make a fuss.' What he'd said seemed suddenly to strike him, because he had said it again. 'Yes,' he had said, as if to himself, 'they do make a fuss.' And he had suddenly seemed very pleased with himself. 'Yes, that's it!' he had said, and smiled. Sophia couldn't see what he was so pleased about because it didn't seem that brilliant a remark.

'Uncle Paolo was quite pleased when the balloon came down,' she said to Seymour, 'because he thought the Germans would make a fuss. Grandfather was cross with him. "Was that what he wanted?" he asked. "Was that what it was all about as far as he was concerned?" And Uncle Paolo said: "Yes." And Grandfather called him a twisted son of a bitch. And Uncle Paolo stormed off, and Mum was very angry with Grandfather and she stormed off, and that's why I remember it,' said Sophia.

A *dghajsa* had just pulled in below them and the passengers were disembarking. Among them was a group of sailors.

'Hello, sir!' said a voice which Seymour recognized. 'Going to the match this evening?'

It was Cooper, and along with him, as usual, were Corke and Price.

'I might,' he said, remembering that Chantale had said something about being on duty that evening with the St John Ambulance at a football match. 'Where is it?'

'Birgu,' said Cooper. 'Not far from the hospital.'

'Who is it between?'

'A Navy side and a local team.'

'A return match?'

'No, no, they haven't played before. They are from the Bormla end. About halfway up the table so not bad. I reckon, though, that our lads are better. *Amethyst* is in and we've a strong team out tonight.'

'I may well be there.'

'We'll look out for you, sir. And see that you get home all right,' said Cooper, with another semi-insolent grin.

* * *

123

Seymour had been over to the hospital that morning to check on a few things.

'A fractured knee-cap,' said Macfarlane. 'That's what he was admitted with. It normally clears up on its own but this time the bone had been splintered and they thought that some of the splinters might have to be extracted so we kept him in.'

'It sounds a bit serious.'

'Not that serious. But, yes, on the heavy side as football injuries go.'

'Do you get many football injuries?'

'It's the next best thing to a war, as far as the Navy is concerned. They come ashore, all full of pent-up testosterone, and football is a good way of discharging it. So, yes, we do have quite a few.'

'Any idea how the injury was incurred?'

'Through a tackle, I understand. But you really need to ask someone else about that. He'll have told the doctors, or you could try asking your friends.'

'My friends?'

'The famous three. Cooper, Corke and Price.'

'They saw the match?'

'They try to see *every* match, as far as I can tell. And then they come here and talk it over with their mates in the wards.'

'I know they were friends with Turner. I didn't know they were visiting Wilson as well.'

'Oh, yes. He was the one that started them coming. But then when Turner was admitted they started going to see him as well. And then it spread. They started visiting all the other sailors in the hospital. It was rather touching. They made a thing of it. Visiting the sick. They were in here two or three times a week. I was rather impressed by the way they stuck at it. Particularly in the case of Wilson, because Vasco was in a bed nearby and made himself unpleasant, as usual. I used to keep an eye on them because I felt it could easily end up with him getting the same treatment as Turner: a broken jaw.'

'He's not that keen on the English.'

'No, but it was more that he is very keen on football. He and Wilson used to argue about it all the time. The trouble was that Vasco knew more about football, even English football, than Wilson did, and it irritated him. It irritated the others, too, when they were visiting.

'Of course, you expect a bit of banter about football when it's men but this was different. It had an edge to it. And it happened every time. Every time that they came in. He would *always* say something about football. Either about the football here – usually the Navy football – or about football in England. And usually it was not just saying, it was *taunting*.

'It got so bad that I felt I had to stop it, so I moved him to the other end of the ward. But that made it worse. He would shout down the ward and they would shout back. So *everyone* could hear, and *everyone* got involved! Of course, I read the riot act and threatened to put Vasco in a cubicle on his own. Things got a little better. But then Wilson died.'

'And they stopped coming?'

'Well, actually, they didn't. I still used to see them hanging around. Visiting someone else, I suppose. Or maybe they just thought that the hospital was a cool place to go!'

Standing there in the Upper Barraca Gardens, looking out over the harbour crowded with English warships, and out further to the incredible blue Mediterranean, empty except for just a couple of ships laying a trail of steam across the horizon, Chantale suddenly felt a moment of release.

It wasn't so much release from the constraints of being with Mrs Wynne-Gurr's St John Ambulance party, although it was nice to get away for a moment, as release from a general feeling of tightness that she had been carrying about with her, it seemed, for ages. She knew what it was. The tightness was England. And it wasn't just the tightness of the crowded East End streets – heavens, the streets of Tangier were crowded enough! – as the way in which the sky closed down on you, shutting you into the closed, tight little horizon of greyness.

Here, the sky opened up and carried on for ever, merging its blueness with sea which was equally blue, and still, so still. This morning the sky was subtly different from what it had been the day before. Mrs Ferreira waking up that morning had pronounced it colder and had stipulated that Sophia was to wear her jacket. Grandfather – surely not? – had put on a scarf.

And, yes, the day had seemed colder when Chantale had stepped out into the street. Of course, these things were relative and later Grandfather would remove his scarf and his jersey and go about shirt-sleeved as before. And Sophia would be racing around in her thin summer dress. But there definitely was a difference in the air.

Or was it not so much a difference in the feel of things as in the look of things? The sky, that beautiful blue sky, seemed somehow whiter, the sun gently muted.

Chantale recognized the feel of the day at once. It was one of those mornings that were treasured in Tangier, when the heat was less intense, lifted its burden, and lots of things came alive. Birds, especially, attacking any stretch of water with revived alacrity.

And, suddenly, Chantale felt a great ache inside her at all the things she missed, all that she had forgone when she had moved to England: the subtle changes of the sun and light.

No, she would not go back, she knew that. But it was nice occasionally to be reminded of it. And here in Malta she was reminded of it. It was a different way of life, which you knew from the inside.

The English had come to Malta, just as the French had come to Tangier, and imposed their way of life. On the surface, they had won out. But, underneath, was a buried life which had continued for centuries and would go on regardless.

126

They might call it the Grand Harbour but Chantale had seen the other name which was on all the maps: il-Port-il-Kebir.

Perhaps it was the slight change in the weather that had prompted it but Mrs Ferreira had announced that morning that she was going shopping with Uncle Paolo to see that he was properly 'fitted out' for his return to the big ships. Chantale had soon grasped that this was the tradition when a member of your family put to sea, and even Grandfather did not demur. Nor, surprisingly, did Uncle Paolo, except for a token demurral that he was now old enough etc. But Mrs Ferreira was firm.

'Debra can't do it, so I must!' she said, and Uncle Paolo bowed his head in acquiesence and arrived shortly after breakfast.

Mrs Ferreira had prepared a list. But she didn't need to, really, since she had proposed similar lists before, for her father, brothers, and even for Paolo himself. In any case, a list was hardly necessary when everyone knew what you needed when you put to sea. But making a list was clearly part of it and Mrs Ferreira got a great deal of pleasure from making one. It helped to bind the family together, she told Chantale, to remind the family that it was one.

This was particularly necessary in the case of Uncle Paolo, she explained. Because of the unfortunate start to his life and his subsequent moving around, not just from family to family but from country to country, he had never properly put down roots. Mrs Ferreira was inclined to attribute to this cause the fact that he had never married. If he had married, she said, it would have settled him.

For, at the age of forty, he was still in her view unsettled. 'He doesn't know where he belongs. Of course, he belongs here, but he doesn't seem able to recognize it.' If he had recognized it, she said tartly, he wouldn't be playing in the Birgu band but for 'our band'. To Mrs Ferreira this was a kind of betrayal: but Chantale thought it was perhaps a case of kicking against the pricks of family as far as, in

Malta, you could decently go. Paolo obviously had a strong attachment to his family. Whenever it gathered, he gathered, too. But Chantale sensed an uneasiness there, a kind of tension, as if he felt that because of his mother's marriage he could never be fully accepted into it.

Chantale wasn't sure whether that was true. Certainly there seemed to be some special tension between Paolo and Mrs Ferreira's father; but Mrs Ferreira seemed determined that if there was any such tension she would personally do her best to overcome it.

The normally genial Lucca was plainly disheartened.

'He's still at it,' he said.

'At . . .?'

'Questions,' he said. 'All yesterday and then all this morning. Well, I don't mind answering questions. It's his job, after all. But within reason. I mean, I've got a job, too, and this is only part of it. When am I going to get the rest done? Every time I look into my office I see a bigger pile of paper on my desk. I soon won't be able to see the desk at all. Forms! Please to fill in this one, Herr Lucca, my Government requires it. And this one. And that one. "But this one is not right, Herr Lucca. It has not been correctly filled in!" "Where has it not been correctly filled in?" "Here and here!" "Where was I standing at 3 p.m on Saturday, June the 3rd? Christ, I don't know. I stand in all sorts of places." "But this is a vital moment, Herr Lucca. This is when the balloon started to come down!" "Ah, then. Well, at that point I was watching to see if any other balloons came down." "Ah, you had suspicions, then?" "No, I was just watching *in case* any of the balloons came down." "But you were watching? Where, then, were you standing?"

'In the end I told him I was standing by the Old Customs House. Well, it was as good a place as any. The fact is, I moved around. I had to. There were other things to see to as well as balloons. A fight between *dghajsas*, for example. Where the Governor was to stand. But his wife couldn't see! Could she move –? Yes, but if she did then I would have to move – and so on. Not to mention the drunks coming out of the bars. And so on.

'Then he wanted to know about security arrangements.

'"Look," I said, "we weren't bothering too much about security arrangements. I mean, Christ, it was just balloons. And they were up in the air. What we were worried about was what would happen if they ran into each other. I mean, they could, couldn't they? There were so many of them. Security? No, what concerned us was traffic control."

'"Traffic control?" he says. "But that would be on a different form."

'And he ferrets in his briefcase and produces another form. "Please to fill this in," he says. "By tomorrow morning."

'"Traffic control?" I say. "Are we talking about balloons? Because we don't reckon to go in for traffic control of balloons much. Or are you talking about *dghajsas*? Because that was what was likely to cause the trouble in the harbour."

'"Both,"' he says. "Both. But *dghajsas* are boats, yes? That would be on a different form."

'Then he says, "But that is not important. What is important is the security on the ground. At the launch site. Can you tell me that, please. The security arrangements there. How did you control access to the balloons? What system of permits did you use? Did the technical staff have identification badges?"

'"Look," I said, "this was not a Grand Prix event. It was just balloons over the harbour. A spectacle. A bit of fun. For everybody."

'"Ah, no," he said. "People can get injured. Or even killed. At spectacles. Precautions have to be taken. All I am asking is what they were."

'Of course, we had made *some* arrangements, and I tried to tell him what they were. And he grew sniffier and sniffier. I thought his nose was going to rise up right over his head. And all the time he was writing. He wrote everything down.

'Well, later in the morning I got a chance to take a look

at some of the things he had written. And it made we mad. "Lack of system," he had written. "Typically British." "But we're *not* British," I felt like shouting at him. "We're Maltese! And we've got our own way of doing things, our own systems. They may not be yours but on the whole they work." But I thought I'd better not because the boss had already been on to me. "This German business is a hot potato, Lucca," he said. "And it's getting hotter every minute."'

'Well, I'm sorry to hear this,' said Seymour.

'You should be,' said Lucca. 'Because your turn is next. He wants to speak to the Englishman in charge.'

'No, no, no,' said Seymour. 'I am afraid you are under a misapprehension, Mr Backhaus, I am not in charge. I am merely a detective assigned to the case.'

'A naval detective?'

'No, no. I don't think we have naval detectives. I'm from Scotland Yard.'

'Ah, Scotland Yard? So London thinks this is important, yes?'

'Well, I wouldn't quite say that –'

'London is concerned, yes?'

'Well, naturally. Suspected murder is –'

'And the Navy, the Navy, too, is concerned?'

'Yes, I'm sure they are. Two of their men, after all. And on board one of their ships.'

'Ship?' Backhaus shuffled his papers. 'It says nothing about ships here.'

'The hospital is a ship to them. It is a naval hospital. In the Navy it counts as a ship.'

Herr Backhaus was silenced. But only for a moment.

'A ship? Yes, yes, I can see that to them – in terms of responsibility, yes. I can see that. It would, yes.'

He thought.

'But that would make it even more important to them!' he said. 'They would see it as something aimed at the heart of the Navy!'

'What?'

'Herr Kiesewetter's balloon. Would they not see it as a threat?'

'No, no, not much of one. They're pretty robust.'

'Think, Mr Seymour! Think! You have the whole British Mediterranean fleet before you. Including its very latest vessels. The Type XK 115 – does that not mean anything to you, Mr Seymour? I assure you it does to the British Navy. Would they want foreign observers studying it from the air?'

'But, look, they can study it perfectly well from the land! If you just stand up in the Upper Barraca Gardens – or anywhere along the harbour front –'

'But study it, Mr Seymour, really study it! Closely. From above. An unimpeded vision. Would they be so happy about that? Might they not be . . . concerned, Mr Seymour? Concerned? At least just a little?'

'Well, I can see what you are saying. But aren't you over-doing it? Anyone could perfectly well observe these ships from the land with a telescope. Why are you making so much of observing them from the air?'

'It is not I who am making too much, Mr Seymour. It is possibly others.'

'The Navy?'

'You said it, Mr Seymour. Not I.'

'But that's ridiculous! Are you suggesting that the Navy –?'

Mr Backhaus held up his hand. 'I am suggesting noth-ing, Mr Seymour. But there are questions to be asked, are there not? A balloon comes down, a German balloon, in a British port. For no apparent reason. Its occupant, hitherto perfectly fit, and not, apparently, injured during the descent, is taken to a hospital where he suddenly dies. A British hospital, a British naval hospital. British doctors. British nurses –'

'Maltese.'

'Are there not questions to be asked? I could go on. The balloon. Herr Kiesewetter is a very experienced bal-loonist. He cares for his balloon, he is very careful with it.

He examines it all the time. Of course, he examines it. His life depends on it. And so, normally, do his technicians. He has flown many times before, all over the world. Safely. But this time there is something different. The technicians are British. And suddenly the balloon is not safe. Why is it not safe, Mr Seymour? Are there not questions to be asked?'

'There are, indeed,' said Seymour, 'but the questions you pose cover only part of the picture. As I understand the drift of your questioning, you are suggesting that the British Navy may have had a hand in the death of Mr Kiesewetter. But may I remind you that his death is only one of a group of deaths that I am investigating. Are you really suggesting that, in addition to murdering Mr Kiesewetter, the Navy also murdered two of its own men? Because if you are, unless you can produce some more substantial evidence in support of your suggestions, I would hesitate before advancing your suppositions, whether in Berlin or London, or indeed, anywhere else. Because I fear they would not be taken seriously.'

Chapter Nine

Sophia and Felix had discovered soon after they met that they had problems in common. One of these, of course, was their projects, which weighed on them increasingly as the time for delivery approached. The other was that they both came from families whose lives were determined by a nearby hospital. The one thing that both of them were resolved on was that when they grew up their own lives would be different: they were both firm that they would have nothing, but nothing, ever to do with hospitals.

In Felix's case the issue was simple: should he become a doctor or not? His father was a highly successful ophthalmologist who found his work completely satisfying and saw no reason why Felix shouldn't find that, too. Felix's mother had harboured an ambition in early life to be a doctor herself. That ambition she had had to set aside because of family objections but much of her life now was devoted to compensating for it by other means. As far as Felix was concerned, she differed from her husband only in the idea – she was not narrow – that Felix might become an obstetrician rather than an ophthalmologist.

Felix, however, was having none of it. As he had pointed out to Seymour when he had met him in the Upper Barraca Gardens, his father didn't seem to have much of a life. He went off unpleasantly early in the morning and came back ridiculously late in the evenings. He was always busy and never seemed to have time to do anything interesting. What sort of life was that? Where, asked Felix, gloomily aware of the burden of his project pressing upon him, was freedom?

This was an issue for Sophia, too. Her mother worked all hours in the hospital dispensary and her father, who was a steward on one of the Navy ships, often wasn't there at all. The burden of minding the younger children often fell on Sophia. While she didn't mind this, up to a point, there were frequently other things that she wanted to do. Besides, looking around her, she had the uneasy feeling that what she was seeing was her future, that this would go on being her life after she left school. Life was suddenly threatening to narrow down. Where was freedom?

Behind this, too, for Sophia, there were other, larger issues of freedom, issues you became aware of, she said to Chantale, as they walked together through the Barraca Gardens, only when you had a foreign power occupying your front garden. No doubt Chantale had had exactly the same thoughts when she was growing up in Morocco. (Chantale, who had, was not, however, entirely happy with Sophia's assumption that all this, in Chantale's case, must have been centuries in the past.)

Sophia herself was determined not to allow herself to be boxed in, in any of the ways apparently destined for her. The trouble with older people, she confided, was that they accepted things too readily. Her family, for instance, had all finished up working for the British, mostly in the hospital. Even Uncle Paolo had done his stint. Well, she would not. She would show them. And especially her grandfather, who persisted in asking what she would do for money, a question which, in Sophia's view, showed the mentally circumscribed state of the older generations in Malta.

Not that she minded her grandfather, really. Her arguments with him, and the desire to prove him wrong, had been a great spur to her intellectual advance. And, no doubt, to his.

What, then, asked Chantale, slightly terrified, was Sophia herself thinking of doing when she left school?

Well, said Sophia, she thought she might become a journalist and expose the iniquities of British rule. And then she might stand for the Council and expose them again.

134

Felix had been slightly terrified too, when Sophia had confided these ambitions to him. It sounded all too much like his mother.

Big questions made Felix uncomfortable. No doubt big questions were raised during his history lessons. But somehow the flow of the lesson passed over them and the last thing that would have occurred to Felix was that they were real questions. But now, suddenly, according to Sophia, they were real and all about him. They even surrounded his project. What Felix had hoped to spend his time on was working out how the little bits of metal that together formed a Hospitaller Knight's coat of mail were joined together. But now, according to Sophia, the Knights Hospitaller were just a bunch of thugs! It was as if his project had suddenly leaped up and kicked him in the face!

And behind this, as always with Sophia, there were lots of other questions. What were the Knights *doing* in Malta? What right had they to be there? And what were the British doing in Malta? And what right did *they* have to be there?

Felix was a logical boy and had to admit the force of these questions. Clearly, he had some thinking to do. He felt he had moved on a long way since he had arrived in Malta.

Sophia, too, felt that she had moved on in her thinking. It wasn't that she had abandoned her position of general rebellion: it was just that it was turning out to be more complicated than she had supposed. While she was still committed to denouncing the British, somehow there didn't seem much point in denouncing Felix. He so clearly did not know any better. It was obviously a case less for denunciation than for re-education, which, generously, after consideration, she was prepared, in Felix's case, to undertake.

But were the British all like that, she wondered? In which case, she had a big job on her hands.

The balloons had long left the Marsa racecourse but the grey patch of Herr Kiesewetter's deflated balloon still remained, guarded by an indolent policeman. The two technicians also remained, required to stay by police and court order. When Seymour got there they were sitting moodily beside the lifeless grey.

'Still here?' said Seymour brightly.

'Still bloody here,' said one of the technicians, the older one, George.

'And likely to stay so,' said the other technician, Joe. 'At least for the next few years. Until they get this sorted out.'

'No movement?' said Seymour, although he knew there was no movement.

They shook their heads. It was an unsatisfactory position for them to be in. They were allowed a little money by the Governor for food and lodgings and necessary expenses, some of which the Maltese authorities hoped to recover from the Germans but that would require negotiation and that could continue for a long time. Meanwhile, the technicians sat and contemplated their problems.

'No one else here?'

'They've all gone on to Stuttgart. That's where the next big ballooning event is taking place.'

'And we won't be there,' said Joe.

'And you would have been there?'

'Oh, yes. Kiesewetter liked us. We've got a good reputation, you know.'

'There are others who'd like us,' said George.

'But not if we've got to stay here,' said Joe.

'Reputations go,' said George.

'If you're not around,' said Joe.

'It may not be long,' said Seymour encouragingly.

They looked up with interest.

'You're getting somewhere, are you?' asked Joe.

'Somewhere,' said Seymour.

They shrugged.

'So what are you doing here today?' asked Joe.

'Checking on the things I missed the first time,' said Seymour.

They laughed.

'That's what you've got to do,' George said. 'Check, check and check again.'

'Which you did,' said Seymour.

'Which we did.'

'And yet someone slashed the balloon.'

'We've gone over it a hundred times,' said George, 'asking when it could have happened, I mean, we were here the whole time.'

'That morning,' said Joe. 'We started early. Before seven. Didn't even wait for breakfast. Got here and stayed here.'

'Until lunch, when we went off for a pint.'

'We were practically done by then.'

'Just a few things left,' said George, 'which we knew we could do in time for the launch.'

'And there was supposed to be a policeman on guard,' said Joe.

'We reckon that's when it must have happened. We reckon he wandered off.'

'Bloody Maltese!' said Joe.

'He swears he didn't. That Inspector gave him a right going over but he was adamant he'd been here all the time. And kept his eyes open the whole time.'

'To be fair,' said Joe, 'he could have been round the other side.'

'It doesn't matter to other people as much as it matters to us.'

'We'd checked just before leaving,' said Joe. 'Gone over it with a fine-tooth comb. Every inch. There was nothing – I'll take my oath!'

'We left it four-fifths inflated. We just needed to top it up a bit when we got back. Wouldn't take a moment.'

'And the thing is,' said Joe, 'it looked all right. When we got back. You can tell, you know. Just by the look of it. If you're really experienced. But it looked all right.'

'He must have done it,' said George, 'just before we got back. So when we inflated, it wouldn't have been apparent.'

'Not at first. It would have gone up all right, and looked

pretty good. It was only after a bit that you would have noticed.'

'And we did notice,' said George. 'I said to Joe: "That doesn't look right!"'

'I thought he needed to open the valve. And I reckon he thought that, too, because we saw him look up and then start fiddling with it.'

'But by then the rent was stretching and opening up. Quickly. So he had to think about coming down.'

'Which he did. And managed all right. He was good, in his way, was Kiesewetter.'

'One of the best we've had.'

'No flies on him. He always knew what to do.'

'And, of course, he did get it down all right,' said Seymour.

'Died in the hospital,' said George.

'Bloody Maltese,' said Joe.

Seymour went over to the solitary policeman left guarding the remains of the balloon.

'Seymour,' he introduced himself. 'From London. Scotland Yard.'

'I know,' said the policeman. 'I've seen you with Lucca.'

'Were you here guarding at the launch?'

'Not exactly here,' said the policeman. 'Over there.' He nodded towards the bandstand.

'You were keeping an eye on the band?'

'That's right. One of them.'

'How many were there?'

'Two and a half.'

'What was the half?'

'Marsa. But they don't count, really. Besides the other. They're tiny. But they wanted to be here. They're nothing, though, compared with the others.'

'Birgu, Valletta – was there another one from the Three Cities?'

'No. Just Birgu.'

'Was there any trouble this time?'

'No, no. People's minds were on the balloons.'

'No trouble, but a hell of a noise? Was that it?'

The policeman smiled. 'Dead right. That was it.'

Mrs Wynne-Gurr was pushing on with her programme. This afternoon the St John Ambulance ladies were meeting a local branch for tea and cakes and profitable discussion and then they were going on with the branch to observe it performing its duties at a local football match. The match, as usual in Malta, was being played in the evening when it would be cooler.

Chantale was not very interested in football, nor, for that matter, in tea and cakes with the local ladies but, having committed herself to the Ambulance, she felt she had to go along. Mrs Wynne-Gurr had allowed them a free morning and Chantale had proposed to spend it with Seymour. A swim and then coffee? And then, perhaps, a gentle stroll through the streets of Valletta?

No such luck. Duty, as Mrs Wynne-Gurr reminded them at the end of the tea and cakes, called.

Chantale's spirits revived slightly when they got to the football ground. It was a lot smaller than the Marsa race-track, just a local field, and there was a friendly hum about it. The crowd was just over a thousand and included many children and mothers. Even here, though, there was a band.

Only one, however. Chantale hoped that indicated that there would be less of a spirit of rivalry and hence fewer serious cases for the St John Ambulance to deal with.

She was stationed this time quite near the band. When the local ladies had put up their two tables, and erected a little tent that they had brought, there was time to look round. The ladies began chatting with people in the crowd whom they knew. Chantale looked over towards the band. There were people there that she knew, too, some of whom had been at the Ferreiras' picnic at Marsa. There was Uncle Paolo, for instance, this time with a trumpet held up before him. And there, yes, was Luigi, also with some sort of brass instrument. Yes, thought Chantale, that was right, for this would be the, or a, Birgu band, to which they both belonged.

Paolo saw her looking at him and said something to Luigi and they both smiled and gave her a welcoming toot on their instruments. Everything was more relaxed than at the Marsa racetrack.

The band began to play, with gusto but without giving the impression, so marked at Marsa, that they were playing *at* someone.

Of course, they were playing against someone here, too, thought Chantale: the British Navy. But there was less edge to it because there was less sense of an opposition. There were sailors here, dotted about in the crowd, but so few of them that they were almost invisible, and, certainly, inaudible against the band.

Seymour had been counting the sailors, too. He was standing next to Inspector Lucca, whom he had encountered at the entrance, keeping an eye open for potential trouble-makers.

'But there'll be no problem tonight,' he said to Seymour. 'There are too few from the Navy, and there isn't a band to stir them up. You really need two bands to get the crowd going. This is too easy for the Birgu band. So they'll be holding back, even though it's the British.'

The sides were evenly matched and not at all unskilful.

'Good game,' said Inspector Lucca, at half time. 'Could go either way. I think I'm going to wander around. If there is any trouble, this is when it will be. And at the end, of course, depending on the result.'

The St John Ambulance had barely been called on. During the half-time break several ladies came up from the crowd and chatted. Chantale suddenly found that Paolo and Luigi were beside her.

'Not so busy today?' said Paolo.

'*Much* quieter,' said Chantale.

'That worries me,' said Paolo. 'It means that we Maltese hate each other more than we hate the British!'

140

'Is it as bad as that?' said Chantale. 'You really hate the British?'

'Yes,' said Paolo shortly.

'And you?' Chantale said to Luigi. 'Do you hate the British, too?'

'Oh, yes,' said Luigi. 'Anyone who is not Maltese.'

'Is this just in football terms?' asked Chantale.

She could see he did not understand her.

'Generally,' Paolo said for him.

'Yes, generally,' said Luigi.

He was not too bright, thought Chantale.

'How's the wound?' she asked.

'Fine, fine,' said Luigi. 'It's nothing.'

'You did a good job,' Paolo said to Chantale.

'I don't really know much about it,' confessed Chantale. 'It's just that I've done it once or twice before.'

'Not in England,' said Paolo.

'No, in Tangier.'

'Tangier's a good place,' said Paolo. 'I might go there.'

'You wouldn't like the French,' said Chantale. 'They're everywhere. Like the British here.'

'But in Tangier they're fighting the French!' said Paolo. 'Here, no one does anything!'

'There's less fighting in Morocco than you might think,' said Chantale.

'Not enough?' asked Paolo.

'Well –'

'I ask because you are an Arab.'

'Half Arab,' said Chantale.

'But you're on the Arab side. You must be.'

'I like the Arabs,' said Chantale. She laughed. 'So did my father. Perhaps too well.'

'Ah, yes. It was like that, was it?'

'They loved each other. My father and my mother. It would be better if it was always like that.'

Paolo was silent.

'It wasn't like that with my father and mother,' he said.

'She was Maltese and he was Arab?'

Paolo nodded. 'That's right, yes.'

141

'I'm sorry it didn't work out.'

Paolo shrugged. 'It just made it complicated, that's all.'

'It *is* that, yes,' said Chantale: 'complicated. You don't know which side to lean to. I find myself agreeing with both, with both the French and the Arabs. And also disagreeing with them. That, maybe, is why I drifted away –'

'Like me,' said Paolo.

'– to England.'

'Ah, England,' said Paolo.

'Don't you find that?' asked Chantale. 'That you're on both sides, Libyan and Maltese?'

'Well, yes,' said Paolo.

'But not the British,' Chantale laughed.

'Not the British,' said Paolo seriously.

'Why?'

'Because they're British and not Maltese. And because they've taken over Malta. And because, well ...' He shrugged. 'They look down on us. Whichever you are. Maltese or Arab. I worked on a ship. A Navy ship. As a steward. And they treated me like dirt! "I am as good as you!" I said. But they didn't see it like that. And in the end I had to go.'

Seymour, walking round the pitch at half time to stretch his legs, came upon Cooper, Corke and Price.

'What do you think of it, sir?'

'Not bad,' said Seymour. 'Not bad at all.'

'Better than usual,' said Price. 'We've been able to put a proper team out.'

'*Amethyst*, I think you said?'

'There's three *Amethyst* players and they make a difference.'

'Got to the finals in Hong Kong,' said Price.

'Not bad, then. But the other side's not bad, either.'

'Them Maltese is tricky devils!'

'Do you see a lot of matches?' asked Seymour.

'Try to,' said Corke.

'Then you're probably the blokes who can help me.

There's someone in the hospital that I'm interested in, who got injured in a match. I wondered if you saw it?'

'What match was that, sir?'

'I'm not sure of the match. The man was named Wilson.'

'The one that was murdered, sir?'

'That's right.'

'Bad do, that!'

'He'd been injured in a match. I wondered if you saw it?'

'We did, sir,' said Price. 'Corkey and me. Not him,' nodding at Cooper.

'I was somewhere else,' said Cooper, 'doing something much more interesting.'

He laughed.

'And not too far away,' said Price, laughing, too.

'You could have come along,' said Cooper.

'We were more interested in the football,' said Corke. 'But, yes, we saw the match, sir.'

'Did you see how he got injured?'

'It was a foul. Their bloke went in on him.'

'Hard,' said Corke. 'And late.'

'It was meant,' said Price.

'He knew what he was doing when he went in like that,' said Corke.

'A bit of ill feeling, was there?'

'More than a bit.'

'Previous history? They'd played against each other before?'

'It wasn't that,' said Price.

'No?'

'He was a mate of the other one.'

'The other one?'

'The one Bob got involved with.'

'Bob?'

'Bob Turner. Him who had his jaw smashed.'

'Ah, yes. The one in the other ward.'

'That's right. He got murdered, too.'

'Bastards!'

'Sorry, can I get this straight? The one who went in on Wilson was a mate of the one who broke Turner's jaw?'

143

'It might not have been him who broke it. But he was there, all right, and the one who went in on Wilson was there with him. I saw them talking when I went in.'

'They were mates?'

'Yes.'

'And what you're saying is that Wilson's injury in the match was a carry-on from the fight in the bar?'

'Yes.'

'So it all comes back to what happened in the bar?'

'Yes, that's right.'

'And what actually started it in the bar?'

'Well, we was in the bar, and Terry had just joined us –'

'After my recreation,' said Cooper.

'– and this little bloke comes in, and he sees Terry, and he stops dead. Then he says something to one of the other Maltese. And the Maltese says something to Bob, and Bob says something back, and that's how it all started.'

'With the little bloke?'

'That's right. I reckon he's a trouble-maker, because after that we didn't see him –'

'He'd gone for his knife,' said Corke. 'I heard him say it.'

'Well, I didn't hear anything because by that time it was a general barney.'

'That was when Bob got hit,' said Cooper.

'I did see that,' said Price. 'At least, I saw him go down.'

'He wasn't up for it, really, because by that time he'd already had a skinful.'

'He wasn't big in it at all, and yet he was the one who got his jaw broke!'

'And that wasn't the end of it, either,' said Cooper. 'Because I don't reckon they left it at that.'

'Meaning?' said Corke.

'They went after them even when they was in hospital, didn't they?'

The half-time interval came to an end and Paolo and Luigi rejoined their band. It struck up and, soon after, the second half began. The St John Ambulance stand had a steady,

144

though small, trickle of visitors. Most of them seemed to be children with bruised knees. A few women had had 'turns'. There was nothing serious; no stabbings on this occasion. Feelings, thought Chantale, were not very high, despite the sentiments that Paolo and Luigi had given utterance to.

And yet the match was closely fought. Coming towards the end, the score was two-all. The band raised its volume, the Maltese supporters urged on their team to a final effort. But the Navy held out. Two-all it remained, and that was the score at the final whistle.

The crowd began to disperse.

'Now's the time,' said Inspector Lucca, 'if there is going to be any trouble.'

He stood on a box to see better.

'All right so far,' he said with satisfaction.

Most of the sailors had prudently left just before the end. There was no show of defiance from either side. The players had left the field shaking hands. There seemed to have been no 'incidents'.

Cooper, Corke and Price, typically, had not left before the end. Seymour caught sight of them pushing towards the exit, but peacefully. They appeared to be talking animatedly, but, he guessed, about the game, going over key moments.

On the far side of the pitch the Birgu band was breaking up. After a final blaze of music they had started to pack up their instruments. They began to melt into the crowd.

Seymour looked around for Chantale. She was helping the St John ladies to pack up their stall. He went across to help carry.

They made their way towards the exit, too. It was a small gap in a fence and the crowd funnelled together to get through it.

Seymour, carrying the Ambulance's small card-tables, was approaching the gap when he saw Cooper, Corke and Price ahead of him. The crowd had slowed down almost to a stop and they were awaiting their turn peacefully.

Suddenly, there was an interruption in the flow. People began to move aside and there were a few shouts.

He saw Lucca pushing his way through the crowd.

The crowd swirled and then parted and in the gap he saw the three seamen again, no longer trying to get out but drawn up together and standing shoulder to shoulder in a short line.

Opposite them was a little group of Maltese and in the group, shouting angrily, his face contorted with rage, was Luigi.

'You watch it, mate!' Seymour heard Cooper say.

'I will kill him! I will kill him!' Luigi was shouting.

'It's that little bloke again!' said Price, surprised.

'What's your problem, mate?' said Cooper dangerously.

'I will kill you!'

'You'll have a job!'

People were trying to pull Luigi away.

There were warning cries.

'He's got a knife!'

The crowd broke away, and suddenly there was Luigi on his own, going towards Cooper with a knife.

'Watch it, mate!' said Corke urgently. 'He's got a knife!'

'Use your boots, Terry!' cried Price.

They pushed forward beside Cooper.

Luigi, though, was on his own making short stabbing motions in the air with his knife. Suddenly, he lunged forward.

And was caught, equally suddenly, by someone who put an arm round his neck.

'I will kill him! I will kill you –' shouted Luigi, struggling to get free.

'You're not going to kill anybody,' said Inspector Lucca.

'Put your boot in, Terry!' cried Corke. 'Now! While you've got a chance!'

'Cut it out!' shouted Seymour. 'You three! Stand back!'

'I'll bloody get him!' said Cooper.

'He's under arrest!' shouted Seymour, pushing the card-tables before him. 'You keep out of it!'

'He's under arrest, Terry!' said Price, warningly.

'I will kill him!' shouted Luigi, struggling in Lucca's grasp.

'Where the hell are you, Rico?' cried Lucca.

'Right here, boss! Right here!' said someone forcing their way through the crowd.

'Help me with this crazy bugger!' said Lucca.

'And you lot get out!' shouted Seymour. 'Get out! Get out of the ground! At once!'

He pushed the table between them and Luigi.

The seamen wavered. Then Cooper shrugged.

'All right, then,' he said. 'This time.'

The other two linked arms with him and began to move away.

'Let me get at him!' shouted Luigi. 'I will kill him!'

Cooper stopped and made a movement as if he was going to come back.

'Keep going!' shouted Seymour. 'You other two, get him out!'

'Come on, Terry,' Price urged him.

They pulled him, unwilling, away.

Suddenly, Lucca cried out.

'Boss!' shouted Rico.

Luigi fell heavily to the ground.

'The bastard got me!' said Lucca, surprised.

'I've bloody got him!' said Rico. He bent over Luigi and Seymour heard the clink of the handcuffs going on.

'Get the knife!' whispered Lucca.

'I've got it, boss,' said Rico. 'I've got him, too. Boss, are you all right?'

'I'm all right,' said Lucca. 'It's nothing. But I'll remember this, Luigi, you daft bastard,' he said.

Luigi, from the ground, began to whimper.

'Sorry, Benito!' he said. 'Sorry! I didn't mean to get you.'

'Well, you bloody got me, Luigi,' said Lucca. 'And I shall remember that! Get this daft bastard away!' he ordered.

Rico heaved Luigi on to his feet.

'Luigi,' he said. 'You don't have a knife any more. But I have a truncheon. And if I have any trouble from you, I'll beat the hell out of you! Now, get going!'

He pulled Luigi off through the crowd.

'Jesus!' said someone, as they went through the gate. 'What was all that about?'

'Can we have a look at that, Benito?' said one of the St John ladies.

'It's nothing, it's nothing!' protested Inspector Lucca.

'We've got someone here who knows about knife wounds. Let her have a look at it.'

'I don't –' began Chantale, but allowed herself to be pulled gently to one side, out of the way of the crowd. Lucca was pulled, too, still protesting.

Someone in the crowd found a chair and pushed the Inspector into it. Chantale bent over him and began to examine the wound.

'I can get him over to the hospital,' said Umberto, who had suddenly appeared. 'It's just round the corner.'

'That would be a good idea,' said Chantale. 'It would be best to get a doctor to look at it. I just want to stop the bleeding.'

'Pad, Miss de Lissac,' said one of the St John ladies.

'Bless you, ladies!' said the Inspector. 'I always knew, Margarita, that you weren't just a waste of time!'

'I wish I could say the same about you, Benito!' retorted Margarita, proffering the pad. 'Still getting yourself into these schoolboy scrapes! At your age!'

Chapter Ten

Early the next morning Seymour went to the Police Headquarters to find out how Lucca was.

'He's all right,' said the man at the desk. 'He's a tough old bird. It'll take more than this to kill him. In fact, he's come in as usual. He's in his office. Why don't you go along and see him?'

Seymour found him sitting behind his desk.

'No, I'm all right,' he said. 'It's sore but not painful. He did an incompetent job, as usual. Waved it around but missed all the vital places. He probably never really meant to hit them anyway.'

'I admire your broad-mindedness, Lucca.'

The Inspector shrugged.

'Well, I know the little bastard,' he said. 'He's mostly piss and wind. Never actually does anything when he gets to the point.'

'He stabbed you, though.'

'He probably didn't even know it. When he's put on the spot, he waves that knife around. They all do round here. But it doesn't mean anything. It's to frighten people. More than people frighten him, which is quite a lot. Especially in the case of that big sailor, who is about twice the size of Luigi. So when he went in on him, Luigi pulled his knife.'

'I don't think he actually went in on him. I was watching them. They were leaving peacefully.'

'Were they? What the hell was Luigi doing, then?'

'I think I know,' said Seymour.

* * *

149

Luigi, small before, seemed to have shrivelled even since the previous day. He was sitting on his bed in the cell, his head in his hands, but jumped up when he saw Lucca.

'Benito!'

He rushed forward and clutched him.

'Benito,' he said, looking at him anxiously. 'You're all right? I didn't really look when you came in before, I was in such a state. But you really are all right, are you? Jesus. I wouldn't have – you've got to believe me, Benito, I would never – Benito, I'll light a candle for you!'

'Well, thanks, Luigi,' said Lucca.

'I really will! Two!'

'Now, steady, Luigi!'

'And ask God to forgive me my sins.'

'Well, that's a good idea, Luigi.'

'Even the thought! I'll ask him to forgive me the thought. What I was doing, I don't know. He made me mad, that Englishman. Just the sight of him. I would have killed him, but I would not do anything to hurt you, Benito, I really wouldn't!'

'Well, thank you, Luigi.'

'You believe me, don't you?'

'All right, then, yes, I believe you.'

'Oh, thank you, Benito! Thank you!'

'I believe you didn't mean to do it, Luigi. But you bloody nearly did do it.'

'I lost my head. When I saw that big Englishman –'

'Yes, well, that's not right, either. You can't go round sticking people with a knife. Whoever they are.'

Luigi hung his head.

'Luigi,' said Seymour, 'exactly why did you want to kill the big Englishman?'

Luigi shook his head slowly from side to side and did not reply.

'Come on, Luigi,' said Lucca. 'Why did you want to kill him?'

Luigi continued to shake his head and said nothing.

'It was your girl, wasn't it?' said Seymour. 'He had gone with your girl.'

Luigi's eyes flashed.

'I will kill him!' he said.

'Tell us about this girl,' said Lucca.

'She was my girl,' said Luigi. 'Before she was his!'

Lucca shook his head sorrowfully.

'It happens, Luigi,' he said. 'It happens!'

'Did you know what went on in the hospital?' said Seymour. 'In the cupboard?'

Luigi's eyes flashed again.

'It was wrong!' he said. 'She was my girl. She shouldn't have gone with others.'

'What do you think I was doing in there?' said Cooper aggressively.

'I know what you were doing in there,' said Seymour. 'I just want to know the rest.'

'The rest?'

'You were in the cupboard enjoying yourself while your mate was being killed next door!'

'No, I wasn't! I'd got out by then.'

'How do you know?'

Cooper went silent.

'How did you know?'

'I didn't know. Not at the time. I worked it out later.'

'You must have been in there when it was happening.'

Cooper's face worked.

'Christ!' he said. 'Christ!'

'Did you hear anything?'

'No!'

'See anything?'

'No! Christ, if I had . . .'

'If you had?'

'I'd have fixed him. I'd have fixed him good. But I didn't see anything, *anything*. I just crawled out and got out of the place fast.'

'And you didn't see anything?'

'No, nothing!'

'What time did you go into the cupboard with her?'

'How do I know?'

'Just tell me!'

'A bit after midnight,' said Cooper sullenly.

'Was there a nurse on duty?'

'She had her back turned – Suzie knows the ropes. She went in first, then beckoned to me. I went on hands and knees, so I was below the level of the beds and the nurse couldn't see me.'

'You'd done it before?'

'Yes. I'd done it before.'

'With the others? After you'd done the visiting?'

'Sometimes. But not usually in the cupboard. She knew other places. She's an artful bitch, she is.'

'In daytime? After you'd done the rounds of the wards?'

'Sometimes.'

'But this was at night. How did she know you were looking for her?'

'She works in the laundry. We sort of looked in earlier.'

'But she did not do it there?'

'No. She came out.'

'Let's go back to the night Wilson was murdered. Was there anything different about it that night? From the other nights?'

'No.'

'You went in just after midnight and you were in there for how long? About an hour?'

'Less. It doesn't take long.'

'And then you came out.'

'Yes.'

'On your hands and knees?'

'Yes. It was dark. They dim the lights, see, at night. There's a sort of light there, but it's by the nurse, and she's usually sitting at her table.'

'You saw her?'

'Yes.'

'And nothing else?'

'Just the usual. People sleeping.'

'Was anyone awake?'

'Not as far as I know. Except, perhaps, that bugger, Vasco,

who's always got his eye on you. But I was looking out for him and kept my head down till I was out of the ward. Look, there was nothing different that time. Nothing! It was quiet as the grave. It was later, later, I'm telling you, that it happened. By then I was out of the place.'

'How did you get out of the hospital?'

'There's a coal chute. Suzie told me about it.'

'That's in the boiler room. Did anyone see you while you were on your way there?'

'Only that daft old bugger who's always drifting around, and he doesn't count.'

'Dr Malia?'

'Yes, that's his name. He's always around.'

'And he saw you?'

'Well – he was standing there, right by the door to the boiler room. I'd have given him the go-by if I could, but I couldn't. He was standing there, right by the door. He seemed to be sort of asleep. Standing up. I waited there for quite a while and then I reckoned that he *was* asleep. So I just went past him. And he didn't say anything or do anything. Just looked at me. But I don't reckon he saw me. His eyes were open, yes, but I don't know that he was seeing much. I reckon he was asleep on his feet. It's like that sometimes when a bloke's on watch. He's standing there, all right, but he's dropped off.'

'He didn't mean to,' said Suzie. 'I'll swear!' she said earnestly.

'He swears that, too,' said Lucca unimpressed. 'I went along to see him this morning when I got in. It was all I could do to stop him falling on his knees and begging my forgiveness.'

'He means it,' Suzie assured him. 'He really means it!'

'Oh, sure, he means it,' said Lucca. 'But that won't stop him trying it again.'

'It's all my fault,' said Suzie penitently.

'Yes, it is,' said Lucca.

'I wasn't really serious about him,' said Suzie.

'Which one was this?' asked Lucca.

'The Navy. I don't know their names. The big one.'

'Cooper?' said Seymour.

'Yes, I think that's his name.'

'The one who was with you that night?'

'I don't like to think that.'

'You said, and he said, that he left before – before anything happened.'

'Yes,' said Suzie. 'That's right.'

'He says he left the hospital at once.'

Suzie was silent. Then she said: 'I expect he did. I'm sure he did. Look, I told you: they were his mates.'

'There wasn't anything between them, was there? Between Cooper and Wilson? The one in the bed? Over you?'

'No, no. I never went with the one in the bed. I knew him, of course, but just to talk to.'

'What about the others? There were others, weren't there?'

Suzie nodded.

'Take those three for a start. There was nothing between them and the two who were murdered, was there?'

'No! They were their mates! And they used to visit them!'

'And they didn't mind about you?'

'No, it was all free and easy.'

'There was nothing that might have led Cooper – the big one – to stay behind that night?'

'No,' said Suzie. 'Absolutely not.'

'What about others?'

'There weren't many,' said Suzie humbly. 'It had got down to those three. There had been more, I admit that. The Navy has looked after me, and I like to look after the Navy.'

'So why are you down to three?'

'The others have gone back to sea. Also, I don't do patients. It's bad for them, the sisters say. And there haven't been any other ones. At least, not in the hospital.'

'But outside?'

'Well – maybe. Occasionally.'

154

'And others, not sailors?'

'Oh, I never see them in the hospital. It's always outside.'

'Luigi?'

'Not even him. I mean, he's different. He's my bloke.'

'Did he come to see you in the hospital?'

'Once or twice. But he doesn't like the hospital. It's too big for him.'

'Does he know about the coal chute?'

'Well, he does, but he doesn't like that, either. It's too dirty for him. He's funny like that. Over his clothes, I mean. He likes to keep them clean.'

She looked at Lucca. 'I've brought some clean ones in for him. That's all right, isn't it?'

He nodded.

'That's okay,' she said. 'I'll leave them at the front desk.'

'Now, listen, my girl,' said Lucca, in a fatherly way, 'I know how it is with you and the Navy. They've done right by you, and you want to do right by them. But you can't go on like this. It's not fair to Luigi. If he really is your bloke.'

'You see, I'm not really sure that he is,' said Suzie. 'Not *really* sure. He's nice but I'm not sure I want to be with him for ever and ever.'

'I appreciate that. But it's landed him in a mess, hasn't it? Not least over me.'

'You won't be hard on him, though, will you, Benito?'

'It's not up to me,' said Lucca. 'This has got to come to court. I can't just forget about it, because too many people saw.'

Suzie hung her head.

'It's all my fault,' she said. 'Can't you tell them that, Benito?'

'Yes, but you didn't have a knife, did you? All right, all right!' he said, and held up his hand. 'I might be able to put in a word. But that doesn't affect the others, does it?'

'What others is this, Benito?' said Suzie, mystified.

'He had it in for Cooper, didn't he? Could he have had it in for anyone else? Those two blokes who were killed while they were lying there, for example? Over you, Suzie, over you!'

'Oh Christ!' said Suzie. 'Surely not! Surely not, Benito!'

'Did you go with them, too?'

'I – I might have, Benito. I don't really know. I like Navy boys. They've been generous to me and I like to be generous –'

'All right, all right,' said Lucca hastily. 'But you see what I mean? If you'd gone with them, and if Luigi knew, might he not have slipped into the hospital and –'

'No, no, no!' cried Suzie. 'He's not like that! He gets carried away sometimes, and does crazy things, but he only does crazy things when he *is* carried away! A sort of fit of passion –'

'Yes, yes, all right. But I've got to ask, Suzie, because of the way you've been carrying on.'

'I'll try not to in future,' said Suzie penitently. 'I really will, Benito!'

'Sophia,' said Mrs Ferreira, 'could you do something for me?'

'Sure,' said Sophia, who was nursing the youngest Ferreira child. 'What is it?'

'I promised Mr Vasco I would take a message for him, but I'm running behind time and I don't know when I shall find a moment to do it. Would you take it for me?'

Sophia put down the youngest Ferreira with alacrity. It was not that she minded nursing him, it was just that for Sophia a little domestic responsibility went a long way.

'You see he doesn't fall off,' she said to another sister.

'Hold him for a minute while I get the letter,' said Mrs Ferreira.

She put down the saucepan she was holding and went out of the room.

'I'll hold him if you like,' said Chantale.

'No, no –'

156

'I'll put him down in his cot,' said Mrs Ferreira, returning with an envelope, which she gave to Sophia. 'It's time for his sleep.'

Sophia took the envelope.

'It's to his brother,' said Mrs Ferreira.

'At their house?'

'I promised to give it directly into his hands,' said Mrs Ferreira. 'I think he's working in the yards at Kalkara today.'

'Right,' said Sophia. 'I'll get over there.'

'Kalkara is where they do the boats?' asked Chantale.

'Yes. It's worth a visit.'

'Perhaps I could go with Sophia?' suggested Chantale. 'If she wouldn't mind?'

The Ferreiras' house was small and when most of the family was at home, as it was during the siesta hour, it was very crowded. She could do with some fresh air.

'I don't mind at all,' said Sophia, who, lacking an older sister, quite liked to talk things over with Chantale.

They took a *dghajsa* over to Birgu and then walked through the narrow streets past the Grand Inquisitor's Palace and past the Band Institute with its splendid balcony for the band, until they got to Kalkara Creek, where they turned along the front to where the old boatyards were. The smell of salt and tar suddenly became strong.

'Mr Vasco's brother paints the eyes on the *dghajsas*,' said Sophia.

'I think I've met Mr Vasco,' said Chantale. 'In the hospital.'

'Yes, he's very ill. But that doesn't excuse him, my mother says.'

A *dghajsa* having its eyes repainted was standing on chocks in a corner and a man was working on it with sandpaper.

'Hello, Mr Vasco,' said Sophia. 'I've got a message from your brother.'

The man wiped his hands on a cloth and took the envelope.

'Thank you, Sophia,' he said.

He read the letter and frowned.

'He doesn't know what he's asking,' he said. 'Lying there, he thinks that everyone else has got all the time in the world.'

He read the note again.

'Well, I don't know what I'm going to do about this,' he said.

He stood there uncertainly. 'He says he wants me to get a message round to everybody. But that's not easy to do when they're working all over the place. I suppose I could wait until the next time the band meets. That will be Thursday – they're playing at a christening. But he says it's got to go round at once.'

'Is there a rehearsal before, Mr Vasco?' said Sophia.

'No, we don't need rehearsals when it's a simple christening. But is there really the urgency that he says there is? Just lying there, you know, you think that the world revolves around you, that everything has to fit what you want. But does it?'

He looked at Sophia and laughed. 'Well, that's not something you can answer, is it? I'm the one who's got to make up his mind. But thank your mother for sending on the message so quickly, and thank you, Sophia. How is your mother, by the way?'

'She's fine,' said Sophia.

'Well, give her my thanks, will you? You've no idea what it means to us to know that she sees him every day. We know that if there's a sudden change in his condition, word will get back to us at once.'

'I'll tell her,' said Sophia.

'Thanks.' He looked at her. 'You don't know how he is today, I suppose?'

'I don't,' said Sophia, 'but this lady might.'

He took in her presence for the first time. 'I'm sorry, madam, I –'

'This is Chantale,' said Sophia. 'She's staying with us. She's in the St John Ambulance.'

'Oh, I know about her!' said Mr Vasco's brother.

158

He wiped his hands again and came over to Chantale and shook her hand warmly.

'You're the one who patched up Luigi,' he said.

'I'm beginning to wonder if that was a mistake,' said Chantale. 'He's in trouble again.'

'That stupid bugger's always in trouble. This Benito business?'

'Yes.'

'He should stay out of it. He should *always* stay out of it. I've told him that. It's the little ones who catch it, I said. The big ones never do. So keep out of it. But of course he won't. Doesn't have the sense to.'

He looked at Chantale. 'Sophia says you saw my brother?'

'Yes.'

'How is he?'

'Not well.'

'As awkward as ever?'

'Well . . .'

He laughed. 'I know!' he said. 'As awkward as ever. I'd like to say that it's what he's got that's making him awkward. But that's not true. He always *was* awkward. Awkward, but not stupid. He's like your Uncle Paolo, Sophia: awkward but not stupid. He was like that at school. It got that the teachers always had it in for him. Well, I can understand. He was a bit too clever for them, see? Like your Uncle Paolo. He could get under their skin. It did him no good in the end. He finished up in the shop. Still awkward. It's not the thing to be in a shop either. He puts people off. But it wasn't really his fault. It was the pain. It was getting worse all the time. It will kill him in the end. But meanwhile it drives him on. And makes him drive *us* on.'

He looked at the letter again. 'And so, I suppose, I'll get it round. Tonight. Although, really . . .'

'Everyone in the hospital knew it was the pain,' said Chantale. 'So they didn't really mind. They knew it was not him, but the pain.'

To her embarrassment, he began to cry.

'Thank you for saying that,' he said. 'Thank you.'

He pulled himself together.

'Thank you,' he said. 'Paolo said that you would understand. Because you were an Arab, he said. You would know.'

'But I *don't* know,' said Chantale. 'I don't know what he was talking about. They keep claiming me for one of their own, but I'm not. I'm not even Arab, not completely. And why do they keep picking on that? Arab? I see plenty of Arab influence around here but not many Arabs. Paolo? But he's like me, half and half. And why do they want to claim me, anyway? They don't want to claim you, do they?'

'No,' said Seymour. 'I'm English.'

'So?'

'They see you as oppressed, like them. And me as the English oppressor.'

Chantale shrugged. 'Well, if they do, they're making a lot of it. Too much of it.'

She thought. 'At least, Mr Vasco makes too much of it. There was this incident while I was there. He wanted to send a message to his brother, and it had to be by someone Maltese. And, now I come to think of it, even that was not good enough. The sister offered him Bettina but he turned her down. He said he wanted Melinda.'

'The Maltese was nothing to do with it, then.'

'Oh, it was. At first. It was just that there was an added complication. Bettina's family didn't get on with his, apparently.'

'He's obviously very choosy.'

'He was insistent on it. I think it really mattered to him.'

'What was he sending messages about?'

'I don't know. But it's a regular thing, apparently. In the hospital they seemed to take it for granted. And so did his brother, while I was there.'

'Lots of messages?'

'Yes.'

'Why?'

'I think it may be about the band. His brother talked of getting a message round to the band.'

'But a lot of messages?'

'Maybe he runs the band. Or used to run it. It's the Birgu band and he's a Birgu man.'

'And still running it? From his bed?'

'At least he would have time for it.'

'And, of course, the bands are fiercely, if locally, patriotic. That would tie in with all the Maltese business.'

'But what about Paolo? And Luigi, for that matter. They're not Maltese. Or not completely Maltese. They're part Arab.'

'But they're Birgu. Maybe, so far as the band is concerned, that overrides.'

'Especially if you're a good player,' said Chantale, laughing. 'And, apparently, Paolo is.'

'I want us to put our heads together this morning,' said Mrs Wynne-Gurr, 'and review what we have learned.'

'I don't think I have learned much,' said one of the ladies bravely. 'Not *learned*. Oh, it's been very interesting and I have had a lovely time and everyone has been so kind and helpful. And, of course, the history has been fascinating. That bit about the ladies in the prison! So brave! As you say, a lesson to us all. But as to learning – I mean, what the St John Ambulance does here is pretty much what it does in Godalming. Except for the stabbings, of course. Which I missed because I was on the other side of the racetrack.'

'That is precisely why we should go over what we have learned,' said Mrs Wynne-Gurr. 'To pool our experience. We have had a stroke of luck in having Miss de Lissac with us with her expert knowledge –'

'Not so expert,' said Chantale hastily.

'Certainly wider than ours. And certainly something we could benefit from.'

'Yes,' said the lady who had previously objected. 'I do see that might well be useful. I was talking to Sergeant White the other day and he said things were getting rougher all the time at the Godalming Arms. He said – he actually *said* – that he wouldn't be surprised if it was knives next!'

'Well, there you are!' said Mrs Wynne-Gurr. 'And when the time comes, we shall be ready. Meanwhile, we may be in a position to help our friends the police here with some problems that *they* face. Thanks not least to your endeavours, ladies!'

'Really?' said the ladies, a little surprised but also impressed.

'I believe so. Your reports on your observations in the hospital wards have been very fruitful. *Very* fruitful! When combined with analysis – *my* analysis,' said Mrs Wynne-Gurr firmly, 'I believe that they will help us to point the police in the direction of the person who has committed these dreadful murders. Now, I shall need just a little time this morning to marshal my arguments – *our* arguments – before we *show our hand*. So I would be grateful, Mrs Wagstaffe, if you could chair this morning. If we could split up into small groups first and then come together in a planning session just before lunch, when I hope to be able to rejoin you –'

'A word with you, Mr Seymour, if I may.'

'Of course!'

'I have been reflecting on these dreadful murders, and particularly in the light of the day we spent observing in the hospital.'

'Ye-e-s?'

'I have to own that my first thoughts on the subject were premature and impulsive.'

'What!' said Seymour, stopped in his tracks.

'I attributed too much significance to a similarity I had noticed between these deaths and some deaths I had recently learned about in my own local hospital – the Godalming, you know.'

'Cot deaths, if I remember . . .'

'And the Admiral – I think he was an Admiral – properly reproved me. There *were* similarities. Similarities can be deceptive, however, and I now think I was deceived. Or deceived myself. They were clearly not cot deaths.'

'I am glad you now think that, Mrs Wynne-Gurr.'

'However –'

However?

'– I was right in one particular: my focus on nursing practice.'

'Well, I am not sure –'

'Or nursing routine. You may not be aware of the importance of routines in a nurse's life, Mr Seymour.'

He looked around desperately. Over by the reception desk Chantale was talking to a group of St John ladies. He willed her to come over. She saw him; but merely waved a friendly hand and stayed put.

'A nurse's life is built of routines. When she takes over, she usually goes round the ward. At a certain point takes temperatures, gives medicine. Records. Goes for her break. And the routines are pretty regular. She takes temperatures at the same time, distributes medicines at the same time. Goes for her break at the same time.

'Now, of course, as you will recognize – perhaps have recognized – this is important. For, you see, one of the things that puzzled me – puzzled you, no doubt – was that, on at least two of the occasions when the crime was committed, a nurse was present. Present, or nearby. Or should have been. But if the nurse was present, how could she have let such a thing occur?

'The obvious deduction was that at the crucial time in each case she was *not* present. How could that be? The obvious answer was that the attack was made during her break. But for that to happen, the attacker must have known when the breaks would occur. He must have been in a position to predict it. Now, something very important follows from that, which I shall return to.

'But, first, there is the question to be answered of whether the breaks *were* taken at regular times? Because if they weren't, it would be impossible to know with confidence when they would occur.

'Now, Mr Seymour, as the result of the many observations made by my ladies while they were in the wards, I am in a position to say that they *were*. There was some variation, of course, but it was within quite severely restricted limits. So,' said Mrs Wynne-Gurr, pausing, and with a certain degree of triumph, 'here we have the explanation of how the attacks could take place without being observed: they were made during the nurse's break for refreshments.'

'Well, yes, but –'

'There is, of course, a further point, the additional one I referred to earlier: the attacker knew in advance when the break would occur. And that could come only from a very detailed knowledge of that particular nurse's routine. And *that* will come only from someone within the hospital. Which means that either the attacker himself came from inside the hospital or else he had an accomplice within the hospital. To anyone familiar with hospital routine, Mr Seymour, such as myself, that points to another nurse.'

'Of course, it could be –'

'Yes, I know, Mr Seymour. It could equally be someone else on the hospital staff. So far as the provision of information is concerned, yes, I agree with you, although I think that the detail of the knowledge makes it much more likely that we are talking about a nurse. And something has come up in my analysis of the date that lends support to that conclusion. I wish to check my workings just once again, Mr Seymour, before sharing them with you, since the implications are so serious. But it appears from my analysis that in each case – *including that of the German aviator* – a particular nurse was in close proximity. As I say, I shall need to check my data just once again, but it looks to me, Mr Seymour, that the St John Ambulance will soon be in a position to say, once again, that they have done it.'

Chapter Eleven

When Felix arrived at the Ferreiras' house the next morning he found Sophia still sitting at breakfast with Chantale but with a face like a thundercloud.

'They've turned down my project,' she informed him.

'I thought you hadn't finished it yet?'

'Actually, I haven't started it. We had to hand in the final form of the title yesterday. And they rejected it!'

'They didn't like the Victoria Lines?'

'*I* didn't like the Victoria Lines. So I decided to change it.'

'What did you change it to?'

'"Malta and the Decline of the British Empire".'

'That *is* quite a lot different.'

'It's more in line with the direction of my thinking,' said Sophia.

'Why did they object to it?'

'They said it was too big a subject for a School Certificate project. And that it was too general. (*I* don't think it's general at all. It's very specific.) And that it was tendentious. I'm not sure what "tendentious" means but I'm pretty sure my project's not it.'

'I know what "tendentious" means,' said Grandfather.

'Oh?'

'Writing that has a particular tendency.'

'Well, all writing that's trying to say something has a particular tendency.'

'"Calculated to advance a cause", it says here.'

'What's wrong with that?'

'Maybe they think it's not objective,' said Mrs Ferreira.

165

'That's just what they think. I think it *is* objective.'

'What *is* your cause?' asked Chantale.

'The freeing of Malta. From the British.'

'Yes, well, look –' said her grandfather.

'It *is* rather general,' said Mrs Ferreira, 'for a Certificate project.'

'It's censorship, that's what it is!' said Sophia. 'And I am going to fight it!'

'Could you fight it *after* you've passed the Certificate?' asked Mrs Ferreira.

Seymour went in to see how Lucca was this morning. He found him filling in forms: 'German forms', he called them.

'Just give me a minute!' he said.

Along the corridor Seymour could hear Luigi's petulant voice.

'My clothes!' he was saying. 'I've got to have my clothes!'

'I'll bring you a change in,' he heard Suzie say soothingly.

'I don't want just one change,' Luigi said, almost tearfully. 'I want *all* my clothes!'

'Well, darling, I don't think they'll let you have them *all*. You've got quite a lot of clothes, you know. And there isn't room for them here.'

'I'll ask Benito!'

'I don't think even Benito will let you. Because, look, there just isn't room for them here. Where would you put them? There isn't a wardrobe. And if you put them on hangers, you'd have to hang them all over the place. And where would you hang them from? There simply aren't places. If you hung them all from the window, all together, they'd get crumpled, wouldn't they? And you know you wouldn't like that.'

'This one is all crumpled already. And I've nothing to change into!'

Lucca looked up and sighed. 'What's he worried about? My uniform's all crumpled, too, and Marta says she's not pressing it until Saturday. Saturday is the day she does the ironing, she says. "Put your other one on if you're that bothered." "I can't," I say. "It's too small for me these days." "It's not that it's too small; it's that you've got too big. You've put on weight, Benito. I keep telling you you've got to get it off!"'

'I've told you I'll bring you in another one,' said Suzie, placatorily.

'Bring it in this afternoon!' said Luigi.

'I can't, dear. You know I'm busy.'

'Nobody cares about me any more!' said Luigi tearfully. 'Not even Paolo. He's not been in once.'

'I expect he's busy, too,' said Suzie. 'You know he's got a berth on the *Ascania*? It's putting in next week, and they need stewards. So then he'll be away for a few weeks. So he's got to get his things together.'

'He ought to have looked in on me,' whined Luigi. 'After what I did for him. I'm his mate.'

'So you are, Luigi, and I'm sure he'll look in. It's just that he's so busy. But I'll remind him.'

'And where are the others? No one's been in to see me since I've been put in here!'

'I'll remind them all. Little Luigi is languishing away, I'll say.'

'I'm *not* little! I'm right for people of my build. It's just that other people are fat.'

'Christ!' said Lucca. 'Even Luigi's on to me now!'

'But I'm wiry and I can do things that they can't. Even Paolo says that. "You can go places that other people can't," he said. But I don't want to get my clothes dirty. "I'll pay for you to get them cleaned," he said. But he hasn't. That's not right, is it?'

'I'll mention that to him, too,' said Suzie.

'It's that sailor again, isn't it?' said Bettina.

'Yes, it is.'

'It won't go away, will it?'

'No.'

'He died on my watch.'

167

Seymour smiled. 'You're another Navy nurse, aren't you? Like Macfarlane.'

'We're all Navy nurses here,' said Bettina.

'And every shift is a watch?'

'And if something happens on your watch, then you're responsible.'

'I don't think that's entirely fair. Being a nurse is not quite like being on the bridge. If someone dies when you're on duty, there may be nothing you could have done about it.'

'Or there may have been: I keep asking myself if there *was* something I could have done but didn't do. Maybe when I was doing the rounds I didn't look closely enough.'

'But you did look, didn't you?'

'Oh, yes. I did look. But maybe I didn't see.'

'Of course, you were looking at the patients. But can I ask you about something else you may have seen?'

'Ye-e-s?'

'There's a cupboard at the end of the ward.'

'Ye-e-s?'

'What is it used for?'

'Nothing much. Sometimes the cleaners put their mops in there. But lately they've taken to keeping them at the other end of the ward, where there is a little kitchen. Then they can pick up the water at the same time.'

'So no one goes in much?'

'Not much, no.'

'Do they ever go in?'

'Well . . .'

'Let me put it another way: have you seen or do you know of anyone making use of it for their own private purpose?'

There was a long pause.

'Maybe,' said Bettina.

'Not a nurse.'

'No.'

There was another pause.

'You know?' said Bettina.

'Tell me,' said Seymour.

'I suspected it. And once I caught them. I turfed them out

and told – told her, that she must never do it again. And then I kept my eye on the cupboard, and thought she'd stopped. But – but now you're saying that she didn't?'

'She was in there that night. The night the man died.'

'Oh, my God!' said Bettina.

'And so was he.'

'That's awful!'

'But perhaps not so unusual. He says he left before – before anything happened.'

'But how could he have left? I was there all the time.'

'That, actually, is the point.'

'I don't see how he could have left! I would have seen him!'

'He says he crawled out on hands and knees. You were there but you didn't see him.'

'Oh, my God!' said Bettina bitterly. 'What a fool I am!'

'Well, maybe. But it's hardly the sort of thing you would be looking out for, is it?'

'Still . . .' said Bettina.

'Still!' said Seymour. 'However, it's easily done. But it would not be so easy to miss the other thing that happened that night. Someone else came into the ward. Either from the cupboard or from outside.'

Bettina shook her head.

'She wouldn't,' she said. 'She's not that kind of person.'

'We never think they are.'

She still shook her head.

'Too small,' she said. 'Wilson was a strong man. Not big, but strong.'

'Someone else, then.'

Bettina looked puzzled.

'But I still don't see –' she began. 'How could they have done it? I would surely have seen them. That, I could not have missed!'

'If you had been there,' said Seymour.

Bettina flushed.

'I can assure you I was there!' she said.

'The whole time?'

'The whole time.'

'You didn't take a break?'

'Only the usual one . . . I see,' said Bettina.

'Do you take it at a fixed time?'

'It's not fixed, but I suppose we take it most nights at much the same time.'

'And do you remember –?'

'Actually, I do,' said Bettina. 'I hadn't been feeling too good that night. It was that period of the month. Melinda knew, and she came in and offered to take over for a bit while I went to the rest room and lay down.'

'Ah!'

'But I said no. I said I would hang on to the regular time. And that's that I did.'

'On watch as usual!' said Seymour.

'I'm always on watch,' said Laura. 'And always on guard.'

'Not from me, I hope!'

'From marauding males!'

Seymour laughed. 'I promise I'll be on my best behaviour.'

'So what did you want to see me about?' said Laura.

'Cover at night,' said Seymour. 'For you.'

'I'm on till nine,' said Laura, 'and then the porters take over. We don't really need a receptionist at night. This isn't like an ordinary hospital. Oh, yes, we do have admissions at night, but there are not many of them. And the porters and medical staff handle them between themselves.'

'So if a person comes in with an injury –?'

'The nurse on duty sees them and makes arrangements.'

'And what if they don't have an injury?'

'Suddenly taken ill? The same. The nurse sees them.'

'And someone not ill?'

Laura raised her eyebrows. 'They don't come in. It's outside visiting hours.'

'Drunks?'

'The porters see to them.'

'That might be difficult if there's only one porter on duty.'

'We've not had any problems.'

'Or not any porter on duty.'

Laura looked at him. 'That time –? Mario, you mean? It happened once. It won't happen again.'

'It's that once that interests me.'

Umberto was carrying a lamp. He put it down when he saw Seymour waiting for him.

'Look,' he said. 'I know I shouldn't have done it. He's only a young lad, and he was helping me out. But, listen, I'm the one to blame. Not him.'

'I'm not blaming him. I'm not even blaming you. But there's something I want to know. Who else knew about it?'

'About –?'

'About him being left to cover for you while you were sniffing around your girlfriend.'

Umberto winced.

'You don't need to put it like that,' he said. 'She was on her own and needed comforting.'

'And you were just the man to do that when you should have been on duty at the hospital?'

'Nine times out of ten it would have been all right, I'd checked beforehand. Honestly, I'd checked! I went round all the nurses, the ones on night duty that week. And they all said that no one was going to be in trouble. "So you'll be able to kip all night," Bettina said. Of course she didn't know that it wasn't kipping that I had in mind.'

'So you thought it was all right to leave young Mario in charge?'

'Well, Christ, I didn't know that he'd have to deal with something like this! No one did. And I can tell you, no one was as surprised as me. You get a feel for these things, you know, when you've worked here as long as I have. You can sort of sense if someone is likely to go. But not this time. I couldn't believe it when I heard. But then, afterwards, when I heard the rumours I felt sick. Someone must have got in. Taken advantage of me not being there.'

'Someone knew that you were not going to be there,' said Seymour. 'Who?'

Umberto shook his head.

'No one knew,' he said. 'I took good care.'

'People knew about you and her,' said Seymour. 'They told me. But that was in general. What I want to know about was that particular night. Did you mention it to anyone?'

'No –'

'Berto? He must have known about it.'

'No, he didn't. He knew in general, of course. But I never told him when – There are things it's best not to know.'

'Anyone else? A hint, maybe, that someone could have guessed from?'

Umberto shook his head.

'No,' he said. 'I was careful.'

'Your girlfriend? Did she know you were coming that night?'

'Well, she might have been expecting it. But, look, she wouldn't have said anything. We'd talked it over and agreed. That we'd never let anything get out.'

He hesitated. 'We were thinking of Bella,' he said.

'Bella is your wife?'

Umberto nodded.

'Someone knew,' said Seymour.

Umberto's face tightened.

'I'll need to talk to your girlfriend,' said Seymour.

'No –' said Umberto.

'I've got to,' said Seymour.

He decided to enlist Lucca's aid; not just because he thought he would never find the place in the twisting, narrow, unnamed streets around Birgu, but because he felt that Lucca would be better at eliciting information from the sort of people who lived round there than he would be.

Lucca, of course, knew exactly where to find her.

'Now, Teresa, I need some help from you.'

'Sure, Benito. If I can.'

'Umberto is in trouble.'

She stared at him. 'Umberto?'

'That's right.'

'Is it about us?' she said.

'In a way, yes.'

'Benito, I wouldn't want any trouble to come to him because of me.'

'I know you wouldn't, Teresa. And that's why you're going to help me.'

'I'll try, Benito. I'll really try!'

'You're going to have to think.'

'I'll do my best, Benito. I promise.'

'I don't know if you know about this, Teresa, but one night when he was with you, a man died in the hospital.'

'Yes, I know,' she said. 'He told me about it afterwards. He felt bad about it. He'd left young Mario on his own –'

'That's right, and that's the day I want you to do your best to remember. You knew that Umberto would be coming that night?'

'He hadn't said anything,' said Teresa. 'But I knew.'

'The question is: did anyone else know?'

'We were careful that they shouldn't, Benito.'

'But might you have let something slip out? Without intending to?'

'No, no, because I didn't talk to anybody.'

'Nobody at all, Teresa? Did you go out that day? Shopping? The baker, for instance.'

'No, no, I wouldn't give Umberto a meal. Not at that hour. A drink, perhaps –'

'Beer?'

'Yes. Yes, I certainly gave him that: he likes a glass after –'

'Yes, well, we don't need to go into that. But did you have beer in the house? Or did you have to go out for it?'

'I went out for it. But –'

'Where did you go?'

'The corner shop. Vasco's. Of course, he's not there at the moment, he's in hospital. Martin is looking after it for him. But I didn't say anything to him about Umberto, I swear –'

'Hello, Martin! How's it going?'

'Fine, Benito. Fine, really. I've just about got on top of it now. Although I'll be glad when Vasco gets back.'

'*If* he gets back,' said Lucca.

'It's like that, is it?'

'I'm afraid so.'

'The family will have to think about it,' said Martin.

'Sure. Sure, they will. But that may be some time yet, so you'll have to hang on. Now, look, Martin, there's a thing I wanted to ask you . . .'

'. . . Yes, I do remember that evening and her coming in,' said Martin. 'and I'll tell you why I remember. She came in when I was putting an order together. It was a big order and there were bottles all over the floor. Someone had come in, you see, and said they wanted some beer for the band. It was a sort of celebration, he said, and they'd get through a lot of bottles. He told me what he wanted and I was just putting them together when she came in. He was waiting for the bottles and I was in such a state trying to put them together – I had just started, you see and it was new to me. And then Teresa came in. "Serve her first," he said. "You don't want much, do you, love?" "No," she said. "Just half a dozen bottles." "Enough to see him through the night, is that it?" he said, and laughed. And I laughed, and Teresa laughed. Did she mention Umberto? No, no. Everyone knows about her and Umberto, of course. But she didn't mention him. Just asked for the bottles.'

Laura hauled Mario before him, not exactly grasping him by the ear but certainly with a very determined grip.

'Mario has got something to say to you,' she said.

'It's about that night,' he said.

'Go on,' said Laura.

'I know what they're saying,' he said, on the verge of tears. 'They're saying I let him in. That I wasn't looking out when I should have been. But it's not true! The only time I wasn't there was when they called for me to go to the ward. But until then I was in my place. I'd brought a chair out and stood it in the doorway where I could keep an eye on the entrance hall. I was afraid that if I stayed in the

174

porters' room I might miss something. So I moved the chair into the doorway and sat there. The whole time.

'And I didn't go to sleep. I had my books with me. I had some homework to do. Maths. And then I was supposed to be getting on with my project. Well, I *was* getting on with my project,' he said hastily, with his mother's eye upon him. 'I was making notes. But not all the time. Part of the time I was thinking. Mr Seixas says that that's what you should do. Not just get your head down and write away, Because if you don't think first, it's just a waste of time. And I *was* thinking. So if it looked as if I wasn't doing anything, that's wrong. I was awake the whole time. And working.'

'And keeping your eye on the entrance vestibule,' said Seymour.

'That's right, sir,' said Mario, fixing his eyes on him pleadingly. 'I know what they're saying, but it's not true. I *was* there the whole time, and I was on duty all the time. Keeping an eye open. My mum says if you're on duty, you're on duty and mustn't even blink.'

'That's right,' said Laura.

'Well, I didn't blink. Not at all!'

'It's okay,' said Seymour. 'I think I'm prepared to take your word for it.'

'No one came in. I swear it.'

'They could have come in before you took over,' said Seymour. 'And then just hung around.'

'Why, yes, they could,' said Mario, relieved.

'Now, tell me,' said Seymour, 'you didn't see anyone before – before they called you to the ward. But did you see anyone *after*?'

'No, no. It was all empty. And still. The way it usually is.'

'And when they released you, you went straight back to the porters' room? To your chair.'

'Yes,' said Mario. 'That's right. But I couldn't – I found it hard to settle down. I tried to read but it wasn't easy. I kept thinking –'

'I am going to kill Umberto,' said Laura.

175

'It's not really his fault,' said Mario. 'He didn't know. And he's very sorry. He apologizes every time he sees me.'

'And so he should,' said Laura grimly.

'So you didn't see anyone on your way back to the porters' room, and you didn't see anyone for the rest of the night?'

'No. No one. Except –' he thought – 'except for Dr Malia. And he doesn't really count because you often see him around.'

'At night?'

'Oh, yes,' said Mario. 'I've often seen him.'

'And you saw him on this occasion?'

'Yes.'

'Doing what?'

'Nothing. Just walking.'

'Where?'

'Along the corridor that leads off from the entrance. It goes out to the services. I'd seen him along there before. And so had Umberto. Not doing anything much but just sort of thinking. I think,' confided Mario, 'he might have been measuring.'

'Measuring?'

'He's always doing it. Calculating space. He's got a theory about it. He thinks there is going to be a war and they'd want much more hospital space. He's always at it. I think he's a bit cracked –'

'And you just watch your words, young man!' said Laura indignantly. 'He may have some funny ways these days, but that's because he's old. He's still a very good doctor. Everyone knows that. And let me tell you, my lad, you wouldn't be here if it wasn't for him! That time you had pneumonia – he didn't leave your bedside all night! Nor the next morning. Not until he thought you were out of danger. You don't get them like that these days. And I won't hear a word said against him!'

'I'm not saying a word against him, Mum,' Mario protested mildly. 'I'm just saying I saw him.'

'That night?' said Seymour.

'Yes. Just walking along the corridor like he often does. And thinking. You can tell he's thinking because from time to time he stops and makes a note in his notebook. And sometimes he sort of drifts away. Mentally, I mean. He goes into a sort of dream and stands there for ages.'

'He's thinking,' said Laura, 'and if you did a bit of that occasionally, I'd feel a lot happier, with the examinations coming up, than I do!'

He tracked him down eventually. He was in one of the lower corridors, notebook in hand, standing there dreamily just as Mario had said. But he turned to Seymour politely as he came up.

'Oh, good afternoon!' he said. 'Are you visiting the hospital? Can I help you? It's a vast place,' he smiled, 'and it's easy to get lost. But I think I know my way around still. Where were you making for?'

'The boiler room,' said Seymour.

'Ah, yes. The new boiler rooms. At least, I call them new although I suppose they have been in for quite a while now. They are a big improvement over the old ones, I can tell you. Although they are not quite in the right place. At least, I don't think they are. When you are locating services, you need to think ahead. Will it still be the right location if the hospital changes? If new wards are built, for example? Because they might well be. In fact –' he passed his hand over his forehead – 'perhaps they have been? I don't quite remember. I don't remember things as well as I used to,' he confided.

'There is always change in a hospital,' said Seymour. 'But, you know, some needs stay the same. A boiler room needs to have access from the outside.'

'Oh, yes,' agreed Dr Malia. 'For the deliveries.'

'And there is another consideration these days: security.'

'Or will be,' said Dr Malia, 'with the war coming.'

'Quite so. And you can't have people coming into the hospital, just as they please.'

177

'I suppose not,' said Dr Malia. 'Although I don't agree with keeping people out. It's good for patients if they're visited.'

'I'm with you there,' said Seymour. 'I just worry that sometimes at night –'

'Well, yes,' said Dr Malia. 'There has to be some sort of restriction. Otherwise thieves would strip the hospital!'

He laughed, and Seymour laughed with him.

'Have you seen much of that in your time?' he asked.

'Not much,' said Dr Malia, 'but enough. It's more the vandalism of the equipment that worries me. Some of it is very delicate, you know. You don't want just anybody handling it!'

'You're right,' said Seymour, 'and what worries me is that it is a little too easy to get into the hospital.'

'Laura keeps a pretty good eye on things,' said Dr Malia.

'I'm sure; but when she's not on duty?'

'The others are not quite as good,' Dr Malia conceded.

'And the hospital is a big place,' said Seymour. 'You can't expect someone sitting at the front desk to keep an eye on everything. People could get in through the boiler room, for example.'

'Well, yes, they could.'

'Down the coal chute, for instance.'

'Not easy,' said Dr Malia. 'And very dirty.'

'But I know for a fact that some people have done it.'

'Yes,' said Dr Malia, 'it's not uncommon.'

'You're around the hospital a lot,' said Seymour, 'even at night. I expect you've seen it.'

'Well, I have.'

'I have, too. Only the other night a sailor was creeping out through the boiler room.'

'And you know what he had been doing!' said Dr Malia.

'I think you were there. You probably saw him yourself?'

'I did. I had been down there thinking about the boilers. And I must have dropped off. I do, you know, from time to time. Take a little nap. Well, I think he saw me, and hung back. But – perhaps I did take a little nap, because the next thing I remember was him creeping past. I didn't say anything, of course. I didn't want to embarrass him. And there was no real harm done, was there?'

'Not by him, no. But perhaps by others. Because there may have been another that night. In fact, I think there probably was.'

'Oh, yes,' said Dr Malia. 'I saw them.'

'Them?'

'Yes. There were two of them. I was very surprised when they came out of the boiler room. Because they weren't the boiler men, you know.' Dr Malia laughed. 'Of course, they were surprised too. One of them ran back into the boiler room. But the other one – I thought he was going to hit me, but, of course, he wasn't. He looked at me for a moment and then laughed. "Back to sleep, Dr Malia. Back to sleep!" he said, and then went back into the boiler room.'

'And then?'

Dr Malia passed his hand over his forehead again.

'I don't remember,' he said. 'I get these lapses – perhaps I *did* go back to sleep.'

'Did you know the men?'

'Oh, yes.'

'I wonder if I know them, too?'

'I expect so,' Dr Malia beamed.

'You know, I've forgotten their names!'

'I'm like that, too, sometimes,' said Dr Malia cordially.

'Can you help me with them?'

Dr Malia thought, and then his face clouded over.

'It's gone from me,' he said. After a moment: 'Perhaps it will come later.'

'If it does, I'd be glad if you would mention it to me. I would like to know.'

'Perhaps it will come to you,' said Dr Malia sympathetically.

Chapter Twelve

Carmen, the nurse on the ward where Turner had died, and where the seamen claimed they had seen someone bending over him, was new to the ward. She had only recently qualified and this was her first appointment. So she had not been absolutely certain at first.

She had bent over him and tried to see if he was breathing. What had attracted her attention in the first place was that the breathing seemed so slight. But even when she had looked and listened carefully she had not been sure. Then she had taken his pulse and she had not been sure about that, either. She had thought she could feel something but it had been so weak that perhaps it had not been there at all. Then she had tried his heart.

And then she had run to Melinda in the next ward, and Melinda had come at once and done more or less the same tests. But she had known at once what to do. They had tried resuscitation and Melinda had sent for one of the doctors, who had come immediately. Carmen thought now that Melinda had realized at once that Mr Turner was dead, but they had continued their attempts at resuscitation for – oh, Carmen could not be sure, it had seemed like ages –

But she, herself, had been stupefied, dazed. This was her first death.

Melinda had taken her into the nurses' room and given her some coffee and made her sit down. She had suddenly begun to shake and Melinda had put her arms around her.

And then, when she had stopped shaking, Melinda had

made her stand up and walk back round the ward. She had gone with her and they had looked at every patient.

And then, another nurse had come and taken her place, and Melinda had taken her back to her own ward and made her walk round that, too, talking about all the patients as they came to them.

Then Sister Chisholm had come in and given her things to do and she had been quite busy. And then Melinda had taken her out to lunch.

Carmen was plainly in awe of Melinda. It wasn't just that she was the senior nurse. It was that she was always so calm and confident. She always seemed to know what to do. And although sometimes she seemed a bit brusque, really she was very nice. Just not soft. Carmen thought that perhaps you got like that when you had had more experience. She knew that she herself had not reached that stage yet.

No, she told Seymour, she had not left the ward during her spell of duty. She had not taken a break in the nurses' room. She would have gone there later but there were some things she had wanted to do. There were measurements she had wanted to check. She was still not able to trust herself so she had taken some again.

'Did that entail going round the ward?' asked Seymour.

In some cases, yes. She had been up and about in the ward almost the whole time. So she was sure nobody could have got in. She knew what people were saying.

Did she know what the sailors had been saying? About having seen someone bending over Turner with a pillow?

Yes. She knew that, too. And she just couldn't see how they could have done that. Unless . . .

Unless?

'Unless they saw me,' said Carmen. 'I had been going round the ward, and I probably did straighten a few pillows and move things. I don't remember going to that bed but I could have done.'

Thinking it over, said Carmen – and she had done a lot of thinking it over – she thought that maybe that was what they had seen.

* * *

181

'As a matter of fact,' said Melinda, 'I did look in. I don't think she saw me, but I did. I wanted to be sure that things were all right. She's new and inexperienced. So I was keeping my eye on her. She's fine, or she will be fine. But she's a bit unsure of herself still. Naturally. Especially about the measuring. Actually, she's not great shakes at sums. But she's very conscientious, so she does them again to make sure. And again. And again. And she was doing that when I looked in, so I didn't disturb her.'

'Would she have been concentrating so much that she wouldn't have seen –?'

'Someone come in and stifle Turner? Of course not!' said Melinda.

'Then –? She says she didn't leave the ward.'

'She wouldn't have done.'

Melinda thought. 'Unless –'

She stopped.

'I think I can see how it might have happened,' she said. 'When Mrs Ferreira comes round with the dispensing trolley she sometimes gets stuck along the corridor – there's a door that has to be held open. Usually the nurse in that ward goes along to help her. If Carmen had done that, she wouldn't have thought she was leaving the ward!'

'But it wouldn't have taken a moment, would it? Not long enough to allow someone to –'

Melinda thought again.

'Barely long enough,' she conceded. 'But usually there's a bit of chat. And there would have been in Carmen's case, because Mrs Ferreira knows her mother, and had probably been asked to keep an eye on Carmen for her.'

'Still –' said Seymour. 'Would this have been a regular occurrence?'

'Oh, yes,' said Melinda. 'Every day. Bang on the dot! Mrs Ferreira would be there with her trolley.'

'You wouldn't have had very long,' said Seymour. 'And you would have to know the hospital routines very well.'

'Yes,' said Melinda. 'You would.'

* * *

Felix had developed the art of never listening to his mother. This morning, though, as she was talking to his father over the breakfast table, he suddenly heard something which shot him alert.

'Yes, on Saturday,' she said. 'That will give me the whole of Sunday to get Felix's things together so that he'll be ready on Monday.'

'Ready?' said Felix. 'What for?'

'School,' said his father. 'Remember it?'

'Monday? Next Monday?'

'As ever is,' said his father.

'But I thought that was the week after! I thought I had another week!'

'Felix,' said his mother. 'You are so vague!'

'But – but I shall still be here. In Malta!'

'Not unless you've made arrangements to stay on your own,' said his father.

'We are leaving on Saturday morning,' said his mother. 'Early. If I've told you once, I've told you a hundred times!'

'But ... but ... I can't!' said Felix.

'Well, of course, if you've made private arrangements –' said his father.

'I've got my project to do!'

'There'll be time for you to finish it,' said his mother. 'We've still got four days.'

'But I haven't started it!'

'You've been talking about it for days. If not weeks.'

'But I haven't actually started writing!'

'Then, Felix,' said his father, 'I suggest you start writing pretty soon!'

Much perturbed, Felix went to see Sophia.

He found her still at breakfast with a very long face.

'But, Sophia,' her mother was saying patiently, 'it's written on the calendar. Up on the wall.'

Sophia turned to Felix.

'School starts on Monday,' she said, 'and I haven't done my project. It's supposed to be handed in the first morning.'

'Same here,' said Felix. 'We're going back on Saturday. Now I haven't even started!'

'I will clear the table,' said Mrs Ferreira, 'and then you can both sit down and get writing.'

'I'm still not sure what it's going to be about!'

'Then, Felix, I suggest you decide in the next thirty seconds. And you, too, Sophia, instead of blaming the British, the Government, and your grandfather.'

'What's all this about?' said Grandfather.

'Sophia's project. It's got to be handed in on Monday and she hasn't even started. She hasn't even made her mind up about the title.'

'I thought . . . the Victoria Lines, wasn't it?'

'It's going to have to be,' said Sophia glumly.

'And you, Felix?' said Mrs Ferreira, turning to Felix.

'Well, I had thought about doing the Armouries –'

'Yes, but you said they were closed?'

'You could do it on what you would have seen if they had been open,' suggested Sophia.

'I think you should follow Dr Malia's advice and do it on the Infermeria,' said Mrs Ferreira firmly.

'You'd better ask Umberto,' said Berto uneasily.

'I want to ask *you*.'

'Look, I don't know anything about it. What Umberto does is his own business, I don't ask him and he doesn't ask me. But what I say is, you've got to give a bloke a bit of leeway. All right, maybe not as much as Umberto took, but he thought it was all right. He'd made arrangements –'

'Mario?'

'I'm not saying that was right, the way it turned out. But it's happened before and it's been all right. The hospital has not suffered. And it wouldn't have suffered, normally, because Mario is a good kid and has got his head screwed on the right way and he knows what to do as well as Umberto or me. Normally, I mean. It was just that this time was different. Now, I don't live too far away and he could have come and got me or sent someone, and I would have come running, I really would. Mario's a good kid and he's not to blame, that's what I am saying. And nor is Umberto. We all make mistakes, and he's made one, and he knows it. He's not been the same man. Look, I'll admit it, if that's what you want. We messed it up between us really bad and –'

'That was not what I wanted to see you about.'

'It wasn't?' said Berto, taken aback. 'Then –?'

'I wanted to ask you about something that happened on a different day. The day of the balloons. Now, unlike Umberto, you were inside the hospital the whole time, weren't you?'

'Yes, I was.'

'Well, I want you to tell me about that.'

'About the balloons?'

'About what happened here. When the German arrived.'

'Oh, right,' said Berto, relieved. 'Well, it was a right to-do. Pandemonium. Absolute pandemonium! Never known anything like it. One minute it was as quiet as the grave. I'd been sitting peacefully here. Nothing was happening, so I wandered out to the front to take a look at the balloons. Then I saw one of them coming down, and Laura said: "You'd better get ready, Berto!"

'Well, the next minute there were bloody hundreds in here, all pushing and shoving. "Get them out!" shouts Laura. Easier said than done but I did what I could. Even the bloody band was here! "What the hell are you lot doing here?" I said. But they just pushed past me. Laura came out from behind her desk and grabbed some of them by the scruff of the neck and tried to push them out of the door and I was doing my best, but they were all over the place.

'And then Umberto appears. "Christ, what's this?" he says, seeing the band. "Are you having a party, Berto?" "No, I'm bloody not!" I say. "Where the hell have you been?" "Putting that little German bastard to bed!" he says. "And it's not been easy." "Well, it's not been exactly easy here," I said. "Help me get them out!"

'So he started shoving, and I kept pushing, and Laura was shouting her head off, but it was a sort of deadlock.

185

No one could get anywhere. "What the hell do you lot want, anyway?" shouts Umberto. "We want to see the German," someone shouts. "Is he all right?" "He's having a kip," said Umberto. "The doctors say he's got to rest." "Have they given him a sedative?" asks someone. "I expect so," said Umberto, "and I wish they'd give me one, too."

'"Can we see him?" asked someone. "No, you bloody can't!" said Umberto. "Melinda has got him locked away in the nurses' room and no one is allowed in." "Is he asleep?" asks someone. "Yes," says Umberto, "and I wish I was, too."

'Well, in the end we got rid of them. But it took nearly an hour because by this time they'd got all over the place and we were having to chase after them. But in the end we did it.'

He found Mrs Ferreira making ready her trolley.

'Hello!' she said. 'I'm glad I've caught you. We're having a *fenkata* to send off our St John Ambulance friends from England. You will come, won't you?'

'I would be delighted to.'

'Chantale has got the details.'

'I look forward to it.' He smiled. 'I expect that, deep in your heart, you will not be sorry to see them go.'

'Oh, no, no!' protested Mrs Ferreira, laughing.

'You have been very kind and very patient, but I suspect that sometimes it has not been easy.'

'She means well,' said Mrs Ferreira laughing; and Seymour knew she was not talking about Chantale.

'She was in here the other day,' she said, 'showing me her charts. She wanted to talk them over with me to make sure that she had got them right. Of course, I was glad to, although I was really rather busy at the time. Paolo had just brought his clothes in for me to check over. His sea-going clothes, I mean – he's off back to sea shortly. I insist on him bringing them to me. Like a fussy mother, I suppose. Well, I *am* a fussy mother, and I try to be one for him. Since Debra can't. Anyway, he had just brought them in

186

when Mrs Wynne-Gurr arrived with an armful of charts she had drawn up.'

'So it wasn't a good moment?'

'No. Not that it mattered, because I had plenty of time to do Paolo's things. But I had set aside the morning for that.'

'Did he mind?'

'Oh, he didn't have to be there. All he had to do was bring the things in. He might have stayed and chatted for a bit but when he saw her, he pulled a face and said: "The English!" and hurried off when she got started and he heard what it was all about.'

'I don't blame him,' said Seymour. 'She explained them all to me, too!'

Mrs Ferreira laughed.

'What did you think of them?' asked Seymour. 'Her ideas, I mean?'

'Well, she seemed to have worked everything out. But . . .'

'But?'

She was silent for a moment.

'Things are not like that. Not here in the hospital. She makes it all seem too neat. And . . .'

'And?'

She was silent again, this time for quite some minutes. At last she said: 'And I didn't like the way they seemed to be pointing.'

'What way were they pointing?'

'I think I'd better leave that to her to tell you,' she said. 'Because I simply don't believe it.'

As he was getting into the *dghajsa* he met Lucca. He was preoccupied and seemed not a little distressed.

'He's going crazy! Backhaus!'

'Backhaus?'

'Yes. He wants me to take the technicians into custody. I'll need some evidence before I can do that, I told him. "I *have* evidence!" he said. "Written evidence!" "Written evidence?" I said. "Yes," he said, and waved a letter under my nose. "Let me take a look at it," I said. "No," he said, "it is evidence." "No, it's not, if I can't look at it," I said. Well, he thought a bit and then said: "How can I trust you?" "Look," I said. "I'm a policeman!" "Yes," he said, "but that means you're in the pay of the British."

'If anything makes me mad, that does. "I'm in the pay of the Maltese Government," I said. "Maltese, not British, can't you understand that, you daft bastard?" (I shall deny ever having said that, if it becomes an issue.) "There's a difference between the two."

'"Ah, yes," he said, "but –"

'"No buts," I said. "Maltese!"

'"All right, all right!" he said. "Perhaps I can trust you, if that's the way it is. I'll send you a copy of the letter." "Thank you very much," I said, and would have walked away, but he said: "Wait! I will read it to you."

'So I waited, and he read it to me. At first, I thought it was just another anonymous letter. I get them all the time. I think there are people in Valletta who, when they've got nothing to do, say to themselves: "I know, I'll write to Lucca!" Anyway, this one said, as quite a lot of them do, the British are behind it.'

'Behind what?' said Seymour.

'Behind killing the German. It was something to do with this new destroyer that's in. Kiesewetter's technicians were British, the letter said, and in England's pay. They had sabotaged Kiesewetter's balloon so that it would crash and kill Kiesewetter.

'"Look," I said, "this is nothing new. I've had the idea myself. What I need is evidence."

'"Ah," Backhaus said, "but there is more." The letter went on to say that an agent of the British Government had been seen talking to the technicians at a pub that morning. And that afterwards the agent had gone over with the technicians to Marsa racetrack to see the balloon and tell them how to do it.

'That made me stop for a minute because it was quite specific. It even gave the pub by name. It gave the pub and the time. And the writer said he could supply witnesses.

'Well, that made me think. People who write this kind of letter don't usually go into details. And they don't usually offer to give the names of witnesses. Witnesses, plural. I began to wonder if Backhaus was quite as crazy as I had thought.

'And then he said: "There is yet more!" and looked at me sort of triumphantly.

'And this bit *was* new, and when I heard it I didn't like it at all. The letter said the agent was a woman and a nurse. And that she had been there when Kiesewetter was admitted and had been near him the whole time he was in the hospital. Including when he died.'

'Yes,' said Seymour. 'I think someone is about to make the same point to me. Did the letter say any more?'

'It did, and I didn't like this, either. It said that after Kiesewetter had died, she left the hospital and went straight down to the Navy place, the new one at St Angelo. To report, says the letter, and Backhaus.'

'Well,' said Seymour, 'that ought to be easy to check.'

'And that is just what I am about to do,' said Lucca.

'Yes, we were in the Eagle,' said the technicians.

'Doing what?'

'What do you think? Having a beer.'

'And something to eat,' said the other technician. 'We'd been on since four getting things sorted out for the launch. Making sure that everything was ready.'

'And hadn't had anything to eat.'

'Not even breakfast.'

'And I said to George, we're not going to get through the day if we go on like this. Let's go out for a bite. We're well ahead.'

'Why didn't you find somewhere at the racetrack to have a bite?' asked Seymour.

'They don't do an English breakfast,' said George. 'The Eagle does.'

'A proper breakfast,' said the other technician. 'And a big one. That's what we needed.'

'Two,' said George.

'Two breakfasts?'

'Two eggs. And bacon and sausages. And black pudding, but they don't do black pudding in Malta.'

'I suppose it was getting on towards lunch by this time,' said Seymour.

'Yes, it was. And we knew we were going to miss out on that as well. So we had a beer with the eggs and chips. To put us on.'

'And see us through.'

'Did you check it with Kiesewetter?'

'Kiesewetter was off somewhere.'

'Looking for milk.'

'He'd been on since four, too.'

'Did we check with him that it would be all right? No. Because he wouldn't have agreed.'

'How long were you in the pub for?'

'Three-quarters of an hour. No more. We had to get back.'

'While you were in there, did you talk to anyone?' asked Seymour.

'We certainly did! This beautiful bird walks in. She said she was a nurse and had been on duty all night. And what she wanted was a bit of breakfast, too. "Join the party," we said. So she sat down beside us. But all she had was a cup of coffee and a bread roll. She said she had to go back to the hospital because it was a special day, what with the balloons and the crowds, and that they were sure to be called in at the hospital at some point. But what she needed was to get out for a bit of fresh air.'

'Did she know you were working on the balloon?'

'We told her. She said it must be wonderful to go up in a balloon and see everything spread out below. It is, for the first few times, we said, but then you get used to it. She said how much she would like to go up in a balloon and asked if there was any chance of going up in ours. "You'd have to ask the Herr," we said. "And he'll probably say no, because he's like that." She said what a pity. And we said we could show her the balloon if she liked. She could come back with us.'

'And did she come back with you?'

'Oh, yes. We let her look over it. The balloons were about ready to go by then.'

'Of course, you'd got yours ready before you went to the pub?'

'Pretty well, yes.'

'And it was all right when you got back, was it?'

'Oh, yes.'

'No chance of anyone getting at it?'

'There were police all round it.'

'It was in a sort of roped-off area,' explained George. 'They all were, and no one was allowed to get in.'

'And we'd asked the technicians next door to keep an eye on it for us.'

'In case the wind started taking it or something.'

'But they said there had been no problem and they hadn't had to do anything.'

'There were just a few last things you had to do? Was the nurse with you while you did them?'

'No, no, no! She'd gone off. Wouldn't even make a date with us for the next morning.'

'Went off when the band next door started striking up.'

'There was a band there, was there?'

'God, yes! Lots of them. I reckon you could have heard them from the harbour!'

'They'd made a big thing of it, you see,' George explained. 'Something like this was a big do for them.'

'You don't happen to know the nurse's name, do you?'

'You bet we do, Melinda was her name.'

'Yes,' said Melinda, 'I went to the Eagle.'

'For a drink?'

Melinda laughed. 'When you're on duty? No. For a breath of fresh air, mainly.'

'Talk to anyone?'

'I expect so. Why?'

'Who?'

'Well, a couple of blokes. They said they were technicians on a balloon.'

'Did you know they would be there?'

'No.' She looked puzzled. 'Why would I?'

'I thought maybe you knew it was the place where technicians might go.'

'Well, I didn't.'

'I wondered if you were interested in balloons especially.'

'Not especially. I'd seen them as I was coming in the day before. I go past the racetrack, and there they were. Not ready to go up, of course, but some of them were partially inflated. It was odd seeing them there like that, on the racetrack. Like whales, stranded whales. It was very odd.'

'They took you over to see them, I gather?'

'It was kind of them. I had told them I probably wouldn't see them that afternoon, not when they were up, because I would be on duty. So they said: "Come on up and have a look now."'

'And after?'

'After? Well, I went back to the hospital. I was on duty, as I said. Only just made it.'

'And then, of course, you were very busy.'

'Not at first. But then they brought Kiesewetter in and after that the afternoon just flew away.'

'And after that?'

'After that?' said Melinda, puzzled. 'Well, I finished my stint and went home.'

'Straight home?'

'Well, yes. I'd been on the night before, and this was an extra shift because of the balloons. I was pretty tired.'

'I'll bet you were. I'm surprised they asked you to do the extra shift.'

'I'm the senior nurse,' said Melinda simply.

'Still –'

'Oh, I didn't mind, you get used to that sort of thing. I mean, it was like an emergency, and if it's an emergency, you go on until it's over.'

'And then you went home?'

'Yes.'

'Straight home?'

'Yes,' said Melinda, puzzled. 'As I told you.'

'Well, I'm not sure you told me everything.'

'I'm sorry?'

'You didn't go anywhere else on the way?'

'No.'

'You didn't call in at St Angelo?'

'St Angelo? What would I want to call in there for?'

'That's what I'm asking you?'

Melinda shrugged. 'No, I didn't call in at St Angelo. At the Navy, if that's what you meant. I know some of the blokes there but I didn't go there.'

'No?'

'No. I went past it. Home.'

'We shall check, you know.'

'Hey, what is this?'

'Someone has told us you didn't go straight home.'

Melinda stared, and then thought.

'You're right,' she said then. 'Or they're right, whoever told you. I didn't go straight home. I called in on someone. For about five minutes!'

'Can you tell us who?'

'I can,' said Melinda, 'but I don't know that I will. What's all this about?'

'Kiesewetter.'

'*Kiesewetter*?'

'Just tell us, Melinda,' said Lucca.

'Well, all right, then. If it's that important. I took a message for Mr Vasco.'

'Mr Vasco in the hospital?'

'That's right. He'd given it me that morning.'

'And it was to –?'

Melinda hesitated. 'Well, I don't know if it's any of your business, but – it was to his brother. The one who works in the boatyard at Volkare. My flat's not far from there so I didn't have to go out of my way.'

'We shall check, you know,' said Seymour.

193

Melinda flared up.

'You can check away as much as you like,' she said. 'If you've got nothing better to do.'

'I don't like this,' said Lucca, as they walked away.

'Nor do I,' said Seymour.

'Melinda had nothing to do with Kiesewetter's death,' said Lucca. 'I'll take my oath on it.'

'But that's not the point,' said Seymour.

Lucca stopped and stared at him. 'Not the point? For Christ's sake!'

'Someone is obviously trying to fix her,' said Seymour. 'Now the point is: who?'

Chapter Thirteen

'"The Victoria Lines in themselves are not important; it is the Victoria Lines inside the Maltese that are." How about that for a start?' said Sophia, with much satisfaction.

'Terrific!' said Felix, impressed; and then, after a moment, 'What, um, does it mean?'

'It means that the Maltese have accepted too tamely the rules laid down by the British. Wait a minute, let me get that down.' And then, after a moment: 'Where have you got to?'

'"The Infermeria was built in 1574. It could accommodate seven hundred and forty-six patients. Its principal ward, at five hundred and eight feet, was the longest room in Europe."'

'No arguing with that!' said Sophia; and then, after a moment: 'Don't you think there ought to be? I mean, wouldn't it be more exciting to get into an argument straightaway? I mean, it's a bit dull as it stands.'

'I could put in the bit about the chickens, I suppose.'

'Chickens?'

'They used two hundred chickens every day.'

'Well –'

'Which they ate off silver plates.'

'That is certainly more interesting. But –'

'I suppose there isn't much argument about it,' said Felix despondently.

'Oh, but there could be. "The Hospitaller Knights, brutes though they were, fed their patients well."'

'That is certainly more argumentative.'

195

'I know, I know,' conceded Sophia. 'It makes a statement rather than asks a question. It's always better to pose a question. "What were the Knights doing in Malta anyway?" That would sort of open it up.'

'Doesn't it open it up a bit too far? I mean, take the argument away from the Infermeria?'

'Hmm,' said Sophia.

'I know,' said Felix, suddenly pleased. 'I could start: "How did a hospital on such a grand scale (the length of the principal ward was five hundred and eight feet) come to be built in a place like Malta?"'

'That's better,' said Sophia. 'But – leave out "place like Malta". It makes Malta sound a bit of a dump.'

'We are coming to the end of our sojourn in Malta,' said Mrs Wynne-Gurr, 'and it is time to pull our thoughts together. I have, actually, prepared a draft. Based, of course, on your discussion yesterday morning.'

'But you weren't there!'

'I have gleaned the results of your deliberations,' said Mrs Wynne-Gurr with dignity, 'and incorporated them into the draft.'

'I hope we shall have time to discuss the final draft?'

'We certainly will,' said Mrs Wynne-Gurr. 'I have planned to set aside the next two days for that purpose.'

'Two days?'

'There is much to discuss.'

'I thought we were going to have an opportunity to do some shopping?'

'And to go to the beach.'

'We can do that on the last morning. In the evening Mrs Ferreira has invited us to a *fenkata*.'

'A what?'

'*Fenkata*. A traditional Maltese picnic.'

'Oh, how nice!'

'Rabbit picnic.'

'Rabbit?' More doubtfully.

'And other traditional dishes, of course. It will give us

an opportunity to mingle with our hosts and talk to them informally about Ambulance work, which I am sure you will be only too glad to take advantage of.'

'Someone to see you, Mr Vasco.'

'Oh, him. And him! Well, I don't want to see them.'

'That's not very nice of you!'

'I'm not feeling very nice this morning.'

'Go on like this,' said Inspector Lucca, 'and I'll not say how sorry I am to see you here.'

'You don't care a toss about me.'

'That's true,' agreed Lucca. 'But I do care a toss about some other people.'

'Oh, yes?'

'Melinda, for instance.'

'Melinda? What has she got to do with it?'

'She's in trouble.'

'Well, I'm sorry to hear that. But that's nothing to do with me.'

'Oh, but it is, Vasco,' said Seymour.

'And you keep out of it!' said Vasco.

'But I can't! I'm investigating the murders of two British seamen and a German balloonist. Right here, in the hospital!'

'Melinda is nothing to do with that.'

'We wonder,' said Lucca, 'we wonder if you're right there.'

'You're a fool, Lucca,' said Vasco contemptuously. 'You always were.'

'Quite possibly, Vasco. But still I'm wondering.'

'You've got the wrong end of the stick. As usual.'

'Very probably. But still I'm wondering.'

'You know nothing about it, Lucca!'

'True!' said Lucca. 'And therefore you're going to have to tell me.'

'Me?' said Vasco, surprised.

'She's been carrying messages for you, Vasco,' said Seymour. 'What were they about?'

197

'That's none of your business.'

'To the British Navy. At St Angelo.'

'What?' said Vasco incredulously, raising himself from the pillow.

'So someone has told us.'

'Bollocks!' said Vasco, lying back.

'She took one just after the German had died. From you.'

'You're making this up!'

'She admits it herself.'

'Taking a message?'

'Yes.'

'To the British Navy? I don't believe it!'

'So our informant says.'

Vasco spat contemptuously.

'She certainly took a message,' said Seymour.

'She took a message, right,' said Vasco. 'And from me. But to the British? Never!'

He raised himself from his pillow. 'Never! To the British? Melinda? You're a bloody fool, Lucca.'

'Didn't she take a message?'

'Yes, she took a message. And from me. But not to the Navy – Christ!'

'Who to, then?'

'My brother. You can ask him.'

'But he's in it, too!' said Seymour.

'In what, for Christ's sake?'

'That little group you've got down there around the boatyards.'

'I don't have a little group.'

'Built around the band. For cover.'

'I don't have a little group!'

'What message did you send them, Vasco, after the German died?'

Vasco looked at them savagely but said nothing.

'Was it simply to say that the German had died? That that part of the plan had been successful?'

'What plan?'

'To kill the German. And bring trouble on the British.'

'There was no plan!'

'Ah, but, you see, our informant says there was. And Melinda was part of it. In the hospital, as well as afterwards. So our informant says.'

'Your bloody informant! I don't believe there was one.'

'There was. And what he says is that Melinda had a hand in the killing. And then took the news to your band of brothers.'

'Had a hand in –?' roared Vasco, raising himself from the pillow. 'You bastards! You're trying to pin this on her! Lucca, you bastard, I'm warning you! If it's the last thing I do, I'll see that someone gets you for this!'

'That wasn't the message, then?' said Seymour.

'No, it bloody wasn't! Ask my brother. Ask anyone down there. Look. I'll admit we've got a group there. And, yes, they don't love the British. And if we could harm them we bloody would. But I can't get them to do anything! They just talk, and – and do nothing! That's what the message was about. To kick them up the backside. Get them going. I want to see something done before I croak. But Melinda –! Look, Melinda's never been anything to do with this. She's not even a member of the group. She just carries messages. And she does that because – because she's got a bit of time for me. Unlike you, Lucca. Unlike everybody else.'

He began to cough. 'I know what you're doing, Lucca. You and the British. You're trying to pin it on her. Because you can't find anyone else to pin it on. Well, I'm warning you. I'm warning you –'

Seymour watched him detachedly.

'Well, you're right in one thing, Vasco,' he said. 'Someone is out to fix her. But it's not us.'

Vasco looked up at him balefully but uncertainly. 'Not –?'

'Not us. It's someone else. And I want you to tell me who that is.'

'Shut up, for a moment, Vasco,' said Lucca, 'and listen to him.'

'You don't sleep well at night, do you, Vasco?'

'No, I bloody don't!'

'I think you were awake the night the sailor was killed in your ward.'

Vasco didn't say anything.

'There was a lot going on that night. There were two people in that cupboard for a start. Suzie and one of the sailors.'

Vasco went on lying there, just looking.

'At one point, the sailor came out. Did you see him? On hands and knees. So that the nurse – Bettina, it was – didn't see him.'

He waited. Vasco said nothing.

'I don't think anyone else went into the cupboard. So it was just Suzie in there. But she was there the whole time. While the doctors and nurses were working on the sailor. And then afterwards, when things quietened down, she left. But in between the sailor leaving on hands and knees and the time she left, quite a lot happened. The attack on the seaman, for instance.'

He waited.

'Did you see that, Vasco?'

'No,' said Vasco, after a moment. 'I didn't realize what had happened until afterwards.'

'But you saw something?'

'Maybe,' said Vasco grudgingly.

'You saw a man come in, didn't you?'

'Maybe.'

'He came in when the nurse had gone out for her break.'

He waited.

'Maybe,' said Vasco, after a moment.

'I think you knew him.'

He waited again. Vasco said nothing.

'Would you like to tell me his name?'

'No,' said Vasco, 'I wouldn't.'

'Why not?'

'It's not my business.'

'And you didn't altogether disapprove of him,' said Seymour.

Vasco looked surprised but then gave a little laugh.

'No,' he said, 'I didn't.'

'I think he may have guessed that,' said Seymour. 'Because I think he knew that you were awake and guessed that you had seen him. But he did nothing about it. Why do you think that was?'

'I've no idea,' said Vasco.

'He knew that you were not unsympathetic to what he was doing, and at first he thought you wouldn't tell. But then, I think, after a while, after he'd got away, that was, he thought again. And he thought that perhaps you *might* tell. So he thought he'd better guard against that possibility. Well, of course, he might have killed you too.'

'I'd like to see him try!' said Vasco.

'Yes. Sick though you were, there could have been a problem. Especially as you'd seen what could happen and might have taken precautions. So he thought he would try another way. He set Melinda up and drew attention to her link with you. He set both of you up, Vasco.'

He saw that Vasco was thinking this over.

'How do I know that you're not tricking me?' Vasco said at last.

'You don't. You'll have to take a chance. But meanwhile the spotlight is on Melinda. That's the way he's left it.'

Vasco was thinking hard.

'He knew you were sympathetic to what he was doing. Are you still sympathetic, Vasco? Because he was doing it against you, Vasco. And against Melinda. He was quite ready to sacrifice her. Still sympathetic?'

He could see the internal wrestle.

'Still sympathetic?' he said again.

Vasco was on the brink of saying something. Then he turned over on to his side and said: 'Bugger off!'

But as they were leaving he suddenly heaved himself up on to one side.

'I've always had a soft spot for them,' he said. 'You may not like them but at least they try to do something. Not like my bloody lot!'

Sophia was working on her project at the kitchen table when Paolo came in to pick up his clothes.

'What are you doing, Sophia?'

'My project.'

He bent over her shoulder and read the opening sentence. Then he read it again. And then he sat down and read it yet again.

'"The Victoria Lines in themselves are not important. It is the Victoria Lines in our hearts that are." That's pretty good, Sophia. That's pretty good! It's the Victoria Lines that you carry about with you that matter.'

'You think so?'

'I know so. The Victoria Lines are engraved on every Maltese heart.'

'That's what I think!' said Sophia, pleased.

'I don't know how they get engraved, but it starts early.'

'It's your parents,' said Sophia.

'Your mother is a wonderful woman, Sophia. Don't ever forget that!'

'On the whole she's not bad,' conceded Sophia.

'And her heart's in the right place. You know that, Sophia.'

'Her heart's in the right place. But sometimes she's distracted by realism.'

Paolo laughed.

'Well, that's something that could never be said of me,' he said.

'You've always been an idealist, Paolo,' said Sophia.

Paolo laughed again. 'Oh, Sophia, if you only knew! If you only knew.'

'You want to pull yourself together, Paolo. You're wasted. And it's you who are doing the wasting.'

'You can only do what you can,' said Paolo. 'It comes back to the Victoria Lines. Once they're there you can't get them out.'

'You let them loom too large,' said Sophia.

'Maybe I do,' said Paolo thoughtfully.

He got up from the table and went over to the window and looked out.

'But, you see,' he said, 'there's another question: if you don't do anything about them, can you ever put things right? Can you ever get yourself right?'

202

'I ask myself that,' said Sophia. 'I've asked Chantale that, too – you know Chantale? Of course you do!'

'I know her,' said Paolo. 'Chantale: is that her name?'

'Miss de Lissac is what other people call her,' said Sophia offhandedly.

'And what does she say?'

'She says that in the end everybody has to compromise. That's life. Now, in fact, I don't altogether agree with her. It seems to me that if you really believe in something, you let yourself down if you don't go for it absolutely. But Chantale says you can't go for things absolutely, in the end you always have to compromise. It's the point at which you decide to make your compromise that's the thing. It's a question of balance, she says. And, she says, you nearly always get it wrong.'

Paolo laughed. 'Well, I certainly get it wrong.'

'I may do,' admitted Sophia. 'Sometimes.'

'It's easier for you,' said Paolo. 'You're not an Arab.'

'Chantale is an Arab,' said Sophia. 'She comes from Morocco.'

'And what does she say about that?'

'She says that things are such a mess there that the only practical thing to do now is to compromise.'

'Yes, but what do the Moroccans say?'

'She is a Moroccan.'

Paolo was silent.

'Actually,' said Sophia, 'she's only half a Moroccan. The other half is French.'

'Ah, well –'

'She says that seeing things from both sides ought to make it easier. But that she's damned if it does.'

Paolo laughed uproariously.

'That lady is the only person who really understands me,' he said.

He turned to go.

'But she's wrong, you know,' he said. 'It's too late for compromise.'

After Paolo had gone, Sophia put down her pen and sat

thinking. She sat thinking for quite a while then got up and went out.

As Seymour was walking down the road, the heavens opened. A torrent of rain descended. In seconds the street was awash. In less than a minute the road had become a river flowing downhill to the bend round towards Sliema. It was too much for the bend and for the drains to cope with, and the river become a lake. It had spread now right up to and over the pavements. Seymour, suddenly finding that it was reaching up over his ankles, bolted into the nearest shop, which turned out to be an ice-cream parlour. In which Sophia was sitting.

The parlour was already crowded but Sophia made room for him beside her on a bench. It seemed only fair to the shop to buy an ice cream. He bought one for Sophia, too. Sophia had already bought one but she was able to manage two, taking lick upon lick alternately.

'I am very pleased, Mr Seymour,' said Sophia, 'to see you and Chantale getting on so well. But what does it feel like to you, as an Englishman, to be married to an Arab?'

'Pretty good, actually,' said Seymour. 'Although, I have to tell you, we are not, in fact, married.'

'Aren't you?' said Sophia, with great interest.

'Yet,' said Seymour.

'But you are going to?'

'If I can talk her into it. At the moment, she is holding out for independence. She is still not completely sure.'

'I would be like that,' said Sophia. 'Not completely sure. And holding out for independence. Is that because she's an Arab?'

'No, I don't think so.'

'Because it might make a difference. She might be proud, you see. And reluctant to surrender her independence to an Englishman.'

'She *is* proud,' said Seymour. 'But I'm not sure that my being an Englishman would make much difference to that.'

'Well, it might,' said Sophia. 'You are a representative of an occupying power. At least, that is how it will seem to her.'

'Britain certainly occupies a lot of Arab countries,' said Seymour. 'But it hasn't occupied Morocco yet. Which is where Chantale comes from.'

Sophia nodded, and licked her ice cream.

'She has told me,' she said. 'And from what she told me, I don't think it's very different there from the way it is here.'

'I like to think,' said Seymour, 'that we relate as individuals.'

'That would be ideal,' said Sophia. 'But is it possible? Is it realistic?'

'We like to think so.'

'But you're still not married,' Sophia pointed out.

She gave the ice cream in her left hand another lick; held the flavour, considered, and then gave the ice cream in her right hand a lick.

'Why I'm asking,' she said, 'is that I am wondering about Uncle Paolo. You see, his mother married an Arab and it didn't work out. And it's left him all messed up. At least, Grandfather thinks so. But my mother thinks it's nothing to do with that. She says that they were both difficult people anyway.'

Sophia took another double lick.

'I never knew my Aunt Debra,' she said, 'but if she was anything like my mother, that could be true.'

'I think your mother is charming!' objected Seymour. 'And so does Chantale.'

'Chantale is very generous,' said Sophia, 'as well as being proud. I'm a bit like that, too. And, probably,' she said, mopping up a drip, 'Grandfather is, too. It nearly broke his heart when Aunt Debra moved away to Tripoli. He didn't really mind her marrying an Arab. He says he could have lived with Uncle Raoul. It was his daughter moving away that he couldn't cope with. I have told him,' said Sophia, 'that he is lucky my mother didn't move away, too. And that when I am grown up I shall certainly move away. Grandfather says that the most he will concede is that it would be a mixed blessing. But whenever I say that, my mother flies into a tantrum. They are both,' said Sophia, 'rather alike in many ways.'

She considered her ice creams and then gave both a series of quick licks to reassess the flavours.

'Mother says,' said Sophia, 'that what's wrong with Uncle Paolo is not that he's half Arab but that he's never had a proper family. Aunt Debra died so young, you see. And, anyway, she was over here and Paolo's father stayed over in Tripoli. So it's all been divided, and he's been divided, ever since. And Mother says the family ought to try to make up for it, and she certainly tries to make up for it. And even Grandfather does. Or did, when Uncle Paolo was small. But then Uncle Paolo went away and when he came back, he was very difficult to get on with. Grandfather says he'd become a real pain in the ass. And that,' said Sophia, licking away, 'I'm afraid is true.'

'Perhaps, when he gets back to sea –' said Seymour. 'Perhaps, actually, he needs to get away from the family.'

'I said that,' said Sophia, 'and Mother flew into another tantrum. The trouble is, every time he gets home again, he's got worse! He says it's the British – he's usually on British boats. Grandfather says, for Christ's sake, stay away from the British, then! But he can't. As I say, he's divided. And that makes it worse.'

Sophia was down to the last tips of the cones.

'Mother says he ought to settle down and start a family of his own. But Grandfather says he's not like that. Mother gets cross with him and says, what a dreadful thing to say about a member of your family! And Grandfather, trying to be helpful, I think, says maybe it's just the Arab way. The men putting their arms around each other and all that. And Mother says: will he stop going on about Paolo being an Arab? He's only half Arab, and, anyway, all Maltese have got some Arab in them. Including him, Grandfather. I wondered,' said Sophia, finishing off the cones and looking at the rain pouring down outside, 'how you and Chantale found it.'

'Found –?'

'Mixed marriage.'

'We don't think of ourselves –'

'And what about the children?' said Sophia. 'How will they find it? I mean, will they turn out like Uncle Paolo? I mean, that has to be a consideration.'

'I'm a bit of a mixture myself,' said Seymour. 'We all are. Once you get a little down the line.'

'That also is true,' said Sophia, going over to stand by the door and look out. 'I wonder what Felix would think about it?'

'About –?'

'Marrying a Maltese.'

'It's a bit early to start thinking about that, isn't it?'

'One has to look ahead. And, in any case, it's probably better if I do the looking. Because I don't think an idea like this has ever entered Felix's head.'

'I thought I would find you here!' said Seymour, taking Dr Malia by the arm.

'I usually am,' confessed Dr Malia. 'I feel at home in the hospital.'

'I'm sure you do. Now, look, there's something I wanted to ask you.'

'Please do!' said Dr Malia cordially.

'I don't know if you remember, but when we met last time, I asked you about the people who had come out of the boiler room that night, the night when there were so many people coming and going, and the sailor was murdered. You recognized them, you said, but at the time you couldn't remember their names.'

'I remember,' said Dr Malia. 'They popped out of the boiler room like rabbits. Most odd! And, by the way, Mrs Ferreira is holding a *fenkata*. Did you know? I hope you are coming.'

'I am coming, as it happens. But let's just go back to the boiler room for a moment. You saw two people and recognized them, but you couldn't remember their names.'

'Couldn't I? Oh, dear! I'm rather like that these days, I'm afraid.'

'Can you remember them now?'

Dr Malia thought, then shook his head.

'I'm afraid not,' he said, with genuine regret.

'I thought perhaps you wouldn't. But never mind. Would you mind stepping along here with me?'

'We're going to the boiler room?' said Dr Malia.

'We certainly are.'

Along the corridor, from around the corner, they suddenly heard Luigi's voice.

'Benito, I don't like it here!'

'I don't like it much, either,' said Lucca's voice. 'But you won't have to stay long.'

Seymour and Dr Malia turned the corner.

'Were these the men you saw coming out of the boiler room?' asked Seymour.

'One of them was,' said Dr Malia. 'Not Benito, of course. I know him. But the other one. Luigi. I know him, too, of course.'

'He was with a different man that night. Do you remember the name of that man?'

'I'm afraid I don't,' said Mr Malia contritely.

'It doesn't matter,' said Seymour. 'I think you will when I show you him.'

'I hope so!'

'I don't like it here!' said Luigi agitatedly.

'You won't have to stay here long,' said Inspector Lucca, reassuringly.

Two nurses came along the corridor. They fell upon Dr Malia with delighted squeals.

'*There* you are! We thought we'd lost you!'

'Someone said they'd seen you over here!'

'You're coming, aren't you?'

'Certainly. If you want me.'

'We do, we do!'

'Where, exactly?' said Dr Malia hesitantly.

'Well, it's not till Friday, actually. But we want to tell you now.'

'And every day until it happens! To make sure you remember.'

'Yes, yes. But what is it?'

'And hang a big reminder notice around your neck!'

'Actually, that may not be necessary since Melinda says she's going to pick you up herself and put you under armed guard.'

'Dear, dear! What have I done?'

'We don't want you to miss it.'

'Miss *what*?'

'The *fenkata*! Mrs Ferreira's arranging one. Over by the Victoria Lines. Everyone's invited – nurses, St John's, the English visitors. You're invited, too,' she said to Seymour.

'And you,' said the other nurse to Dr Malia, 'are especially invited. And Bettina's bringing her mother, so you've *got* to come!'

'I would certainly like to see Bettina's mother.'

'I'll bet! Are there any other old flames you would like us to invite?'

'It sounds as if the young flames will be enough,' said Dr Malia.

'Now, Luigi,' said Inspector Lucca, once they'd got him in a quiet room by himself, 'you've got some explaining to do.'

'Benito, I don't like it here!'

'So why did you come here, then?' asked Seymour. 'That night when the two of you came out of the boiler room and saw Dr Malia?'

'He made me!' said Luigi whimpering. 'I didn't want to come. I said it would make my clothes dirty! And it did!'

'Did you go on into the hospital?'

'No, no. I would have lost my way.'

'So you just stayed by the boiler room?'

'Yes.'

'So that you could help him get out? That board's very stiff, isn't it?'

'Yes. You have to wedge it. And he wanted me to be there right beside it so that I could hold it open for him.'

'And you did that, did you, Luigi?'

'He made me. I didn't want to. I didn't want to come at all. And I didn't want to get down that filthy hole, not with my suit on. I knew it would make my suit dirty!'

Chapter Fourteen

Preparations for the *fenkata* were under way. Mrs Ferreira had chosen a spot right beside the Victoria Lines where there was soft grass to sit on and the wall would give protection against the wind, or, if some more rain should come up, against that, too. Tablecloths were already spread and, on the other side of the wall, rabbits, some alive and in cages, others already dead, were assembled. There were going to be a lot of people, with the two St John Ambulances, Maltese and British, the nurses, some staff from the hospital – Umberto and Berto, for instance, and Laura and Mario, working like a slave carrying baskets and boxes over to the picnic spot from the carts on the road. And, of course, the band.

But which band? The Birgu band, Birgu being the place most of the people had come from, or Mrs Ferreira's home band, Mrs Ferreira being host and convenor? This could have turned awkward but, as Chantale pointed out to Sophia, even here compromise was in the end reached. There was a *joint* band.

And, of course, given the large numbers of people, well over a hundred, indeed, more like two hundred, there had to be a corresponding amount of provisions. The number of rabbits, for instance ... Seymour feared a wholesale massacre of rabbits on the island but, apparently, they had already been massacred, years before, and the rabbits were grown for the market. Even so, there were startling numbers of them and Seymour worried now about the cost and whether and how far he should make a contribution. It was totally out of the question that someone as poor as Mrs Ferreira –

He confided these worries to Mrs Wynne-Gurr and she admitted that originally she had shared them. The West Surrey St John Ambulance would do its best but even those redoubtable ladies were daunted. Mrs Ferreira, however, was not at all daunted. The Maltese were used to this sort of thing. The nurses chipped in, the hospital chipped in, the Navy, with characteristic nautical legerdemain and disregard for accounting, switched massively from buying a battleship to funding a *fenkata*, half of Malta, it seemed, threw in a bit and suddenly there were funds in plenty.

In any case much of the chipping in took the form of contributions in kind, most of which came, of course, from the generous Maltese ladies, who produced *pastizzi* galore, the aniseed-smelling *mquaret*, crunchy *kannoli*, *guabbajt*, nougat hard or soft, brittle or chewy, *kwarezimal* almond biscuits covered with honey and nuts, and, especially, for an occasion such as this, the *quaghaq tal-ghasel* that Seymour and Felix had already encountered, a ring of heavily treacled pastry.

And then of course, there was the main dish: the rabbits, as big as piglets, plump and fleshy, not at all like the rabbits that Seymour knew.

Chantale did not know rabbits and viewed them doubtfully: but the nurses, who used up a lot of energy during the day and often the night, and were always hungry, knew exactly what to do with rabbits, and did.

The Registrar of the hospital had brought along an Admiral, and Sophia explained to him her project.

'The Victoria Lines? A complete waste of time? But that's what I've always said!' cried the Admiral impressed. 'An army concept! Useless!' Sophia elaborated her theories of military strategy and the need for a fluid and flexible defence system. 'Exactly what I've always argued!' said the Admiral, and congratulated Mrs Ferreira on having such a remarkable daughter. 'Well . . .' said Mrs Ferreira uneasily.

Felix was deep in conversation with Dr Malia. 'You see,' he explained, 'if you used bunk beds you could double the

capacity of the ward.' 'I've never thought of that!' con-
fessed Dr Malia: and, later, he was heard telling Mrs
Wynne-Gurr what a remarkable son she had. 'Well . . .' said
Mrs Wynne-Gurr, rather doubtfully.

'But where is Paolo?' asked Mrs Ferreira, looking around.

'May I have a word with you?' said Seymour, taking her
gently aside.

'I cannot believe it!' declared Mrs Ferreira. 'Where is the
evidence?'

'There's quite a lot of it,' said Seymour. 'In each case he
was on the spot when the victims died.'

'On the spot?' said Mrs Ferreira. 'But they all happened
in the hospital, and Paolo was never there!'

'Well, he was,' said Seymour. 'Take when Kiesewetter
was killed, for example. A great crowd of people surged
into the hospital after he was taken there. Including the
band. Among whom was Paolo. For a short time there was
general chaos as they spilled around everywhere looking
for Herr Kiesewetter. But Paolo knew exactly where to find
him. Because Umberto had told him, had told everyone.
There was only the question of getting into the room, and
Paolo knew because he had worked in the hospital. He
knew where the porters kept the key and in the general
confusion it was easy to slip the key off the hook and use
it to unlock the door of the nurses' room, which was where
Mr Kiesewetter was sleeping.'

'But the band was not in the hospital when the others
died!'

'No, and that is where the evidence becomes crucial, particularly in the case of the killing done during the night. It
took me some time to figure that out, actually, because there
were several possibilities. First, whoever attacked the seaman, Turner, could have come in through the main entrance.
Umberto, who was supposed to be on duty, had gone off to
see his girlfriend, leaving Mario in charge. Mario is a good,
conscientious boy but he is only a boy and might have been
deceived. He did leave the entrance unguarded, actually, for

a time, but that was when he was called to the ward after Turner had been found. He did think, in fact, that that may have been when the murderer got in, but it wasn't, because of course, Turner was already dead.

'In any case, there was a much more likely possibility. There is a cupboard at the end of Turner's ward used only by Suzie for her assignations. She had, in fact, used it that night to meet another of the sailors, Cooper. She swore that he had left before the attack took place. She knew when the attack took place because, soon after, she heard the doctors and nurses trying to resuscitate Turner. Worried that there might be a search, she left the cupboard and crept out. But in theory there was the possibility that someone else, someone other than Cooper, had been in there with her. Both Suzie and Cooper denied this, but for us it had to be a possibility.

'But there was another, more likely, possibility. Both Cooper and Suzie had left the hospital by an exit through the boiler room. They used the coal chute. But if they could leave, could not someone have come in that way?

'The boiler men told me that would be difficult because there is a stiff board over the chute which would be hard to push aside from the outside, and also it would be hard for a big, or even normal-sized, man to get down there.

'What I think happened was that there were two men, one big or biggish, the other definitely small. The small one came into the hospital earlier in the day, probably by the ordinary entrance, and then concealed himself until the boiler men had gone off duty. Then he entered the boiler room, climbed up the chute, wedged the board open and left. Later in the night he returned with an accomplice, who was, in fact, the killer, and together they were able to enter by the coal chute.

'At first I thought that this was unlikely because, if you remember, Suzie and Cooper had left the hospital earlier in the night using the coal chute, and surely they would have noticed if the board had been wedged. I think that if they did, they thanked their stars and wriggled on. Anyway, they left it wedged open.

214

'That is, in fact, what happened. There *were* two men. We know that because they were seen coming out of the boiler room, by Dr Malia, who has, incidentally, identified them.

'There is also some supplementary evidence. The smaller man, who went up first and wedged the board, was initially reluctant to do so because it would dirty his clothes – he is very fussy about his clothes. He *did* dirty his clothes and was very aggrieved about it. We know this because he complained about it. He said that Paolo – because, of course, we are talking about Paolo as the other person involved – had promised he would get them cleaned. But he hadn't done so. Partly because of that he was prepared to explain all this to Inspector Lucca and myself when we asked him about it. All the more so when we told him why we were asking. It came as a complete shock to him. He had no idea why Paolo wanted to get into the hospital. He is, I have to say, not very bright; and totally under Paolo's thumb.

'But there is yet another thing: Paolo was seen entering the ward that night. By Mr Vasco. Now, Vasco was unwilling to make a direct identification of Paolo as the person who entered the ward; but he made an indirect identification which, along with the other evidence, enables us to say definitely that Paolo, I am afraid, was the killer. More to the point, the way he made his identification gives us a clue to the reason why Paolo killed these three men.'

'I cannot believe this!' said Mrs Ferreira. 'What sort of men are these witnesses? Malia, half crazy and half asleep all the time: Vasco, embittered to the point of madness. And this third one, worried about dirtying his clothes – who is he?'

'Luigi.'

'Luigi! That twerp! He'll say anything!'

'He'll say anything that Paolo tells him to.'

'Paolo wouldn't tell him to say this!'

'For once, confronted with the reality of the situation, Luigi is prepared to go against what Paolo says. Especially since he is being urged to tell the truth by someone for whom he feels as great a regard as he does for Paolo: Suzie.'

215

'Suzie! Well, you *have* made a choice of witnesses, I must say!'

'Maybe. But, in his way, he loves her.'

'And she?'

'Loves him. In her way. Perhaps that is putting it too strongly. She is fond of him and tries to care for him.'

'She treats him like a little dog!'

'You can love dogs. And dogs, in their way, can love you.'

Mrs Ferreira made an impatient gesture. 'Malia, Vasco, Luigi, Suzie – are those the people your case depends on?'

'There is another thing,' said Seymour. 'Luigi is an Arab, or part Arab. Like Paolo.'

Mrs Ferreira burst into tears.

'This is prejudice!' she said angrily, through her sobs. 'He has never been allowed to get away from this. All his life. What he is, we have made him. Our family. All of us. And now we are trying to – we are saying that he is responsible for those terrible things. But he is not! He is not!'

'He has confessed that he is.'

'You have made him do that! You and Lucca between you!'

'He is a sick man.'

'He is *not* sick! We have driven him out. And he behaves peculiarly as a result. Peculiarly, but not . . . evilly. He is . . . different, I grant you that. But that is what we have made him. Inside, he is – I *know* he is! He has a cause. The cause is different from yours, but –'

'I am not objecting to the cause. But in his pursuit of it he has become out of touch with things the rest of us take for granted. There is a line between fighting reasonably for your cause and fighting unreasonably, and it is to do with the effect on other people. Let me give you an example: Melinda.'

'Melinda?'

'Mrs Wynne-Gurr took you through her theories about the murders – tried out her ideas on you. She had worked out that one nurse, the same nurse, was present in the case of all three murders. Melinda.'

'What she suggested was ridiculous.'

216

'I agree. Logical, but ridiculous. And it did not exclude other possibilities. That someone else had also been present. And, as we know, Paolo was. But Paolo was also present – do you remember? – when Mrs Wynne-Gurr outlined her theories to you. He heard, and what flashed into his mind was a way of using them himself. He would reinforce the case against Melinda and safeguard himself – because he couldn't be quite sure that Vasco would not give him away.

'Very cunningly he did so in a way that not only threw suspicion on Melinda but also drew attention to the possible role that Vasco himself could have played in the process. He sent an anonymous letter pointing out, as Mrs Wynne-Gurr had done – in fact, borrowing what he had heard her tell you – Melinda's proximity on all three occasions and adding information of his own – that after the attack on Herr Kiesewetter Melinda had taken a message to say that the attack had been successful.

'The message – and there had been one, although it did not say that – had come from Vasco, thus implicating and, Paolo hoped, discrediting him and anything he might say. But it had another purpose, too. The letter said, falsely, that Melinda had taken it to the British Navy Headquarters at St Angelo, thus implicating them as well.

'There was a further point to this, which was important. It is to do with the reason why Paolo chose to mount an attack on Kiesewetter in the first place. The attacks on the sailors were easy to understand. They were British and Paolo had a grudge against the British. Not only that, the grudge had been inflamed by recent disagreements over football and over Suzie which involved those particular seamen. But why the attack on the German Kiesewetter?

'Something Sophia had said earlier struck me. She said that when they were watching the balloons Paolo had made a remark to the effect that the hospital had better brace its ideas up if it was dealing with a German because the Germans made a fuss about inadequacy. Sophia said he had seemed particularly struck by his observation. I think it was then that he decided to follow Kiesewetter into the hospital and kill him – simply because it would make trouble between England and Germany. And it was this point, of course, that he was reinforcing by claiming that Melinda had taken such a message to the British Navy Head-quarters. The claim was made in the letter to the German Consul, who was investigating Kiesewetter's death.

'It was part, that is, of Paolo's general opportunistic political scheming, an illustration, I think, of the extent to which he had now crossed the line between what was rea-sonable and what was evil. And on that last issue, just think of the impact of what he was doing on a perfectly innocent person, Melinda. Not to mention a rather less innocent Vasco. Who, I think, will now be willing to testify that he saw Paolo enter the ward that night.'

Afterwards, Mrs Ferreira returned to the *fenkata*. It was her *fenkata* and she was never one to shirk her duties. The St John Ambulance ladies were distributed around the table-cloths, sitting with the families whose guests they had been and exchanging vows of eternal friendship and repeated visits which became even more fervent as the glasses of alcoholic lemonade went down. At a certain point the band struck up, the nurses put away their rabbit bones and took off their shoes and began to dance, and the picnic became, in the words, but not necessarily disapproving words, of one of the English St John ladies, 'positively Bacchanalian'.

In the midst of the revels Seymour suddenly saw Luigi, allowed out of jail, under the watchful eye of Inspector Lucca, and the still more watchful eye of Suzie, to play in the band. Luigi was still entirely bewildered but, now in his best, cleaned-up suit, was prepared to blow his heart out for the occasion.

Lucca, benign, but fearful of the opprobrium he knew he was going to suffer from the Ferreira clan, the inhabitants of Birgu, the Maltese generality and probably, once Herr Backhaus had reported home, the German one as well, timidly plucked up courage to ask Mrs Ferreira for a dance. Mrs Ferreira, ever generous and eager to believe the best of people, was prepared on this occasion to waive the usual Maltese treatment for someone they considered a traitor, a knife in the back, and, after consideration, consented. Lucca was, after all, Maltese and from Birgu; and perhaps would do better another time.

Another person who was present was Mr Vasco's brother. He had just been visiting Mr Vasco and reported, with astonishment and some concern, that his brother was unusually quiet. He attributed this, to her surprise, to the influence of Chantale. 'He always had a soft spot for Arabs,' he said. 'He used to say that they were only doing what we ought to be doing. I told him that if that meant doing what Paolo had done, he could count me out. I was a bit surprised that he didn't bite my head off.'

At one point in the proceedings Mrs Wynne-Gurr was observed talking to Melinda. 'I was quite wrong,' Felix heard her saying. Felix was astounded; he had never heard her use such an expression before and thought, first, that he had misheard and then, second, that she wasn't well. Sophia said, however, that it was big of her to say so. She said that it was a very un-English thing to do, and she asked Felix if possibly his mother was not entirely English. Felix, who had hitherto taken his mother's and his own Englishness for granted, was somewhat taken aback. However, he applied to his father who said that there was some Welsh and Scottish and Irish blood in the family, as there was in most English people. 'We're all pretty mixed up by now.' 'Like Malta,' said Sophia, relieved.

The Arab issue was weighing on her, as it was on the whole Ferreira family. The Ferreiras had at once closed ranks around Mrs Ferreira but also, feeling some sense of guilt, around Paolo, too. Indeed, Sophia suddenly started to take up cudgels on behalf of the Arabs. 'Another lost cause!' said Grandfather, and that started the father-and-mother – in fact, grandfather – of a quarrel ferocious even by the standards of Grandfather–Sophia disputes. Somehow, however, it cleared the air and they took to visiting Paolo together, both in his prison cell and later in the special hospital to which he was transferred.

Felix, probably put off by his mother, had never been one for causes lost or otherwise, but now revised his position, having come across Sophia in tears one day. He had, in fact, revised *all* his positions as a result of the Maltese holiday; as, indeed had Sophia.

They handed in their projects on time and both did very well. Sophia had amended her original thesis and now drew attention to the Victoria Lines inside *everybody*, thus earning from her teachers commendation on the balanced view she had developed recently, an observation which made Grandfather choke over his (English) tea. Felix's project had transformed itself, too, into something like a work-study of hospitals, ancient and modern, which left even Mrs Wynne-Gurr shaken.

The real fruit of the change in emphasis came years later after he had completed his medical studies and then switched unexpectedly to hospital administration, in which he was astonishingly successful.

His new work required him to visit St George's Hospital at Hyde Park Corner where he ran into Sophia again. Sophia had found, as had so many bright Maltese girls, that about the only job open to her was as a nurse, and she had been sent to London for her training. There, as well as taking up once more with Felix, she took up the cause of female suffrage; where she met again Mrs Wynne-Gurr, now a prominent lady in the cause, as well as being an experienced knocker-on and opener-up of doors. Some of which benefited Sophia considerably. They were altogether a formidable family team.

Sophia remained in touch with Chantale and continued to give her the benefit of her thinking. And Felix remained in touch with Seymour. He found that the political skills Seymour had honed through years of experience of working with the Byzantine processes of Scotland Yard were an invaluable source of advice in his struggle with the no less Byzantine processes of health care.

PEARC   HLOOW
Pearce, Michael,
A dead man in Malta /
9/16/20 Minor liquid damage noted
LOOSCAN
12/10   - ML/HEI